FIVE BELLS

On a radiant day in Sydney, four adults converge on Circular Quay, site of the iconic Opera House. Each one is haunted by past intimacies, secrets and guilt: Ellie is preoccupied by her sexual experiences as a girl, James by a tragedy for which he feels responsible, Catherine by the loss of her beloved brother in Dublin and Pei Xing by her imprisonment during China's Cultural Revolution. Told over a single Saturday, their stories chime and resonate. A fifth — the figure of a child — is ever present. By night-time, when Sydney is drenched in a rainstorm, each life has been transformed.

Gail Jones lives in Sydney and teaches at the University of Western Sydney. Her books have won numerous literary awards in Australia.

SPECIAL ... **ERS**

This book is published under the auspices of

THE ULVERSCROFT FOUNDATION

(registered charity No. 264873 UK)

Established in 1972 to provide funds for

rese... ... ...s.

R...

T...
Grea... ...n,

You... ...n
by ... y
co...

T...

T...
c/o ... d

94-98 Chalmers Street, Surry Hills,
N.S.W. 2010, Australia

GAIL JONES

◆

FIVE BELLS

Complete and Unabridged

ULVERSCROFT
Leicester

First published in Great Britain in 2011 by
Harvill Secker
The Random House Group Limited
London

First Large Print Edition
published 2012
by arrangement with
The Random House Group Limited
London

British Library CIP Data

Jones, Gail, *1955 –*
    Five bells.
    1. Life change events- -Fiction.
    2. Sydney (N.S.W.)- -Fiction.
    3. Large type books.
    I. Title
    823.9′2–dc23

    ISBN 978–1–4448–1066–0

Published by
F. A. Thorpe (Publishing)
Anstey, Leicestershire

Set by Words & Graphics Ltd.
Anstey, Leicestershire
Printed and bound in Great Britain by
T. J. International Ltd., Padstow, Cornwall

This book is printed on acid-free paper

Memory believes before knowing remembers

William Faulkner, *Light in August*

Where have you gone? The tide is over you,
The turn of midnight water's over you,
As Time is over you, and mystery,
And memory, the flood that does not flow.

Kenneth Slessor, 'Five Bells'

1

Circular Quay: she loved even the sound of it.

Before she saw the bowl of bright water, swelling like something sexual, before she saw the blue, unprecedented, and the clear sky sloping upwards, she knew from the lilted words it would be a circle like no other, key to a new world.

★ ★ ★

The train swung in a wide arc to emerge alongside sturdy buildings and there it was, the first glimpses through struts of ironwork, and those blurred partial visions were a quiet pleasure. Down the escalator, rumbling with its heavy body-cargo, through the electronic turnstile, which captured her bent ticket, then, caught in the crowd, she was carried outside.

There was confusion at first, the shock of sudden light, all the signs, all the clamour. But the vista resolved and she saw before her the row of ferry ports, each looking like a primary-colour holiday pavilion, and the boats, bobbing, their green and yellow forms toy-like, arriving, absorbing slow lines of passengers, departing. With a trampoline heart she saw the Bridge to her left: its modern shape, its optimistic uparching. Familiar from postcards and television commercials, here now, *here-now*, was the very thing itself, neat and enthralling. There were tiny flags on top and the silhouetted ant forms of people arduously climbing the steep bow. It looked stamped against the sky, as if nothing could remove it. It looked indelible. A *coathanger*, guidebooks said, but it was so much grander than this implied. The coherence of it, the embrace, the span of frozen hard-labour. Those bold pylons at the ends, the multimillions of hidden rivets.

★　★　★

Ellie gawked like a child, unironic. She remembered something from schooldays: Janus, with his two faces, is the god of bridges, since bridges look both ways and are always double. There was the limpid memory of her schoolteacher, Miss Morrison, drawing Janus on a blackboard, her inexpert, freckled hand trailing the chalk-line of two profiles. With her back to the class, there was a kind of pathos to her form. She had thickset calves and a curvature of the spine and the class

2

would have snickered in derision, had it not been for her story-telling, which made any image so much less than the words it referred to. *Roman God*: underlined. The Janus profiles not matching. A simple image on the blackboard snagged at her feelings and Ellie had loved it because it failed, because there was no mirror and no symmetry. And because the sight of Miss Morrison's firm calves always soothed and reassured her.

★　★　★

From somewhere drifted the sound of a busking didgeridoo with an electronic back-beat, *boum-boum, boum-boum; boum-boum, boum-boum*. The didgeridoo dissolved in the air, thick and newly ancient.

For tourists, Ellie thought, with no disparagement. For me. For *all* of us. *Boum-boum, boum-boum*.

In the democratic throng, in the pandemonium of the crowd, she saw sunlight on the heads of Americans and Japanese; she saw small children with ice-creams and tour groups with cameras. She heard how fine weather might liberate a kind of relaxed tinkling chatter. There was a news-stand, with tiers of papers in several languages trembling

3

in a light breeze, and people in booths here and there, selling ferry tickets behind glass. There was a human statue in pale robes, resembling something-or-other classical, and before him a flattened hat in which shone a few coins. A fringe of bystanders stood around, considering the many forms of art.

Janus, origin of *January*.

Ellie turned, like someone remembering, in the other direction. She had yet to see it fully. Past the last pier and the last ferry, there was a wharf with a line of ugly buildings, and beyond that, yes, an unimpeded view.

* * *

It was moon-white and seemed to hold within it a great, serious stillness. The fan of its chambers leant together, inclining to the water. An unfolding thing, shutters, a sequence of sorts. Ellie marvelled that it had ever been created at all, so singular a building, so potentially faddish, or odd. And that shape of supplication, like a body bending into the abstraction of a low bow or a theological gesture. Ellie could imagine music in there, but not people, somehow. It looked poised in a kind of alertness to acoustical meanings, concentrating on sound waves, opened to circuit and flow.

Yes, there it was. Leaning into the pure morning sky.

Ellie raised her camera and clicked. *Most photographed building in Sydney*. In the viewfinder it was flattened to an assemblage of planes and curves: perfect Futurism. Marinetti might have dreamt it.

★ ★ ★

Unmediated joy was nowadays unfashionable. Not to mention the banal thrill of a famous city icon. But Ellie's heart opened like that form unfolding into the blue; she was filled with corny delight and ordinary elation. Behind her, raddled train-noise reverberated up high, and the didgeridoo, now barely audible, continued its low soft moaning. A child sounded a squeal. A ferry churned away. From another came the clang of a falling gang-plank and the sound of passengers disembarking. Somewhere behind her the Rolling Stones — 'Jumping Jack Flash' — sounded in a tinny ring-tone. *Boum-boum*, distant now, *boum-boum, boum-boum*, and above it all a melody of voices, which seemed to arise from the water.

Ellie felt herself at the intersection of so many currents of information. Why not be joyful, against all the odds? Why not be child-like? She took a swig from her plastic water-bottle and jauntily raised it: *cheers*.

She began to stride. With her cotton sunhat, and her small backpack, and this unexpected quiver in her chest, Ellie walked out into the livelong Sydney day. Sunshine swept around her. The harbour almost glittered. She lifted her face to the sky and smiled to herself. She felt as if — yes, yes — she was breathing in light.

★　★　★

James DeMello was obstinately unjoyful. Even before the rattling train pulled into the station, he knew in his bones that he would be disappointed. He glanced at the leather hands of the old woman sitting beside him and felt the downward tug of time, of all that marks and corrodes. They resembled his mother's hands, the sign of a history he did not want. So much of the past returns, he thought, lodged in the bodies of others.

James rose from his seat to escape the hands and stood clutching a cold metal pole. The train swung in a wide arc around sturdy buildings and through his limbs he felt the machine braking and the stiffening of bodies encased in steel. When the carriage doors opened he followed the man in front of him, moving towards the down escalator with his hands in his pockets.

At the foot of the escalator everyone swung out onto the quay, a mobile mass, subservient to architecture. Before him were ferry ticket-boxes hung with LED light timetables in orange and people of assorted nations, queuing for a ride. There was a tawdry quality, he decided, and too little repose. A child squealed and he felt an elemental flinch of annoyance; the rest was cacophony and the vague threat of crowds.

Turning to the right, James walked automatically, trailing behind others. There were shop-fronts decorated with arty souvenirs, there were little white tables with empty wine-glasses, there were waiters clad in black aprons and haughty dispositions. It was too early for lunchtime and they were in merely indolent preparation. A man stood with his arms crossed, scowling, emphatically doing nothing. James thought of Sydney as inhabited by a tribe of waiters, a secret society of men and women united by their contempt for those they served, and with rituals of smug superiority and arcane rules. They met mostly on Mondays, when many restaurants were closed, and engaged in ceremonial meals at which they spilled food and swore.

Umbrellas bearing coffee-logos fluttered in the breeze. James skirted one, then another, wondering if he needed caffeine.

Then he saw it looming in the middle distance, too pre-empted to be singular. It appeared on T-shirts, on towels, even trapped in plastic domes of snow; it could never exist other than as a replication, claiming the prestige of an icon. Its maws opened to the sky in a perpetual devouring.

White teeth, James thought. Almost like teeth. And although he had seen the image of this building countless times before, it was only in its presence, *here-now*, that the analogy occurred to him. The monumental is never precisely what we expect.

At an Easter Show, long ago, he had seen the yawning jaw of a shark, the great oval of an inadmissible, unspeakable threat. Death was like that, he knew, shaped in ivory triangles. Death was the limp panic of imagining oneself as raw meat. Or even less than that; just a shape to be ravaged, just a drifting, edible nothing in blood-blurry water.

At the entrance to the carnival tent, a sign read 'Monsters of the Deep' and an old codger with filthy stubble and an aspect of decay ushered him in by lightly touching the back of his head. He can still see the moment, those teeth gleaming in the brown light, bleak and distressing. He can still smell it: the reek of stale tobacco and unwashed clothes, and an acidic stench, as though someone had pissed in a corner. When the tent flap fell closed with a soft *pffth*, sealing him in, James felt sure he would die there, swallowed into darkness as in the belly of a beast. Superstitious and afraid, he had placed his feet in a slender triangle of sunlight falling through the entrance. He glanced from his shoes to the teeth and back again; shoes to teeth, teeth to shoes. He could not look at the shark-jaw entirely, nor could he resist looking. He was a child terrified by what his imagination might suggest.

The stinking man moved up behind him and James felt a hand on his back. He froze there, submissive, and looked only at his shoes, aligned with tied laces in the slash of lemon light. And then, twisting free, James turned and fled. He pushed at the flap of the tent, panicking, and fell forward onto his face.

Why, he wondered now, does time shudder in this way, and return him always to this inadequate boy that he was, in short pants, and afraid, and seeing white teeth in a jagged vision? The experience of a few minutes, years ago, and no doubt an exaggeration.

James turned, pissed off by this ridiculous

memory-siege. No, no, no. Coldplay's 'Clocks' swam into his head: *'closing walls and ticking clocks'* — it was the curse of his generation, to have a soundtrack enlisted for everything.

★ ★ ★

James turned away and walked back down the pier. He saw the Bridge, he saw the ferries, he saw the peach-coloured façade of the gallery of contemporary art; it was hung with red banners advertising something or other. His gaze was listless, remote. Considering these sites unremarkable, dull in his own livid space, James turned his back to the Harbour and retreated to a café, as if he needed to defend himself from what might entertain others. People swept around him, each with their own thoughts, each — the idea was fleeting — with their own apprehension of what might undo a single life, teeth, a touch, a brown space held in time by a gape of open canvas. But the crowd was a collective, and indistinct. They were unconnected to him. They were blithely autonomous. The *masses*, he liked to call them.

In the blue shadows of the café James found an empty chair with its back to the window. He was feeling slightly ill. He was feeling implausible. A waiter with a pumice complexion and a lank pony-tail took his order, professionally cool, and then slid away. One of the secret society, perhaps, a smarmy condescender. Chatter rose with the clack of cutlery and the chink of teacups, the infernal din of the coffee machine and the roar of steaming milk. Beyond that, what was it? The summer of Vivaldi's *Four Seasons* playing in a jangled slur. How he hated this: music treated as a background accessory.

When his espresso arrived with a glass of water, James swallowed a tab of Xanax, sucking down his own misery. Chemistry, he thought, to change errant chemistry. To be neurally synthetic, to be in biochemical kilter, to concoct homeostasis from this haggard sick self. He might look in a mirror and be startled by a handsome return. He might yet recover.

Every sound was amplified; the café was no retreat at all. The glass walls were percussive and strangely radiant. A rack of grimy magazines, from which smooth faces pouted, leant against the wall for the customers' lazy perusal. Everywhere around him James saw detritus — a serviette crushed into a flowery ball, ring-pulls from drink cans, a chocolate bar wrapper, its form origami, torn sugar sachets, food scraps, the bits and pieces of commercial junk people left everywhere in their wake, setting a litter trail, as in a fairytale, to be found in a mythical dark wood.

Someone had left a tiny pyramid of sugar poured on the table. James pressed it flat with his index finger and thought he might sob.

The traditions of the dead generations weigh like a nightmare on the brains of the living. A favourite quote. Karl Marx. 1852.

Even the coffee was bitter.

* * *

Pei Xing had been here many times before, but she loved the elevated train, rattling through a grid of ironwork that resembled the old Waibaidu Bridge, and the press of the crowds, and the echoing noise as people descended to the quay. Westerners, she had heard, were lonely in crowds; but this seemed so wrong, somehow, since there was a vitality, a *chi*, moving between every body, a collective spirit, a complication. Jostling, touching, feeling the population in movement, this was a beautiful thing. No one saw her, she knew; just a nondescript grey-haired woman, and an Asian at that.

Can't tell us apart. All Ching-Chong-Chinaman.

Her parents would not have understood this: living in Australia, finding a home here.

Pei Xing turned with those around her and descended on the escalator. Before her stood a young man guiding his small daughter. He held her hand high as he nudged her forward. 'Careful now, sweetheart.' The child placed her feet gingerly on the moving stairs, watching them all the way down, as if afraid she might slip. She was pretty, her hair divided in plaits in Chinese-style, her face aglow and tremulous with anticipation and excitement. Pei Xing thought she might be from the country, seeing all this for the very first time. There was something tentative in her movements, and something wholly innocent.

Pure heart of the peasant.

It might have been the ripple of a dragon moving thus, these figures sliding on the escalator, and the way they all turned as one body, sinuous and flicking slightly, through the tunnel of glare towards the water.

★ ★ ★

At quay level Pei Xing bought an ice-cream from her friend Aristos. They had known each other a long time and one of her pleasures in returning to the quay was to exchange a few

13

sentences with the old man behind the counter. He had come to Sydney when she had, some time in the late 1980s.

'Hey, China flower!'

'Hey, old fisherman!'

'Still too skinny, China flower.'

'Still too fat!'

The old fisherman laughed. It was a ritual they shared, an idiom of solidarity.

Aristos scooped her favourite flavour — hazelnut — and pressed it with the back of his spoon into a messy double ball. As usual he refused payment, but detained her for a chat. His back was bad again, he said, and the arthritis was playing up. Voula was still nagging for a trip home he could not afford. Eleni was expecting their first grandchild, God be praised. And Dimitris, good-for-nothing boy, still drank too much.

In return Pei Xing said Jimmy was still doing well in his business, a good boy, he tried hard. He was a loyal son. His girlfriend from Hong Kong, Cindy, was a lovely young woman.

When Pei Xing reached up over the counter, she saw the future. Aristos looked vulnerable. Death was swooping towards him. She saw it in an instant: grey wings, a feathery presence, hung over his tired, flushed face. She saw his eyes softly close, as if in slow motion, and a sinking of the supple animate face into a hard fixed mask. She heard a breath exhaled, the tiny wind that separates this life from the next. And in this half-second she saw too how he had laboured and suffered, and how he now entered his intractable dying.

There are things one knows but can never say. There are intuitions that rise up, irrefutably, and one can only bow one's head to Fate and stay sensibly silent. Flesh was always melting away, time was always churning in undertow. The history of peoples, and the slow dragging-under. For all this, the ice-cream, the crowd, the luxurious sunny day, no soul was exempt, Pei Xing knew, from sudden extinguishment. Aristos paused and closed his mouth, as if he had read her thoughts. He smiled, but was sorrowful. 'Ay! What can you do?' he said, shrugging his shoulders with extravagant melancholy, waving his spoon, looking to the heavens, signalling his interrogation of all that lay before him, the ice-cream, the crowd, the luxurious sunny day.

★ ★ ★

Pei Xing looked into the multicoloured tubs arrayed in rows before her. They had

15

beautiful labels: *nocciola, limone, bacio, fragola*.

'You feed people,' she said softly. 'This is good. To feed people.'

It was the only benediction she could summon, this small tribute to his trade. She wanted simply to impart compassion, and to tell him that she knew. His lined face crumpled. His eyes became moist. He knew too, she realised. Ah, he knew too.

Pei Xing said goodbye, perhaps for the last time, and moved away slowly, trying not to consolidate her vision or to grieve in anticipation. Aristos waved, looking like a Greek Orthodox priest. His open palm lifted to the sky and hung for a few seconds in the air. He might have been a saint in an icon, already long gone.

It was Pei Xing's lot to know things in advance, her particular burden. Even as a child she had known things, had seen death arrive early, had read what is yet to come written in the lines of a face. She turned, as one does when one glimpses the future. The body is intelligent in this way, instinctively facing and refuting. She moved from the two teenagers who had now claimed Aristos's attention. There was another old friend, Mary, whom she had wished to seek out. Mary slept with her belongings tucked in a

16

corner under the railway arch, only partially hidden from the visitors to the quay. Her plastic bags were visible, but she was away somewhere, bedraggled and roaming, searching for a drink. The plastic pile looked flimsy, as though it could be dislodged with a sneeze. Pei Xing leant into the waste space that was Mary's home, flinching a little at some rotten decomposition smell, and tucked a ten-dollar note where she was sure that her friend would find it. Then she stood still for a minute, looking again at the plastic bags, the sorry heap of a life, feeling a swelling of sadness for the inverted order of things, for Mary, now lost, her whole life a craving, for Aristos, who would die and be no longer by the water, for his wife Voula, who would weep, and never again see her homeland.

★   ★   ★

Pei Xing waited in the queue and bought a ticket for the ferry. The man in the booth did not recognise her, though she had been his customer many times. She was glad it was one of the old ferries, green and yellow and wooden, like something she might have seen as a girl on the Huangpu River; the newer white ones, sleek and gleaming, were simply not the same. *Supply*, the ferry was called.

17

Finding a seat towards the back, Pei Xing settled in and finished her ice-cream. The boat strained and creaked around her, rocking gently, then lurched away with a throbbing pulse she now and then thought of as human. People settled, talked on mobile phones, sent text messages that reduced the world and its vast feelings to a few shiny codes. All those swift, fidget fingers tapping into enigmatic circuits. All those microprocessed signs and electronic hallos. The man who claimed the seat beside her opened a book-sized laptop. It sounded a pleasant chime, G major, and lit up like a personal lamp.

I am old, she thought, and turned her face to look through the window. Yes, I am old.

There it was, jade-white, lifting above the water. She never tired of seeing this form. It was a fixture she relied on. The shapes rested, like porcelain bowls, stacked one upon the other, fragile, tipped, in an unexpected harmony.

'*He*': *harmony*.

She saw the Chinese character, wheat and a mouth; she saw the flourish of eight strokes of the wolf-hair brush. She felt her father's hand on her back correcting her posture, as he taught her calligraphy. Sometimes he corrected the angle of her chin, with the

18

slightest of touches, with just the tip of one finger, then watched as she dipped, caught the ink, and tried a difficult character.

The monument glided past. Pei Xing experienced the illusion that it was moving and that she was staying still. She looked back to see it floating away, diminishing, becoming an ornament, small enough to hold in the well of her hand. Someone leaning against the railing outside moved to block her view.

Mary, where was Mary? Ah, poor soul. And Aristos, poor Aristos.

Pei Xing felt the tremor of the ferry and heard the murmurous hum of its engine. She closed her eyes. She saw herself as others might: miniature, a Chinese woman with an inscrutable air. A kind of type, or an absence. Then she saw herself from the inside: those layers of self slowly, gently, time-travelling across the water, the child receiving a white thin-lipped teacup from the hands of her mother, the student in plaits taught to sit still with her hands in her lap, the lover opening arched spaces to the engulfment of a man's body, the mother bent, cloudy with joy, over her infant son's head. In the wilderness of leaving Shanghai, these selves had blended and folded; now, in meditation, she was able to fan them apart. This was her habit, these days, to see herself in this way, the concertina of a life in which she saw her own folds and crevices. *I have lived many lives.* There was something reassuring in this, not to be single but many, not to be of one language but several, not to have but one discrete past but a skein, and multiple.

★   ★   ★

She must have dozed a little. When she woke, blinking, the ferry was at the north shore and the passengers were standing and ready to leave. There was a ruffle of bodies departing, voices lifting with their destination, handbags slung, or opened, or reached into for a mobile phone. Mozart sounded somewhere — or was she imagining it? — a trail of Cherubino's aria floating in the air. Outside was luminous. High trees moved in a breeze from the water. There were rich people's houses, and the concave sweep of a steep slope garlanded with creepers and flowers.

The ferry bumped the small jetty of a paradise everyone took for granted.

★   ★   ★

When Catherine stepped from the train, she dropped her ticket. *Fuck*; she needed it to exit.

20

It fluttered under someone's running shoes in the transitional light of the station. But then the ticket rested and she lunged for it, and rose up holding it aloft like a botanical specimen, the papery petal of a rare orchid, found only in railway stations.

On a wet black bough.

She descended on the escalator and moved as one body with the crowd.

'Careful now, sweetheart,' she heard a voice say to a child, and she was filled with poetic impulse and a disposition to tenderness. The child was a girl with sparkly pink clips in her divided hair. Her father held her hand above her head as he guided her forward and down. Catherine watched her swaying dress and her bare legs and the straps of her sandals. Some scrap of memory had been stirred that she could not quite capture.

On ground level — quay level — Catherine looked for it immediately. She asked an Arab-looking man at a newspaper stand; he smiled kindly and stretched his chubby arm to the right. That way, he indicated, without saying a word.

Catherine walked past serried ferry ports and cafés and the casual, milling crowds. There were lines for tickets on cute, old-fashioned ferries, painted uniformly in emerald and gold, and people just wandering, or standing, or having their photographs taken. There was a human statue, stiffly inhuman, posing as a Roman god.

And beyond the farthest, and down a curving wharf, there it was, nestling before her, its folded forms stretching upwards, its petal life extending. The peaked shapes might have derived from a bowl of white roses, from the moment when they're tired and leaning, just about to subside. *Blown*, that strange term, *a bowl of blown roses*. She had not expected intimations of wind and flowers from something so essentially hard and bright. She had not expected to be reminded, obscurely, of her own body.

'Gis a kiss!'

Catherine heard a Scottish accent, a trace of tipsy hilarity.

And then: 'Up shit creek, that car; bloody cactus, that's what, done for, I reckon mate, trade it or what? yeah? what-do-ya-reckon? eh? what-do-ya-say?' Spoken in an overloud voice to a mobile phone.

Catherine loved Australian accents, the way they rasped in the air. The conversation unrolled in a friendly snarl. There was French, too — she recognised the syllables she had first heard as a schoolgirl in Dublin — and fragments, what was it? — of sing-songy Mandarin. Catherine saw a young man lunge for his girlfriend. He took her by the waist, swung her around, and kissed her dramatically, with a succulent smack. He was the Scot, another visitor, like herself. He wore a NYC cap on his head and had the indiscreet, restive confidence of someone newly in love.

And that was when she thought of it: *beauty like a kiss*.

On a day such as this, a bright January day with light pouring from the heavens, when the blown quality was not disintegration but a token of completion, when other lives seemed everywhere to open and effloresce, it was easy to believe there was an eroticism in the address of something beautiful. This was it, arousal, the pause of a new pleasure, the comfort of a sudden connection, intimate and unanticipated. In a kind of instinct of humility she bent her head, then raised it again, and saw the petals anew.

★   ★   ★

Catherine found herself thinking of the lover she had left. She thought of Luc's mouth, its fleshy appeal, and the ragged scar on his upper lip, the mark left by playing with a corkscrew as a child. It was a sign by which she knew him, the groove that was his wound.

When they made love her tongue sought it, with a pre-emptive kiss. She thought now of her lips swooping his chest, tasting his skin. She thought of her hands clasping his cool buttocks on a warm humid night; how lovely, in general, men's buttocks were, always unspoiled when other parts began to sag and discolour. She liked to watch him sleeping, face down, the way he hooked an arm under his body, the sweet and somnolent compression of his face. Even his snore had appealed, resonating in the depth of his sleep, making the sheets quiver, making him serious, somehow, older and more vulnerable. Catherine felt lusty here in public, standing at a distance from the monument. Beneath her sight-seeing was this mayhem of remembered touch.

And there was something else. As Catherine paused, she saw, to the left, the Bridge across the water, and the harbour, and a small ferry, chugging away to the north. Bridge, water, harbour, ferry: all were ablaze, all illuminate. This part of the world collected light as if funnelled double-strength from the sun. Perhaps some refractive quality of the water, or those shining petals, perhaps the geography of sheltered spaces or the winking skyscrapers on the far shore, perhaps these together contributed to an increased incandescence.

Catherine fumbled in her bag for her sunglasses, thinking of Luc's pale shoulder, glimpsed from behind. She felt the brush, ghostlike, of an unshaven kiss. Elvis Costello's 'I Want You' trailed mournfully through her head.

How did Australians cope with all this light?

★　★　★

As Catherine sought a patch of shade and put on her sunglasses, she felt a fleeting nostalgia for dull sky and objects fogged over. Her mother's sad face flickered into remembrance, framed by a cheap nylon scarf and squinting in sea-spray. It must have been Sandymount, and the sea like liquid ash. It must have been just after. A week, no more. Midwinter. Mourning winter. Chrysanthemums, not roses.

It was like a still from a fifties' black and white movie — the woman's face turned just so, panning to the light-sliced ocean, the tone Irish, miserable, and a strained soundtrack, a Bach cello. This scene may have been fiction, but it was already ineradicable.

And now she looked across the wide, encircling stretch of the harbour, the enormous glaze of sun-fire and surface-dazzle stretching into the distance, and wondered what she was doing here, in Sydney, in Australia. Restlessness had caused her to move across the planet. The job offer was a year-long placement, but it was enough; she had felt the need to flee London. She could not have stayed there, with Luc, becoming heartless in the mire of her grief. She hoped he would forgive her, and join her, and understand why she had fled. The calm of their lives had been destroyed by her obdurate mourning. It had deformed their conversations, interrupted their contentment, filled to the brim all the spaces between them. It was eleven months now, and still she could not free herself.

* * *

Catherine noticed the tiny human shapes of climbers moving in a line upon the Bridge. They were cartoon-like in their simplicity and vaguely nonsensical in their endeavour.

How small we might appear. Going nowhere, just up and down again.

Flags waved at the summit of the bow, like a mountain conquered. There was not a single cloud. The sky was a high dome.

I beheld the Bridge.

Beheld. Where did that come from? Since

the death there had been incursions of stray vocabularies, as though current language was worn and deficient. *Hearken*. That was another. *Hearken*. It suggested gold-leafed manuscripts, lovely decrepitude, and paper so brittle it must be held behind glass.

Catherine turned away, almost tearful, from a jumble of associations she could neither disentangle nor inspect. How confused this place had made her, this Circular Quay, turning on the curve of lost time and unbidden recurrences.

Catherine glimpsed the Scottish lovers retreating along the wharf. They were almost skipping. His arm rested around her shoulder and hers slid along his waist. The utter fit of their bodies was a beautiful thing to behold.

2

It was a kind of tropical summer, cool in the dawning, steaming up as the sun rose, raining in late afternoon or at night. Ellie had not expected Sydney to carry such moistness, such skin scent and sensuality.

That morning she pushed open the sash window, lifting against the resistance of weathered wood and time, feeling grateful to have found an old apartment so close to the city centre. It had the semi-dark, compartmentalised feel of Deco buildings — all deep red brick and shadowed nooks, cosy, European, reproducing a foreign shade remembered slant-wise from elsewhere. But the apartment suited well; it fitted the austerity and quiet inwardness of her bookish life. It was not a slab of a high rise, glassy and tough, such as bordered the freeways that curved down to the city and the harbour. Instead there were Moreton Bay figs, jacaranda and eucalypts with shedding bark; there was birdsong — currawongs and honey-eaters — sounding above the buildings, and a scale of life beyond traffic-roar and the pitch of distraction wrought by cities. From here, in the bathroom, from the small window above the basin, Ellie could see the rooftops of her suburb, the TV dishes and antennas. She could see the renovated additions, the solar accessories and the rusted corrugation on the poorer houses. The whole vista of mortgages, families, graffiti in laneways, the desire for a second car, a bigger life, and the meaning of it all. Just visible was the spire of an abandoned church. It pointed to the sky like the aerial to a lost wireless code.

Ellie would discover today that she will never escape James. He was pressed into her life as they pressed together as fourteen-year-old lovers. Into her memory. Now and for evermore.

Ellie would recall, with sharp clarity, as if she had prised a fading photograph from a powdery album, dear Miss Morrison, her seventh grade teacher. Although she had not thought of her for years, she will carry her all day, close as a new baby.

Ellie will be troubled by the newspapers — the war going on in Iraq, the cruel atrocities, the violence that had persisted beyond any war-monger or peacenik reckoning. For all this, her anticipation of James, her childhood recall, the disturbing continuity of tales about war, Ellie was predisposed, this Saturday morning, to joy. She woke each day to the world, not expecting catastrophe. She woke in blue light, to a damp clear morning, and before the sun was a lit fuse in the gap between the curtains she had already found five objects of interest to consider and contemplate.

★　★　★

After rain during the night everything was bright and cleansed. There were still isolated pools of water, holding the sky in a sharp shine, and a fresh beaded gloss to the trees and the creepers. From next door a frangipani tree, an old twisted monster, sent fragrance into her rooms as a local blessing.

Ellie had gone out early to buy the newspapers and found herself skipping over puddles and hurrying beneath dripping leaves. At each step she scuffed a fallen blossom. Frangipani stars lay everywhere, and sprinklings of jasmine; the browning petals of crêpe myrtle had washed across the road and filled up the gutters. It was the world in a benign organic dissolution. Ellie collected a few of the frangipani blooms to place in a bowl on her table, holding them gently against her chest as she walked, her papers tucked in an awkward roll beneath her arm. Such a simple garnering. Such a fine clear sky. She was empty-headed and happy. She felt the frisky vague euphoria of a new day in a new city.

In the bathroom Ellie applied kohl to her eyes and pink to her lips. She would be meeting James later on, after all these years, and was self-conscious in anticipation of the severity of his judgement. Her enhanced lips looked tarty and over-emphatic, but suitable for a harbourside lunch and the exhibitionism of Sydney cafés. She would go to Circular Quay early, since she'd not yet seen it, and wander about, *lollygagging*, as her father would say, so that she could look out when James came, and watch him unobserved. She would *lollygag, people-watch*, wander the city, finding the pleasure of eddying crowds and the wayward motions of human traffic, their tidal sweeps at traffic lights, their rhythmic currents of locomotion, doing nothing-in-particular until it was time for their meeting. Six weeks. She had been living in Sydney for six weeks and had not yet seen the Quay. The business of finding her apartment, the settling in; now James's email had given her permission to take a day to sightsee.

Ellie made herself coffee and spread the Saturday papers on the table. There were the usual horrors. The war in Iraq, bombings in Afghanistan, the rapacity of large powers and the subordination of the small. There was a photograph on the front page of a distraught woman in a headscarf, bending in torn, rigorous grief over the body of her son. It was generic and familiar. She was a no-name mother who had lost a no-name son, the convenient portrait of another attack, and selected because the contortion of her face, and her anguish, and the plea of her uplifting hands, told in dumbshow what exceeded the journalist's skill.

Death's enormous sickle.

History would record this time as one of relentless repetition. How many images of grief might the reader of any newspaper see? How many scenes of blasted terrain, or medics rushing headlong with a stretcher on which lay a figure beneath a sheet, too small, too anonymous, and too deathly still? How long would they *mean?* Ellie thought of the Japanese photographer, Hiroshi Sugimoto, who photographed movies inside the cinema. He left the shutter of the camera open in the dark auditorium and the film exposed for the entire length of the screening. The result was not a wildly complicated superimposition of images, but simple white-out, pure light, a flare of nothing. Too many images, layered together, left only a blank. She imagined Hiroshi Sugimoto gazing at his photographs

32

in a gallery, marvelling at the mystery of what excess might delete.

★　★　★

From somewhere in the streets beyond a siren sounded. Then another, following, in a high panicked drone. Ellie wished to protect herself from what might overwhelm her mood. She read only the first two paragraphs on Iraq, then sought the national news. The stories were still of the change of government and the 'honeymoon period' of inauguration (how strange, she thought, this sexual connotation). But there was optimism about, and the sense of a new beginning. The youngish Prime Minister, his moon-face beaming, looked pleased with himself, like a school prefect dressed in his blazer, receiving a prize. Ellie was always struck by how many male politicians retained a little-boy visage. Or managed to look poignantly dazzled at their own *ex cathedra* announcements, insisting to the TV spotlights on the innocence of a feckless decision. The microphones looked like listening insects, leaning to suck up the nectar of scandal. Now the government had changed. One might yet be permitted to expect reform; and one might yet be disappointed.

Ellie extracted the book review supplement of the newspapers. These she would save for later, for a casual perusal of the wordy dimensions of the world, the unremitting, mock-heroic, making-of-sense. She had no money these days to buy new books, but for now there were libraries, which she cherished, and these compact descriptions of other worlds.

★   ★   ★

One of the workers in her local library looked like Miss Morrison. Why had she not made the connection before? And both, in weird likeness, resembled the Queen of England, that abnormally stiff face, that taut string of a mealy mouth. Miss Morrison would draw on the blackboard and write fancy words, underlining them with an oversized oak ruler that clacked as it struck. When Ellie recalled her now it was often in a static rearview, the woman of indeterminate age communing with her own messages, turned away, serious-minded, her back to the class. In their small country-town school, with James sitting beside her, the children were tempted by an impulse to mock, but somehow constrained and respectful. Away from school, however, James could be cruel. He was the child

— there is always one — able to parody others. For the guilty enjoyment of his classmates he mimicked Miss Morrison's hunched-over posture, he copied her rather high-pitched voice, he pretended to underline words on an invisible blackboard, turning back to face his classmates with a grimacing smirk.

★ ★ ★

Ellie folded the newspapers and drank the last of her coffee. Frangipani scent hung lightly in the room. Another sundrenched day, the kind that might sell a city. The kind that might signify package-holiday amusements, with volley-ball on a beach, frolicsome children and the shadows of palms quivering over impossibly bright water. Still, Sydney surprised her. Would it always visit her in this way? Would Circular Quay match up to its own publicity? Ellie touched her coloured lips, wondered about her hair, then was annoyed at these traces of vanity she had tried to eliminate.

★ ★ ★

As she rose with her cup to the sink Ellie recalled James and Miss Morrison figured intimately together. James had developed a nosebleed in class and Miss Morrison was tilting his head back, her left hand placed on his forehead, her right holding a cloth, soaked red, clenched securely beneath his nose. It was a sort of tableau: the teacher solicitous, commanding, taking control of the child's body; the boy morosely compliant, embarrassed by his bloody nose and the spectacle of his submission. Miss Morrison had clamped him down, held him there, and his classmates looked on with malicious fascination. Ellie had wanted to say something, or be a nurse, or put her own hands to his face, clammy and loving, but instead she sat in her place watching with the others, silently commiserating.

James often developed nosebleeds. It was one of those afflictions that undermine the gifted, seeming to make them like everyone else, vulnerable and common. James took to carrying a wad of handkerchiefs and would disappear from class at the very first spot of blood. Ellie had felt a kind of frightened pity; the boy otherwise a class star, an intellectual champion, streaming with blood in some dank, hidden corner of the school, his head upturned, his throat draining with fluid, his mouth tasting the trace of something sour and internal like death. Each time James returned to the classroom he would not meet anyone's gaze, but resumed his smart-arsed, cocky manner, showing off his learning and wittily denouncing his peers. Miss Morrison found him irritating — Ellie could tell — but retained the distant affection clever children inspire. Once there was a vulgar fleck of blood-spatter across James's chequered shirt; no amount of bravado erased it, or reinstated his power.

And now here was Miss Morrison, cradling him, holding his head like a mother. James had the drowsy, abandoned look of a child feeling faint or swooning, without will, falling inward, becoming limp and yielding like a plant. It was a vision that bound them like a fresco, varnished and cracked with age, shining its meaning through time as from beneath the archway of an Italian church. Ellie resisted the word *pietà*, but it hung around nevertheless, dignifying what was, after all, a very ordinary distress.

Miss Morrison looked beautiful then, in the way tenderness is beautiful, a kind of indication of the soft collapse into which one might be held. Ellie was surprised to consider her teacher in this way, but found that her childhood was full, in retrospect, of exactly this tenderness, which she missed, and wanted to recall, and had found in the sleepy roll into someone's arms that precedes a slumberous, post-coital confidence. Her former lover was a gentle man and she dreamt of him still, wanted him still. There was no conclusion in the matter. There was no cessation of desire. True feeling does not conclude; this much she knew.

★　★　★

James had tracked Ellie down through a mutual friend, who wrote a small lifestyle column for the daily newspaper. Ellie had not seen him since they were fifteen or so and was curious as to why, out of the blue, James now wanted to meet.

He had been a handsome boy, and tall — another high-school predictor of success — but she had also known the James who had lived half a block away, the single child of an abandoned mother. He was the boy who rode his bicycle alone and seemed to have few friends. She remembers him pedalling up and down the street in the grainy lavender dusk, doing wheelies, raising dirt, disappearing as nightfall grew. The shape of a boy. A lonely figure. Even then she saw a muted torment in his repetitious route, and in the meaningless display of skids over gravel.

Sometimes she would hear his mother's

voice calling for James; she was bidding him to his dinner, wanting his company, calling in Italian for her son to return to her side. There were times when the calling went on and on. Ellie knew where James hid when he wished not to be discovered, but would never have told; it was part of their pact. In the small space between schoolday's end and dinner, in which children might recover themselves, might find somewhere beyond the confinement of a desk and mean regulation, James would have returned to their hideout, *our hideout*, so that when he was not riding the street he was private and self-possessed.

Adults underestimate the degree of solitude required to counter school-life. Whole populations of schoolchildren crave to be left alone. Everywhere. Millions of them. Just to be left alone. So that they can find in sulky noise or quiet the refuge they have lost.

★　★　★

Between mockery and mastery, James made his way, and when at the end of tenth grade he won a scholarship to a boy's school in the city, no one was surprised to see him leave. His mother was proud and heartbroken. Ellie saw her living a contracted life, lingering near the letterbox in her dressing gown at the end of the day. She'd not bothered to dress, nor to separate daytime from nighttime. Her face looked worn to a frazzle and her manner was infirm; her matted hair flew up around her sad, rather doll-like face. She developed a gesture of tying and untying the cord of her dressing gown so that her hands were a flurry of agitation and could not stay still. She spoke to herself in Italian, further marking her foreign state, announcing to everyone that she had returned to the country of her birth and was immured there, alone, tethered elsewhere by words. People gossiped, or despised her, or took pity in mostly blunt and unhelpful ways, taking her hands so that she burst into tears from a human touch, leaving food on the verandah that she refused to eat. The Country Women's Association tried to organise her into shopping excursions and social activities. Eventually Welfare had to be told: the woman, Ellie heard, was *a danger to herself*.

★   ★   ★

One day James's mother was no longer there. Ellie waited, and watched, but she did not return. She stared at the letterbox, as Mrs DeMello had stared, feeling a secret collusion.

'Loony bin', neighbours said. 'She was

chucked in the loony bin.'

And Ellie imagined a mute, desperate place, full of people bereft in the ways in which Mrs DeMello was bereft, their faces lined nervously at barred windows, their eyes sick with betrayal.

Ellie wished she had answered when Mrs DeMello had called for her son in the dusk. She knew by then what it might mean to have a call unanswered and to feel one's voice not ringing as it should. And to have been part of this woman's unhappiness, knowing that James had also left her, had been affrighted by what he had disclosed and the intimacy they had developed.

Although Ellie missed James, she could tell no one about it. There was no summary of the overlap of two young lives, or of what they did, or where they hid. After he left for the posh school James had never written, or been in touch. He was simply gone. Nor did he answer letters or revisit their town. Only when he won a university scholarship did they learn the dimensions of his success and the public achievements of his shining life. Ellie's parents read the article from the local paper on the phone, but by then Ellie was also living in the city, at another university, and leading another kind of life. She resisted, as much as possible, the effort of imagining him elsewhere.

★ ★ ★

In her apartment Ellie looked up from the table. A tall tree outside the window had produced an illusion of swinging light upon the wall. She'd not noticed it before, how for a brief time each day the shadows at a certain angle might project a light-show effect. Most days she had been working, whether studying in a library, or serving as a waitress in Gallo's café on King Street, and this fleeting holiday vision gave her pause.

Outside was seamless sunshine, promising a hot day; in here, swamped by memory, her rooms existed in another light, as if the power of remembering itself had altered the physics of her surroundings. This idea charmed her. This counter-time of James's return that splashed light in its own theatre.

Ellie sat looking at the watery radiance of moving shapes. It occurred to her then, irrelevantly, how bloody James was, how in recollection he was often not a school star, the clever kid, the 'genius', they once had called him, but one of the walking wounded. And another return: James flustered, his head lowered, his eyes downcast. James covering his ears with his hands as he read, as if holding his head together. James not meeting her gaze. James closing himself in.

★ ★ ★

James slept badly in the room at the hostel. The bed was lumpy with the thousands of other bodies that had preceded him, their exertions, their tossing and turning, their own dragnets of haunted dreams, and the room was full of exhausted air and the trace of furtive cigarettes. The small window was stuck open, but the atmosphere was still and stale.

When, in late darkness, he finally slept, something disturbed his self-enclosure that turned out to be rain, sliding into the room with gentle insistence and a light tapping sound, as if infant fingers were drumming or prying open his sleep. Rising half-blind in the half-light he had fumbled at the window, but he could not dislodge the frame and found himself leaning his face there, in a kind of dizzy spell, neither asleep nor awake, peering down into the black, rainy canyon of George Street. It must have been, he guessed, about 3 a.m. Up the street, just beyond sight, was the sandstone town hall, its façade beer-coloured in a strip of spotlights, and beyond that the shopping block that looked like a nineteenth-century exhibition hall and had a dumpy statue of Queen Victoria squatting at its entrance. On his side of the road, less salubrious, was a line of small stores that marked the beginnings of Chinatown — cafés for noodles and yum cha, Vietnamese bakeries, pawn shops, pubs, more backpacker hostels.

A bus rumbled along the street with the stray vehicles of a Friday night, but the pedestrians had thinned out, fleeing the rain. There were a few desperate hookers smoking beneath umbrellas and a single druggie, trying to score. One of the women wore heels so high she looked as if she was constantly toppling, correcting her balance, then set to topple once again. This display was contrived to make you want to catch her, James thought, to stand Jesus-like, arms open, as she sexually subsided. That sense of drama-tised risk and the anonymity of her body. Oneself a saviour. A car appeared from nowhere and slowed as it approached. James watched the woman leave the shelter of her friend's umbrella and lean into the car window. There was something about how she leant — from the waist, like a doll — that called forth his pity.

James felt the rain on his face. It was cool

and light. He sensed a camaraderie with others awake at this time, the desperadoes of the city and its working drivers. The stragglers, lost and wandering. The sleepless. The deprived. Country guys like him, maybe, who found all this city shit too much and way too overwhelming. When an ambulance sped past, its siren moaning, James thought it emblematic of big city life: there was always an accident or crisis, there was always somebody bleeding or spilling their guts.

He kept telling himself he had come to Sydney to speak to Ellie, to save something of his past, to atone and to tell her, but there was a desolation and finality about being here, *here-now*, in this rainy, woeful darkness where he felt truly himself.

★　★　★

James must eventually have slept again because at nine he found himself waking. The name *Magritte* hung on his lips. It flared in his mind, then left. James felt groggy from too many pills and late-night vodkas, unfocused, dull. The day was already hot and the damp of the night was evaporating, and he roused himself because he had to walk down the hallway to piss. It was a queasy visit. The tiles were hospital green and the walls were grubby. He saw spiders beneath the pipes and the stains of other men's emissions and the morning light that poured though a barred window and should have cheered him up was instead the garish inspiration for an early headache. As he shaved before the mirror above the sink he avoided his own glances. How many men shave thus, not wanting to see themselves? In the lopsided tilt of his head he was hiding from what might be revealed. Loss of faith. Loss of face. Some closing down of what once he might have dreamed or become.

★   ★   ★

Back in his room James swallowed a handful of vitamins and analgesics, miming the crazy doctor on television, ceaselessly self-medicating. For a few seconds he considered returning to bed, locking himself in a winding sheet, shutting his eyes against the day, refusing the real-time of the city for a dead-beat retreat. But he rose and moved from the gloomy interior — *Ellie, Ellie* — watching his feet on the uneven stairs.

The young man at the reception counter had also had a bad night and looked even more sordidly wrecked than James. He held up a palm, like a Catholic priest, in a silent greeting. Might be gay, James thought. He had the grey-skinned appearance of someone who lived in a capsule in a 1980s film, a sci-fi with drooling aliens and constant threat. Or of someone drowned, drained away, lost in watery depths. The pallor of the man's face shone sad and unholy. James nodded hello, wishing not to think of priests, or drowning, or B-grade movies, and stepped quickly onto the street, so as to avoid any small talk.

★   ★   ★

René Magritte; his favourite painter.

At fourteen Magritte had gone with his father Leopold to the banks of the river Sambre to identify the body of his mother, Adeline. She had committed suicide by drowning and he stood there, solemnly and silently holding his father's hand, a dutiful son, a reliable good boy, as they fished her slim body from the chill grey water. It was 1912. It was the end of his boyhood. Leopold had a face full of capillaries and was florid with crying; his knees failed, he released his hold, he crumpled before the corpse like a puppet articulated. But pale young René simply stood and looked. René was the strong one, emotionally composed. Cloth covered his mother's face in a wet sucking shroud.

Her dress had reversed as they pulled her from the river feet first, and yet he knew her from the brown shoes on which she had replaced a non-matching buckle and the signet ring on her middle finger that had once been his grandmother's. When they peeled back the skirt and made her decent, she was grimy with river-silt and pretending to sleep. Her cheeks were sallow, caved in, her eyes were closed, and René felt his heart heave and capsize at the sight. Her face. His mother. Death deep enough to wallow in.

It was not long after that, the soon-to-be-Surrealist began his first job, working in a wallpaper factory, designing repetitions. It was easy, to repeat. Any loose flourish would appear whole if chained in a repetition. Any single flower became many, any rough abstraction a pattern. There was a solace in blueprinted and easy decoration, the sweep of ink through a silk screen and the moist sheets carried away, the regularity of the copies and their filling up of parlours and bedrooms. He could have gone on like this forever, wallpapering the surface of things, printing the same image again and again.

Later, when Magritte was an artist in Paris reinventing his own past, someone pointed out that his most disturbing paintings were of figures blinded or covered in cloth, and he knew then — as though responding to an accusation — how he had converted her, how he had made his mother Art, how everything stored away and given art-form was reborn as another repetition.

★　★　★

James paused in the busy street, looking around, looking lost. Sydney, Saturday morning. January. George Street. Why, after all these years, was he thinking again of Magritte? Why did this recovery of Adeline seem so like his own memory?

There were shoppers speeding into department stores and broad-spectrum hubbub. The buses sounded like thunder hurtling towards the Quay. Cars glowed in the morning glare and were burning and purposeful. Aware of the tenacity of crowds intent on a summertime bargain, James saw how they moved in urgent surges and breaking waves, the hiding place they offered, the self's liquefaction, the mad sense of being sucked inside a flexible organism. He walked without direction but was not really there. He was somewhere in the Belgium he had invented as a child from a book, somewhere in silvery light, by the grim river Sambre. Being René, the strong one. Being *the dutiful son, the reliable good boy*.

★ ★ ★

Lives of Modern Artists: James's mother gave it to him for his fourteenth birthday. He had been shocked to realise that the boy René standing on the riverbank was exactly his age and that René's father, Leopold, was employed as a tailor. James's father had been a tailor in the Old Country, his mother said, before they came to Australia and he found himself labouring on building sites, steering wheelbarrows of wet cement along angled planks, shovelling, hauling, crippling his frail tailor's back. It was no surprise he had left them. He was *lost* here, his mother said. There was no work for a tailor when everyone was building houses.

James heard a tone of forgiveness in her steady voice. She met his gaze. Her face across the kitchen table was alight with this rare disclosure. She had been beautiful, he realised. His mother had been beautiful. And there was no taint of bitterness, or recrimination. She might still love him, James vaguely thought. Perhaps feelings of this kind do not conclude.

★ ★ ★

In the city of Naples beautiful Giovanna had fallen in love with handsome Matheus, the tailor. They had gone on an adventure together, floating across the ocean on the good ship *Oriana*, and found themselves in Fremantle, Western Australia, feeling stranded. They knew almost immediately that something in their marriage was wrong; but in those days couples endured, sometimes to despair. As if in resistance to migrancy, Giovanna learned almost no English and maintained a prideful and fierce isolation. Matheus joined his *paisano* for drinks and local advice. He worked hard, learnt English, took his wife to the southwest following an Italian building team. He demolished himself in physical labour. In this country in which men need not talk at all, except of workaday details over a beer or two, Matheus gradually grew silent and then he was gone. Giovanna had seen him retreating for years, becoming thin and stretched as a Giacometti sculpture. One day he stretched into nothingness and slipped over the horizon.

★　★　★

James was almost three years old when Matheus disappeared. He had a recollection only of being swung upwards onto his father's shoulders, and the terror of such height, the

51

sheer demented panic, that made him clutch to save his life at handfuls of black curly hair. There was no face, or clear memory, just this swoop upwards into the sky and the feel of large hands surrounding his body. *Matheus* was a name and a legend, the man he was told he resembled. And who had lifted him like that, the better to see the world. Only recently he had learned of Matheus's brother, Leo, living somewhere in Melbourne, with his own life and family. But it was too late for all that. It was too late for that version of Italian happy-families, arrayed with identical faces at a long sun-speckled table piled high with pasta and wine, raising glasses, as in an advertisement, to the appreciation of olive oil. A man with a moustache, a plump mama, the family commercially jolly. Above them the leaf-light of grape-vines, like a net of open hands.

★   ★   ★

Lives of Modern Artists taught James how calamitous artists' lives were — and how interesting, compared to his own. He had stored the book under his bed as if shameful knowledge was held there, but knew essentially that it was the art-life he secretly daydreamed, this promise of making meaning without needing a single word. The promise

52

of Europe and of shadowy spaces, of a life grievous but endurable, the record of which might exist in a gallery somewhere, detached and valuable, impersonal and illustrious, stylish, pure. He flicked through the pages of the book until they were worn. He knew all the artists' portraits, and self-portraits, and their most famous images. Even when he discovered he had no aptitude for drawing or painting, he still held onto this desire for an artistic life. As a teenager James developed an ambition to be hired as an extra in a movie. He knew now that this was a symbol of his accurate sense of mediocrity, that he would never exist at the centre of anything.

★　★　★

Beneath all, beneath all the sound and fury, lay the sensation of being swung into the air as a human helicopter, to rest perched there, at an absurd height, his hands deep in his father's hair. This heft and turn in space, profoundly remembered, lay at the base of all that James was and of his dangerous imbalance. Memory was not in the prefrontal cortex, or the hippocampus, or the cerebellum, or the amygdala — how he loved this vocabulary saved from his days as a medical student — but in the space into which an infant might be lifted and turned. All he retained of his father was enclosed in that curve.

Ellie too was stuck fast in movements of James's body and her own invisibly encircling presence. There had been others since, of course, the usual one-night stands, casually without meaning, and a few of them serious, possibly life-partners. But only Ellie persisted as his father did, in this deeper-level recollection, deposited like radium in the substrata of his cells.

★   ★   ★

They had been fourteen years old when they first made love. It astonished and moved him to think of it now. It was not audacity or expertise but lustful curiosity; kids, they were just kids. They flung themselves uninhibited into each other's bodies because each knew so little of what they should do. It was a collision of vague intentions and truly naive. They had laughed, played around. They had tumbled creaturely, like kittens. They had relished a kind of delinquency they knew implicitly to be occurring. And now, as he approached Ellie after all these years, James hesitated before the traces of her persistence. Even in distracted moments he was recovering memories of her body and her words.

The mystery of their pact was contained in the derelict building where they met, the fusty brick office of what once, years before, must have been an iron foundry. Their *hideout* they called it, as if they were sexual criminals. There was an upturned paint-can on which they set a candle, a few sticks of furniture strewn about, and a single exploded chair, its horse-hair stuffing gaping. This chair returned in dreams, oversized and with menace. It was the kind of anachronistic, lumpish object that theatre students might have adopted to symbolise East German deprivation. There was a panel of almost intact glass sheets through which the boss must once have surveyed the men in the workshop, but each pane had become dingy and opaque with dust. Ellie and James had resisted writing their names; both understood the need for secrecy. They laid a blanket on the floor and *hid out* together, too happy to bother with the inlaid dirt or heart-enclosed initials, too far gone in their junior hunger to be merely boyfriend and girlfriend.

★　★　★

James thought of René Magritte's painting called *The Lovers*. It was a portrait of two

55

enshrouded heads, both swathed in grey cloth. The obliteration of detail was surely all the artist could bear. Adeline, a milliner, used to sew well into the night, and her son no doubt remembered her fingers in lamplight on a curved rim of felt, or pressing the dome of a head-shape onto a faceless wooden mould. He no doubt remembered the precise arc of the needle looping into wool and the angle of her back as she leant forward, to gather more light.

There were many, many hats in Magritte's paintings. And there were huge apples in living rooms, pipes that were not pipes, trains emerging from fireplaces, reflections not where they should be, day and night coexisting. His images were of displacement and his figures were all verging on erasure. Particularity would have killed him. Realism would have killed him. The buckle. The maternal ring. The circular stain of river mud, the thumbprint of death, that lay in the shallow dip just beneath Adeline's bottom lip. It was because James understood this that he could contemplate seeing Ellie again. For all that she was an intangible sequence of gestures and moves, it was specificity he yearned for, the tiny details he had known of her, the beloved face uncovered. In his case, he knew, the details would save him. The ideas were too large. The space a drowning might make, the milky-green water closing over a face, was a tremendous, vile and unassimilable thing.

* * *

In downtown George Street a car alarm sounded. There was the rumble of a plane in the far distance, slowly descending, and James noticed, all at once, the traffic's strident roar. In the petrochemical haze he glanced upwards at the ugly mixture of geometric steel, the plate-glass of sparkling skyscrapers, the rude banners of retail. The whole of central Sydney seemed to be bearing down on him, the way slapstick buildings collapse — *phoof!* — around a smiling fool. James considered sliding into the aisle of a store or an alley. But instead, instinctively decisive, he turned and walked in the other direction.

The train, he decided. He would catch the train to Circular Quay.

* * *

In his jumpy discomposure, the short walk uphill to Central Station was easier to negotiate. Magritte fell away. The River Sambre. The drowned mother. The shadows

57

of what he had been. James was fixed upon Ellie as he recommenced his walk, heading westwards.

He saw posters in Chinese and the large diagram of a foot, its pressure points outlined in fine script with a remarkable degree of complication, then a shop selling Buddhist artefacts in which most items appeared to be red. That a store for objects of religious devotion might exist in the inner city seemed hopeful, if anomalous. Peering in he saw altars, incense, a row of cross-legged Buddhas, all made of what appeared to be crimson plastic, and various dangling embroideries, the purpose of which he assumed to be prayer, released wavering into the spiritually receptive air. James would never have entered such a store, but found himself glancing in with interest. A shop assistant looked up and smiled at him; James blushed and turned away. Further along two men's faces leered at him through the window of a pub; he found himself blushing once again. Then there was a string of cheap frock shops, all staffed by petite Asian women with swaying hair; and beyond were food stores — Thai, Chinese, Indian, Vietnamese — more than could possibly be sustained on a single street. Worlds were converging, he thought. Australia was Asian. He saw how various it all was, the zeal of many nations, the emporia of many merchants, the international energy that pulsed between languages and countries. The translations were less of words than of these perplexing combinations: shops, peoples, signs and wonders.

In another life he might have loved it. But James was disintegrating, he knew. He was becoming fissures and gaps, as if something in his body had torn. Time past was leaking in, and shame, and regret, and too much irksome reality. He continued his walk through the city, hearing her name in his mind: *Ellie, Ellie; Ellie, Ellie*. The name he sighed in his sleep. As though she was a Buddhic chant, or a compass alignment, or the talismanic code to a forgotten world. As though the sound of her name was a kind of inward music.

★　★　★

Pei Xing had woken that morning thinking of Boris Pasternak's *Doctor Zhivago*. *Yuri Andreyevich Zhivago*, the poet-doctor. Apart from her father, the first man, though unreal, she had ever loved.

Before she opened her eyes she had felt him in the bed beside her. It was as if he had flown through the window from the Russian cold to find warmth beside her body, to nestle his dark head between her small breasts. He appeared as he did in the famous film version — played by Omar Sharif — those enormous brown eyes, that air of sexual distraction. The first seconds were snowy, image-confounded and fabulously arousing; and she might have been holding his face in her hands, so sure was his incarnation.

When Pei Xing realised she was awake she found that her cheeks were moist with tears. *Doctor Zhivago* had been her father's favourite novel and his most famous and prestigious translation. Though dangerous and counter-revolutionary, a target for the Red Guards and the Mao Tse Tung Thought Propaganda Teams, he had cherished it, with tortured obstinacy, until his very last breath. He liked to quote a section from the opening about '*inward music: the irresistible power of unarmed truth, the powerful attraction of its example*'; and even now she remembered the whole paragraph, though she had once striven to forget it.

'We all possess an *inward music*,' he had told her, sounding like a teacher. 'Every person on the planet. Every single one of us.'

Inward music. What was that? she had often wondered.

Her father was prone to announcements. Every now and then he dispensed an aphoristic sentence, or felt obliged to comment, in italics, on literature or politics. What others might have derided, Pei Xing found endearing.

★ ★ ★

Her father owned a Feltrinelli first edition, in Russian, from 1957. And then one in English, Harvill, from which he wrote his translation. She had watched him work night after night at his desk, in the glow of a brass lamp, with English-Chinese and Russian-Chinese dictionaries by his side, and a Great China brand cigarette dangling from two fingers. She imagined the trade in meanings as a kind of game, in which tokens shaped like mahjong tiles were exchanged and switched. Signs moved from one world to another, clacked together, made new sequences. A man in Bolshevik Russia became virtually Chinese; a world unfolded from a paper envelope. This game existed in the borderless continent of her father's head. She could see how he concentrated: 'cher' in Russian, 'neve' in Italian, 'snow' in English, until he arrived at the sound 'xue', and then the character: the radical symbol for rain, the strokes for frozen, the little block of marks that revealed the transition from alphabets to ideograms. As he removed his glasses and rubbed the bridge of his nose, Pei Xing felt a pure, focused pang of love.

She considered her father the most intelligent man in the world. She competed with her brother for his attention, but somehow knew that her bookishness gave her a clear advantage.

'There are many words for snow,' her father announced. And he tilted his head back and chuckled, as if he had just told her a joke.

★   ★   ★

In the bonfire the Red Guards lit in their lane in 1967 *Doctor Zhivago* was aflame in the pile of books deemed ideologically treacherous. Pei Xing watched the book-burning with her parents, who were forced to kneel in mute witness. Her father's face was bruised and her mother looked absent.

The immolation of books took longer than expected. Sometimes a book would flip open page by page, each separately blackening, curling, igniting, disappearing, and still there were more pages rising softly underneath. The pyramid of paper seemed for a time to resist its own fire, so that a Guard poked at the smouldering mess and called for kerosene. When at last it flared up, with a kind of fierce luminosity, everyone was relieved that the event was at last consuming itself. And because she could not look at her parents' faces, and because she was afraid, and because history had become this incredible will to erase, Pei Xing watched the bonfire with devoted attention. It was impressively bright.

The past never left her. Her parents were always there, always kneeling, the last time she saw them alive. The pile of books was perpetually burning.

And the seductive Yuri Andreyevich Zhivago seemed almost more real to her than her own parents, since he lived on robustly in cinema and words, and since his own life story had a definite, well-described conclusion. This was something her father believed in, that fiction might eclipse life. It pained her to think of it now, how distant he had become, how vague and how replaced. Her mother was more present: the ministrations of food and comfort, the Guangdong folk-tales, the sound of her piano as she practised a Brahms piece, or a Bach. These memories greeted her more frequently, and more often in moments of happiness.

★ ★ ★

It had rained during the night but the sun was now shining. The day was fast heating up. Pei Xing rose, splashed her face, and went immediately to the kitchen to prepare her Dragon Well tea. There was some cold sticky rice left over in a bowl in the fridge; she covered it with condensed milk and slices of mango and ate her breakfast standing up, as she always did, looking as though searching into the far distance.

Beyond the window above the sink lay the broad sprawl of Bankstown and the outer western suburbs. Mighty trucks were rumbling along the freeways with homicidal speed; there were houses of dubious design, with utes on the front lawns and chunky letterboxes made of bricks; there were factories and steelworks and a huge hardware store, the size of a jumbo-jet hangar, spread over an entire block. A mattress factory and a glass factory stood absurdly side by side. *Aussie Mattresses. Down Under Glass.*

In the shopping centre beside the train station there were dozens of small businesses with signs above the doorways in Vietnamese and Arabic; these Pei Xing found particularly enchanting. She loved to look directly into the faces of people on the street: men with powerful forearms and forthright eyes, and women in hijabs and scarves walking together in friendly clusters. Their children all looked plump and smiling and for some reason reminded Pei Xing of nutmeg. Then there were Vietnamese at the fishmongers on the corner, a meeting place of sorts, and casual groups at the Pho shop, who all seemed to know each other. This version of Australia was Asian and Arab. These people moved in an aura of their own, not afraid to claim space; and among them were other populations, migrant as she, each pulled from another history and cast up at the bottom of the world. On the street Pei Xing always felt cosmopolitan. She felt she was moving among friends in a spacious new world. She thought people from the Middle East, especially, were very exotic. She tried not to stare.

★　★　★

Conspicuous beneath a sun umbrella, Pei Xing walked the streets of Bankstown to catch an early train. She looked at the signs above the stores and saw again how beautiful a script Arabic was, how different from Chinese characters, and from English translations. There were cursive waves and dots and ultra-precise dashes, like flags. There were suggestions of Mecca and arched windows and the spaces a mosque might contain. How might 'snow', she wondered, appear in an Arabic script? How might desert peoples write the word 'snow'? Would it be imagined as flying sand?

It had occurred to Pei Xing more than once that she would like to learn Arabic, so that she could speak fluently to her neighbours and chitchat with the small children who played in the stairwell of their ugly block of flats. She could address the women in headscarves and ask what they thought of this place, and where they worked, and what kind of food they ate and how it was prepared. Her son Jimmy had tried to persuade her to move to the suburb of Ashfield, to the large Chinese community in which he lived. But Pei Xing liked it here, near the western Sydney University. Here she had a little work teaching her own language, and here, one day, she might yet learn Arabic.

★   ★   ★

At the train station Mr Nguyen was settled in his glass booth. Ignoring the ticket machines that looked like the robots of an unfortunately boxy future era, Pei Xing preferred her friend, and his hasty chat.

'Mrs Chang!'

'Mr Nguyen!' She folded her umbrella.

'Hot enough for you?'

It was a rhetorical question. Pei Xing had teased him before about the battery-run miniature fan that he held to his face. It was of pastel pink plastic and shaped like a rocket ship. It blew his fringe backwards into a glossy black fin.

'You sound Australian, Mr Nguyen.'

'I'm trying,' he responded. 'The usual?'

Mr Nguyen knew that each Saturday morning Pei Xing made the long journey to Circular Quay, then to the North Shore, to meet someone from her past. He was too polite to ask any details, but recognised her reticent dignity and the lifelong habit of privacy. He had said once that she reminded him of a schoolteacher from his childhood in Saigon and Pei Xing accepted this disclosure as a verbal gift; the remembrance she inspired in him was spoken with affection.

'The usual. Circular Quay.'

Mr Nguyen brushed at his fin, in unconscious grooming, as he produced the ticket.

★ ★ ★

These simple exchanges sustained Pei Xing. People put too little faith in modest

67

conversation, she thought, and in what was known but remained silent or impossible to express. The veneration of small sentences, or a gesture, or even a single word; this was the fabric of civility, the basic social contract. One could die without it.

Mr Nguyen reminded Pei Xing of no one in particular, but his face was generically kind and his tone solicitous. How did this kindly intelligent man end up here, locked in by timetables, and piles of change and an airless booth?

The train station was noisy and busy, all brutalist steel, echoing with voices and the severe acoustics of hard tubular spaces. Rubbish blew along the platform, a McDonald's carton for fries, a jangling aluminium can. Without hesitating, Pei Xing picked up both and deposited them in a metal garbage bin hanging from a pole. Waiting passengers watched suspiciously and with blank incomprehension.

★   ★   ★

The train from Liverpool approached, slowing its roar, screeching to a halt; and when Pei Xing boarded, something that persisted as a trace from early morning returned as a complete image.

Once she had sought her father at his desk and found him missing, then located him smoking on his bed, an ashtray balanced on his chest. He was lost in thought, gazing at the ceiling. Music was playing from the gramophone — something moody with wailing trumpets. The light was yellow; it was always yellow in her parents' bedroom. This easy vision: of the great man at rest, a small blue brass and enamel vessel moving fractionally with his breath. The cigarette, Great China, dangling from two fingers. As a girl she had been caught by the quietness and solemnity of the moment, the knowledge that he had not seen her, his contemplative self-sufficiency, the mixture of aloneness and distance her spying implied. Children tell themselves things in a summarising mode: she told herself then, 'I love my father.'

Perhaps love rested more in images than in words. There was no memory of him speaking at this time, or even acknowledging her presence. It was a quiet, folded moment, entirely her own.

★　★　★

Two young men, both wearing hoodies despite the heat, sat directly in front of Pei

69

Xing and began talking in loud voices. One wore a pattern of human skulls on his fleecy jacket; the other had the tattoo of a Chinese character, *fate*, just visible on his neck. Odd to see these characters appearing as fashion on the skin of young men. Decoration Chinese. Empty Chinese. Pei Xing looked out the window and watched the buildings of Bankstown slide away.

★ ★ ★

Her father, Chang Yong, had met her mother, Nan Anyi, in London some time in 1935. He had been at Birkbeck College in London, studying for a doctorate in English Literature; she was a student of piano, at the Royal Academy. They met through a mutual friend, Wu Xingfu, who was one of those energetic expatriates for whom linking with others was an exciting and essential duty; he was always organising get-togethers in pubs and picnics in parks. Londoners gazed at the motley crowd of Chinese students, incurious as to their histories but also — they sensed — dimly hostile to their presence.

Chang Yong owned a Box Brownie camera, his prized possession, and there once existed a series of cheesy photographs of their group posed before various London landmarks, the lions in Trafalgar Square, rows of pansies in Hyde Park, the twisty decorated gates of Buckingham Palace. There was a particularly askew image of Yong and Anyi standing with palace guards in their pillar-high bearskin hats; both look dwarfed, innocent and silly with pleasure. They had their chins raised to Wu Xingfu as he took the photo; he must have been kneeling in order to show the comic dimensions of the guards. Soon after there was a formal photograph of their marriage, also by Wu Xingfu and also slightly off-centre. The couple were standing on the steps of the registry office in Camden, both now unsmiling, as was the convention. Anyi wore a tailored suit and her hair was styled as a black sea-shell in a neat wavy bob, glistening as if wet; Yong wore pinstripes and a self-consciously slanted fedora. They were glamorous, and they knew it. What the photographs told Pei Xing was that they had loved each other, that London had emboldened them, and that they saw, in their nascent marriage, limitless days ahead.

★ ★ ★

None of these images survived the Cultural Revolution. None of their group. Wu Xingfu, who had a doctorate from the London School of Economics, was murdered in the early days, after being expelled from Beijing Normal University and denounced as a 'rightist and snake-demon revisionist'. A son of the 'landlord class', educated abroad, there was little he could say in his own defence. His wife, who worked as a doctor at the Peiping Union Medical College, renamed the Anti-Imperialist Hospital during the Revolution, committed suicide a few days after she learned of his death. Pei Xing had seen a note in the newspaper announcing Wu Xingfu's posthumous rehabilitation under the Deng regime, during the long weeks and months in which she searched lists for her parents' details. She read the names of the dead carefully, with filial piety. Her greatest fear was that she would look forever, with utmost care, and never find them.

*   *   *

Her parents' names at last appeared. Pei Xing's first thought was for herself; that she was no longer 'politically black', that she could now leave the country. Chang Yong and Chang Anyi were both rehabilitated, twenty-two years after their disappearance. Their names appeared in a list in the paper, in the column of political resurrections, and a formal letter from the Public Security Bureau followed.

Pei Xing felt nothing when at last she read it. She applied for the return of their property and possessions, and received instead a small amount of money. Then she wrote to her brother in Australia asking if she might join him. When she went to the Xuijiahui office for papers for herself and her son, she had difficulty speaking of a 'family reunion' without betraying excitement. The official behind the desk, a stalk-thin man with the face of a dried peach, wrote down her birth-date — 26th December, Chairman Mao's birthday — and raised an eyebrow and smiled. Pei Xing was accustomed to comments on the auspicious date of her birth. But the official said nothing. He signed the papers. He handed them over. Pei Xing left the office briskly, and without pausing to thank him.

★   ★   ★

There is a section of *Doctor Zhivago* that is full of snow. Zhivago is with his wife, Tonya, travelling in the freight truck of a train, and the journey is remarkable for the snowfall that impedes their progress and enters the hero's thinking as a series of metaphors. The snowflakes begin as woolly but thicken to a white stage curtain as wide as the street, one slowly descending and swinging its fringe. Snow is a swirling fire in the headlight of the train. Snow covers the land as a child in a cot, his head beneath an eiderdown. And then there was a section her father had read to her. Zhivago is lying in the stalled train, hearing a sound like that of a waterfall, and realises all at once that spring is in the air, the time when the snowflakes turn black as they fall to the earth.

The poet thinks: *transparent, blackish-white, sweet-smelling, bird-cherry.*

Pei Xing remembered this phrase because her father taught it to her like a poem, after he had discussed the translation of 'snow'. When she was in distress she recited it: *transparent, blackish-white, sweet-smelling, bird-cherry.* There were so many — mostly improbable — words for snow; the melody of the phrase mysteriously nourished and sustained her.

★　★　★

There was no distress here, here and now. There was just this unbidden recall and the suburbs of Sydney flashing past. But what Pei Xing saw from the train was mostly

74

unbeautiful. The backs of houses with their collapsing fences, the power-lines, the graffiti, the drifting glimpses of mortgaged lives. There were car bodies, rusted out, and the tangle of weeds around rubbish, riotous greenery and lush urban wastelands. A shopping trolley had been tossed with guilty haste into a gulley; it looked like an animal cage as the train whizzed past. More graffiti, scrawled in puzzling, illegible messages. A young man, perhaps, a bold young man, had climbed wire fences at night to ego-mark the city and try, with a ritzy signature, to make it his own.

Pei Xing did not enjoy this train journey and often buried herself in reading. But motion she liked. She liked a sense of moving forward.

★   ★   ★

Catherine Healy woke that morning to dazzling light. To be in a city so shining. A city so bright. She stood on the small balcony, enwreathed by warm air, her face lifted to the sunshine. There never was a light like this in Dublin. Not on the sunniest day.

Catherine had woken by eight in the apartment in Darlinghurst, which was situated, obscured, behind a vast Coca-Cola sign. There

75

was a glimpse of William Street, leading to the city, but no Harbour view. Here, everyone asked: *do you have a Harbour view?*

She wanted to ring Luc just to say: my, but the sun shines! And by dark there's this billboard, old-fashioned kitsch, a fluorescent wall of shifting crimson stripes and curly white lettering, like something from an all-American movie, directed by Altman . . . and it stands out for miles and miles, my own personal landmark, my own electric advertisement . . . and who would have thought it, a girl from the Pearse Tower, a girl from Ballymun . . .

⋆　⋆　⋆

In the air hung diesel fume and petrol stink and the roar of traffic streaming down and up the slope of William Street, to and from the centre. Catherine had been in Sydney for only two weeks, and her accommodation was borrowed and temporary. Someone from the newspaper office where she worked had invited her to flat sit; she would soon need to begin looking for a place of her own. But in the meantime she liked this fake version of camping, living with unfamiliar furniture and knick-knacks, and someone else's clothes hanging in the wardrobe. It was like a holiday, or a dream, or something that allowed her to feel contingent and uncommitted. When she thought of her four sisters and her mother back in Dublin, and her dear brother Brendan, God-rest-his-soul, she believed she was the free one. The only one who had escaped.

Catherine rose, showered, and pulled a loose indigo sundress over her head. She surveyed herself in the mirror briefly and decided against lipstick. She would have breakfast on Macleay Street, then walk back to the train station. She would visit Circular Quay, she would become a Saturday tourist, she would acquire a sun-tan.

★　★　★

Beside a fountain that resembled a dandelion, a sphere of rent water, ablaze and extravagant, Catherine drank a glass of soy latte and picked at a flaking croissant. There was a waitress in black trousers and dreadlocks who was casually chirpy and a clientele of good-looking, mostly youngish couples, the kind who start the day at the gym, or walking fast with a tiny dog. Tracksuits, ponytails, a perky little cap — they were everywhere, this tribe, in Ranelagh and Rathgar, in Camden and Notting Hill, in Potts Point in the sunshine with the Saturday papers.

Catherine would sit here quietly considering her good fortune, as though some part of her felt it was ill-deserved, like a lottery win, mere chance, that made her instantly enriched. She enjoyed the astonishing weather and the nature of her freedom. Might a migrant feel this way? For all that trailed behind, lost families and countries, there was a sense too that a new sky might cast a light of revelation. The fountain beside Catherine blinked and she found it a contemplative object. Mammy would love this. And Mary. And Philomena. And Claire. And Ruthy. Especially Ruthy. And Brendan too, before the accident took him and he ended up, before his time, at Glasnevin Cemetery.

Catherine experienced a momentary longing for sponge cake and potatoes, saw the ring road stretch out, all grey desolation and over-sized lorries, charging devil-may-care through rain-slick and blur.

★　★　★

The man sitting closest to Catherine flapped open his paper and she glimpsed the front page. Another bombing somewhere. This much she knew, that there were always bombings. On Catherine's tenth birthday,

12th October 1984, the IRA bombed the Grand Hotel in Brighton, hoping to assassinate Margaret Thatcher, and her birthday was ever after linked to this history, usurped, really, by politics and men and the absolute shite of all that bombing. For days it was in the papers and on the television screen — five dead, nothing of course compared to Iraq now — but Catherine discovered then how all she had longed for on her birthday meant nothing in the wider scheme of things. Being the second youngest of five sisters was bad enough; she would always feel overwhelmed by the designs of others. But this was the day she began to think about Irish politics, to think about a history that was other than Irish-eyes-a'smilin'. She and Brendan, who were close, though he was five years older, huddled together imagining the birthday death of Margaret Thatcher and considering like grown-ups the meaning of life.

A few months earlier Brendan had marched against the visit of President Reagan to the village of Ballyporeen. Catherine was the only one at the dinner table who spoke in Brendan's support, even though she did not really understand what the demonstration was about. Mam slammed down the serving spoon on the tablecloth and said *there will be no politics in my house!* And Da had just sat there, eating his peas, and the others had all giggled.

Brendan and Catherine were the serious ones, the clever ones, Mam said, when she was in a better mood. Brendan was on the television; you could see him in O'Connell Street, shouting at the top of his voice with the other rascals, making a holy show of himself and wanting to be famous. He was shouting that Reagan was a warmonger and feckin evil and would bring Star Wars to the world, zapping innocents from the sky. Catherine was thrilled to see him there, in the streets, doing something noisy in the centre of Dublin. Familiar city images flashed past, and before them his face, floating in a crowd whose mouths opened and closed in unison.

Her big brother, ah lovely, and with the gift of the gab.

A few days later Brendan showed her a newspaper article that said Reagan had presented a paperweight to the Irish President: he thought this hilarious. He mimed the presentation, put on an incompetent American accent and mocked the weightiness of what was needed to hold down the bothersome papers of the state. Catherine had to shush Brendan when his laughing became hysterical — Mam would want to know what they found so funny. But it was a wonderful moment, when they knew their complicity, when they leant against each other's bodies and decided wordlessly and instantly, in sibling love and in the apprehension of a shared future, that they might form a team.

★   ★   ★

In Sydney, people on the streets seemed contented and relaxed. Perhaps it was the sunshine. Perhaps sad people hid. Catherine thought of the fourteen-year-old mothers begging at the end of O'Connell Bridge, their pallid skinny babes resting sideways in their laps, and decided there's nothing of this here, no girls ruined before their time, or none that were obvious anyway, not sitting where everyone could see them, showing off their sorry lives. There were no frazzled wives with vertical lines between their eyes, standing in cold slanting rain outside Dunnes Stores, moaning with their shopping. Or those who had made it in IT, sweeping the city in sleek European cars; or the tough-looking men with shaved heads and leather jackets and south Dublin confidence.

Catherine realised that she was missing her home. Even though she had been living in London since she was twenty-two, Dublin, which she visited annually, was still her default comparison. She had left Ireland just after the murder of the investigative reporter, Veronica Guerin, when she decided journalism would be better pursued abroad. Here now, her comparisons were still with her own city. In the Holy Spirit School she was always the top student in her class, just as Brendan was, in the Holy Cross, and some time around her tenth birthday they both knew they would leave. Catherine lived in anticipation of the day she would take the ferry at Dun Laoghaire and sail over the waters. Away from her entangling sisters and the misery of Ballymun housing, away from North Dublin sorrow, which was unlike any other, away from the ring road that strangled them and lassoed them all in. To dirty London, as it turned out. City-of-Sin, Mam called it. City-of-Sin. But it had to be better, they reasoned, better than dreary Ballymun.

★   ★   ★

Catherine ordered a second coffee. The dandelion fountain was surprisingly captivating. White ibis with curved black beaks long as a scythe, and potbellies, like old men, were treading the puddles beneath the fountain, unmindful of café-goers and shoppers passing by. You could kick them like a football if you were so inclined, since they barely flinched as human legs passed their way.

Two young travellers, probably from Sweden — blonde girls with skimpy shorts, tanned legs and exclamatory manners — took turns having their photos taken in front of the dandelion. Carefree, the word was. Their parents were probably executives of Volvo or owned rental property in Iceland and were off now, on a yacht, sailing a sparkling fjord, communicating only sparsely and by electronic mediation. But Catherine had dragged her past and her family with her. They hung around. She thought of them often and with a kind of doleful, compelling concern. Most of all she thought of Brendan, though he was no longer in the world, and it was a riddle to her how powerfully the dead continued, how much space they took up with their not-here bodies. Brendan lay trapped in her atoms and in the folds of her brain, he had infiltrated, somehow, the way damp entered the clammy rooms of those stinky old flats in Dublin, leaving blotches like blossoms and streaks going nowhere.

Catherine would ring her mother soon, or perhaps send a postcard of the Opera House. Or of the Bridge, or Bondi Beach, or a cute kangaroo, aerodynamically leaping. Filial piety, that's what Father Maroney would call it. *Dutiful daughter*.

★ ★ ★

Last Saturday, her very first in the new southern world, Catherine swam in the ocean. Instead of heading off to see the monuments, she had decided to find holiday indulgence and enjoy the hot weather. She watched children leaping in the surf and sun-worshippers posing their brown bodies, stretched unselfconscious, on the new-moon arc of Bondi sand. It had been a day awash with light, rather like this one, and the sound of the sea falling onto the shore was nothing like home, but a kind of joyous *plash!* as the water curled and foamed and dispersed, a blue muscle, turning, and a commodious body one might rest in. She wondered if this was how sex felt for a man, to be surrounded, to be held, to be dashed somewhere, gasping.

Luc, she decided, would love Bondi Beach. All that flesh and the mystery of such an immersion, one's body buoying, the currents, the kiddie-excitement of a breaking wave.

She had seen the body-surfers flying prone on the angle of a swell, following the ridge of the water, their heads bonneted by froth. Energy and massive churn pulled them to the shore. She had seen children no older than eight fly towards her on blue boards. They lay on their bellies and held out their heads like turtles, and smiled as they fled past. Everyone's face was bright; everyone glistened and was animated.

And she had seen a woman her age swim directly towards the horizon, her arms turning in assured and rhythmical strokes. There was a moment of envy; to swim like that. And a moment of terror. To go so far out, to push the body into distance. As she lolled in the churning shallows Catherine resolved to take swimming lessons. She would be *that* woman, on a kind of journey, going far out into the ocean.

★ ★ ★

In the summer of the year following Catherine and Brendan's political deal, their mother took them to the village of Ballinspittle, to see the moving Madonna. Not the others, just them. They needed a miracle, Mam said, to show them back to the Way.

Children in the village had witnessed the outdoor statue of Mary opening and closing her eyes and moving her hands in the tiniest wave, and their fervour and testimony attracted pilgrims by the thousand. All over

Ireland people had heard of this marvel, and then all over the world. Some said Our Lady had actually taken a step forward, in a diamond of white light, radiant with grace; others that it was a nod or a blink or a wee tilt of the head, a body-message to the faithful. The Spirit was among them; it had only to be witnessed.

On an overcast day in July, Mam, Catherine and Brendan boarded a chartered bus full of nuns to take them to the miracle in County Cork. Brendan and Catherine sat together at the back of the bus, feeling ill with the journey and shuddery with every bone-shaking jolt of the road, and were surprised by how loudly the nuns chattered and the topics of their conversation. Mam sat up the front with an old biddy and looked particularly pious. It felt like forever.

When they arrived in Ballinspittle they found the place invaded: 'Every Irish eedjit is here,' whispered Brendan; 'every sad fuckin headcase.' Pilgrims were everywhere, spilling out of cars and buses. A public address system, from which prayers were broadcast, was in full crackly voice. There were little stalls, selling holy objects made of plastic, and toilets set up at the base of the statue. The Virgin Mary was disappointing, truth be told. A figure in cast concrete, ringed with eleven light-bulbs that signified her halo, she stood quietly in her little grotto, twenty feet up, and seemed obdurately disposed not to move at all. Catherine and Brendan stood where they were told and looked up at the statue. But nothing moved. They stood for ages and ages, with Mam looking too, and stood even when rain began to fall and others went for shelter.

'It takes patience,' Mam said. 'It takes patience to see what is true in this world.'

Mam bought them each a keyring souvenir of the event, and some Lourdes holy water for Gran, and a little badge with Mary's face, but her children could tell she was mightily disappointed.

'We didn't go in the right spirit,' she said softly. 'Our hearts weren't open.'

Catherine hugged her mother and wished for her sake that the Virgin had danced a jig and blessed them all in a strident yawp. Or better still, just raised her white hand in a silent gesture, the way the priest does, quiet-like and calm and well-understood, at the shuffling, slightly sorrowful end of the holy mass. Just that: the simple, direct, loving code of the hand. It would have sufficed. It would have offered her mother meaning.

Mam hugged her back. It was a rare moment of concord.

Brendan also felt sorry for Mam. 'It was

me,' he said meekly. 'I spoiled it for you.'

He glanced at Catherine to show that he cared for his mother, though she knew of his scorn and his atheism and his belief that Mam was merely gullible and had wasted their money. She loved her brother for that pretence, for trying to comfort Mam. And for the fact that he cared what his little sister thought.

★   ★   ★

In the evening Catherine saw her parents take a small glass of sherry together — another sign that all was not right with the world. Illnesses, wakes, these were the sherry occasions. They spoke together in low, hushed voices. Da smoked a cigarette. Catherine knew her mother was describing the trip and the nuns. She was telling him of the low-wattage halo and the little stalls selling trinkets; she was reconvening the details so they would make a good story. Da nodded and looked serious. In the yellow light of the kitchen there they were, her parents sharing a trip they could not afford, entering into the limited circle of their own experience, having never moved beyond Ireland, and little beyond Dublin.

Only years later did Catherine realise what

an important event this was for her mother, to journey with other souls to perform an act of witness, to see her own credulousness multiplied among the faithful, all looking at the same time in the same direction, all waiting for epic-scale confirmation and a fan of light from heaven. Afterwards, Mam spoke often of Ballinspittle, so that eventually the sense of failure fell away, and what replaced it was a tale of communal hope and the ardent wish to see something not on the telly. Her tone was solemn and prayerful: *ah, you should have seen them, all lookin' there together, all eyes fixed on her face, and the faith of it, and the love, even when the rain came down, and we all stood there together, patiently waiting, patiently waiting in the rain for her holy sign.*

After Ballinspittle Catherine and Brendan were linked inseparably. It marked the understanding that they were truly alike. The older girls bothered her less, content to know Catherine was peculiar, and the youngest, Ruthy, only seven years old, was sure her big sister was special because she had been taken to see the statue. Catherine had given Ruthy the moving-Madonna keyring, and was pleased to see how treasured it was. Mam seemed to worry just the same, but practised a measured forbearance, apparently resigned.

Catherine felt her relinquishment as a kind of relief; she was liberated now into a career of self-understanding.

★ ★ ★

Catherine paid for her drink and left the café. The dandelion fountain shone. She paused and gazed into it. A sixties' object for sure, when water features popped up everywhere in modernist cities, smoothing crude box-shapes and ugly façades, nostalgic for genuine and replaceable nature. This liquid dandelion stood alone, a memorial, perhaps. Not beautiful, exactly, but buoyant somehow, light, luminous and strangely sensual. There was something in the falling of fine water drops that reminded Catherine obliquely of snow; and snow reminded her of the story Brendan loved above all others.

At his funeral she had read from James Joyce's *The Dead*. She had stood before the casket, in front of all those people, and Mam crying her eyes out, and her sisters with their hankies, and the priest just behind her, hovering with disapproval, and read the last paragraph of James Joyce's short story. The congregation in Our Lady of Victories looked distracted and confused. Some thought she was gone in the head to read out this something-or-other, blatant and disrespectful and certainly unreligious blather, but it was what Brendan would know, his literary world, and what he would have liked. And how did it go, now, the section about snow falling general, all over Ireland? Over the plain, over the hills, over the dark Shannon waves; then over the cemetery where the beautiful young man was lying buried? And that fellow, Gabriel his name was, looking out the window:

His soul swooned slowly as he heard the snow falling faintly through the universe and faintly falling, like the descent of their last end, upon all the living and the dead.

Upon all the living and the dead. This was how Brendan haunted her, visiting at unexpected moments, falling over her, as if from the sky, smoothing her own definition. So that Catherine might be rising from coffee in a good mood and remember his funeral, so that she might be walking in the sunshine in another country entirely, so that she might be heading for the Opera House or wishing she had written to her mother, and think suddenly, irresistibly, of the intimate presence of snow.

3

Their connection began when they were both nine, and together watched her father with the axe. Under the pepper tree he raised it high, and brought it down on a scraggly white chicken, which he had tied, just one loop, with a rope to the chopping block. Father was unsure of his aim, perhaps, or worried that the bird would flap away. But in the act itself there was no trace of uncertainty or worry, just irreproachable gravity and the blade fast-falling, just the *whoosh* of an intention sharper and heavier than most.

Only seconds before, the doomed chicken was making a throaty, moaning sound, inert but for its roving and nervous eye. Ellie saw it blink, and blink again, and wondered if chooks had thoughts or memories, or heard songs in their heads, as she often did. She held James's hand tightly and pulled him close. In the olive-green light of the backyard he looked nervous and afraid. His face was pinched, his mouth was firm, his brown eyes were moist and suddenly huge. Clouds flew above them, wind, a single bird.

Then the axe-blade fell. The chicken's head

popped off — no big deal — but when her father untied the body a ghastly thing happened. The body writhed a little, uprighted itself, then lurched away in a swoony, directionless run. James laughed, but looked terrified. As the headless chicken ran past he bent down and swooped it into his arms. He clutched hard, trying to still it, trying to make the lively body die. His eyes entreated — who knows what? — and filled with tears. Ellie could hear her own rapid breathing and knew that time was rocking into shape as water does, pooling around this boy's face and his blazing desperation.

When her father prised the chicken from James's grip his shirt was bloody and bespattered. The boy shook and began to cry, and Ellie opened her arms and took him gently into her child's embrace. She knew then, even with her own heart galloping and her senses all alive, that she was the calm one, that in the circle of killing she could watch and somehow know not to recoil. She knew too that there was a gap between death and life, a remnant vigour, a kind of puzzled searching.

Do humans search like this, looking stupidly for what is missing? Would a human body run? Crazy-like, with no head?

Ellie was possessed by this idea, its

exhilarating horror. As an adult it will occur to her that this was her first moment of philosophy, when she found in the world a seductively bamboozling question. Yet in the vast stillness of the moment she saw the answer in James's face: *yes*, crazy-like-with-no-head, a human would still search.

★ ★ ★

Ellie decided to walk to Central Station, take the train to the quay, and then return on the bus. She wanted this walk down-hill through the Saturday crowds, already trailing out of coffee shops and cycling past with the newspapers, already responding with like heart to the glorious weather. Faces evanesced before her, rose up and fell away, and she thought of the negligent flicker of perception that negotiates any crowd, of how in the champagne morning light they were all caught in flux and lustre, igniting, appearing, lit with energetic purpose. In the grounds of the local primary school a market was being established; Ellie could see stallholders setting up trestle tables and unpacking their wares. They were holding cardboard cups of coffee and lightly chatting. It would be a good day. Even from across the road you could hear optimism ringing in their voices. But

Ellie was still thinking of James at nine years old, and of herself, self-centred. She hadn't really cared for his suffering. She had wanted high drama.

★   ★   ★

Her mother was suddenly there, surveying the mess. 'Bloody hell,' she said, 'what were you thinking, Charlie?' Ellie noticed her father become submissive at his wife's reproach. He was still holding the chicken, its feathers mucky with gore, the event a crude wreckage, and the head forgotten, ridiculous, in the sawdust beside the block. Ellie saw him pass the upside-down carcass from one hand to the other, then wipe his left hand on his trousers, leaving a faint greasy smear. They exchanged words, her parents, and then her mother seized James by the wrist and dragged him away. Ellie saw in her mother's glance that she was also stained; holding James she had printed chicken blood onto her clothes. So there was the blood-print, the sky, her father dangling the chicken. Images lined up for her memory, for the future, for wild or idle surmise, this little collection that made up the blunder of the moment, and of James's pure fear, and of her own shameless sense of triumph.

In this pause lay the inkling of a net of relationships. Ellie registered with sure judgement the range of her affections: she loved them all — *loved* — her mother, her father, her school-friend James, all of them caught in this drama with the headless chicken that would not do the right thing and straightaway, as it should, just lay down and die.

★   ★   ★

Ellie was in the kitchen, dressed in a clean cotton blouse. She had tucked her hair behind her ears, and sat silent, watching, fiddling with the hem of her skirt. James had been on his knees, vomiting into a plastic bucket, but was now perched on their high stool, not yet settled, with a glass of water in his hands and her mother leaning towards him. She was soothing, whispering words that Ellie could not quite hear. They would be the right words; her mother was good at that. They would be words gathered from the air, or so it had always seemed, and fitted into just the right sentences, in just the right order, and spoken just right, like a special trick, like the way a dog knows when to nuzzle you and when to stay far away. She recognised the low tone of voice and the lovely comfort residing there. James was hectic with crying and barely consolable. He had the glazed look of a child too small for the enormity of all he'd seen. His shoulders hunched, he trembled a little. Ellie's mother plucked at a box of tissues and handed him fat, floral bunches.

Like James, Ellie was a single child. She learnt only as an adult of the brother who preceded her, dying of infant leukaemia at the age of four. William, his name was. Her parents had never spoken of William, but their devotion to her was his ghostly bequest. They loved her double and found her existence adorable. Ellie watched her mother's attention as she calmed James and offered him an arrowroot biscuit, as he nibbled around its edges, like a storybook rabbit, as he brushed the crumbs away, like a girl, she thought meanly, like a scaredy-cat girl, and began gradually to see where he was and what a bother he had made.

In her watching Ellie glimpsed her mother's power, this remaking of damaged things and events within words, this placing of sentences, carefully, as a balm over a wound. At last her mother straightened. She lifted James under the armpits, hoisted him upwards and straightened him too.

'Time to go home,' she said. She untied her

apron, folded it swiftly, and held an arm out to show that Ellie was allowed to accompany them. The kitchen light was pale yellow; it was always yellow in the kitchen. Every kitchen in the world, thought Ellie, is always yellow. James and her mother both had round yellow faces.

★　★　★

They had walked the gravel road of their seaside town, passing Mr Anderson-with-the-large-belly who was outside watering his garden, flailing the plastic hose, this way and that, like a private game or an emblem of his own distraction; past the Covichs' (who were divorced) and the Hallidays' (who were Catholics), and the Maloufs' (who were from Lebanon, wherever that was), past the empty block in which Patterson's Curse flourished its purple blossoms (Dad said it could kill horses, so Ellie thought it magnificently dangerous), to the end of the street, where there was only James's house, an unrepaired weatherboard, half-falling down, with holes in the roof that let the rain in (James had told her) and beyond that, the sand dunes, the coast, and the true-blue Indian Ocean. The house had a wretched, decomposing look, as though it was caught in a process of unmaking that affected no other house on the street. The verandah had planks of wood missing and a broken rail, and an iron roof, rusted orange, that was peeling away. One of the side-walls was crudely patched with a warped sheet of three-ply. It looked like a blister, just hanging there. A surprisingly vigorous rosemary bush grew by the letter-box. Ellie watched her mother tear a woody stem in an absentminded gesture, rub the little leaves together and sniff at her fingers as she passed.

When Mrs DeMello opened her door she saw only a blazon of red. She let out a cry and fell to her knees before her son, then reached and pulled his thin body towards her face.

'He's not hurt,' mother said quickly. 'It's not his blood.'

But Mrs DeMello sang: 'oh Dio, Dio, Dio.'

'Chicken,' mother added, in what must have been an incomprehensible explanation. But still Mrs DeMello did not acknowledge the visitors. She buried her face in her small son's belly. Ellie was excited to see a grown-up so disarrayed. It was a kind of guilty pleasure; the sight of Mrs DeMello weeping, even before she knew what had happened, and the way her face reshaped, and James staring dizzily ahead, mystified, unfocused, embarrassed by his mother's possessive display.

'Italians are different,' mother said later. 'They have passions,' she added. Ellie would wonder over this statement for the next few years.

But then she saw that burst of feeling as something she might desire. To be clutched at like that. To be seized by an adult as if you might be the one to save them. Ellie glimpsed behind Mrs DeMello her orderly house. Although ramshackle outside it was impeccably tidy inside. There were doilies on every surface and plaster ornaments of lap-dogs and prancing horses and figures in puffy historical dress, rimmed in stiff lace. There was a Jesus on the wall, showing off his lolly-pink heart, and an old velour armchair with a crocheted cream cover. In so ruined a space lay foreign oddity and decorative excess.

'Oh Dio, Dio, Dio.' Still chanting, still distraught.

Then at once Mrs DeMello rose up, uttered a hasty thank-you, smothered in tears, and pulled James inside. She banged shut the door.

'Well I never,' said Ellie's mother. 'You can't tell with some people.'

As they left Ellie grabbed at the rosemary

bush, twisting free a twig. She crushed it as her mother had done, and breathed in its scent.

'Rosemary,' her mother said casually. 'Rosemary for remembrance.'

★ ★ ★

Afterwards James did not talk to Ellie for three years. Mostly he was alone, but for a time, when he was eleven, he hung out with the tough kids, the bully, Col Harper, and Kev Andrews and Blue. Ellie saw how James used his wit to entertain them and didn't squirm when they gave him Chinese burns or knuckle-punched him in the upper arm. They liked to whack other kids behind the knees, so that you buckled and fell forward and were scared they might kick you when you were down. For a while she seemed to see them everywhere, skinny boys with mean streaks, in their striped T-shirts like their hearts, Ellie thought, remembering those comic books in which prisoners wear stripy pyjamas. They were rowdy and rude, a collection of trouble-makers. They invented war games and shot at each other and died rolling in the dirt, clutching their bellies, scowling with enjoyable, make-believe agony. They chucked stones on old Mrs Taylor's roof and ran away laughing when she came outside. They spat on the ground and looked at their gobs of spittle, proud. They were cheeky in shops and morose in the classroom, swearing under their breath, glowering, planning insurrections.

'Dickhead!' they shouted at the old metho drinker, Merv, who lay half insensible in the park that was only weeds and pussy tails and a tall lonely monument to the First World War. 'Shitface dickhead!'

Ellie felt sorry for Merv. And since in her home no bad language was allowed, she was transfixed by the swearwords, flung spinning into the sky, and by the cruelty of the boys and their bold bad behaviour.

But she also missed James. Until the chicken and the botched slaughter he had been her best friend. She missed what had precariously existed between them, secrets, mostly; secret talks and words and sly imaginings. She knew James wanted to be a pilot when he grew up, so that he could see the world from the sky, he said, and go out across oceans, far, far away, where people were more interesting. He might even visit Italy, where his parents were from, and where he could speak the lingo and see the Coliseum in Rome. 'Two thousand years old, Ellie,' he had whispered, 'just imagine that.

Two thousand years.' James wanted to go back in time, to find another history. Ellie would go forward and be a movie star, she dreamily confided, kissed by handsome men wearing hats and speaking American. Their ambitions were like stories they might some day live by. Ellie thought of a flash-light, its ray erratic in foggy darkness, seeking a pathway. And her own footfall, a child-searcher, sounding as she went.

James had peered into Ellie's face. She knew he saw her freckles and her sunburn and her stringy brown hair, but he did not mock or denigrate or suggest that her dream was impossible. 'I'll speak American too,' he said, leaning close, 'and I'll fly to California, whatever, or to China or Czechoslovakia, and look down from the sky, from way up high. And you can wave, and I'll see you, and I'll wave back; and it will be a kind of spy-code we have, with no one else knowing . . . '

★   ★   ★

Extraordinary to surrender like this, to so cogent a memory. To have her young self returned to her, and the particulars of one day.

It was a trance Ellie walked in, with all the welter of details — the spluttering fear of Mrs

DeMello that for years, absurdly, would denote 'Italian passion', the marriage drama of her parents, one submissive, one strong, the vision of James's face, all alarm and pure shock; and more than that the improbable density of moments she'd not thought of for years — it was an oval-shaped arrowroot biscuit he nibbled, it was a chicken's death, horribly messed, that had shattered their friendship, and all the blood it sent flying, all the irrevocable filth, and James's over-reacting misery and sense of contamination. It was — could this be so? — the mustard-coloured walls of their kitchen that cast everything of that era in yellow light, and the listed names of their neighbours that tinted the yellow memories with affection. And it was the 'Dio, Dio, Dio', a terrible song, that broke through to this white morning and into the hurrying present.

★   ★   ★

Ellie turned left at the Salvation Army charity shop on the corner. The university was to her right, beyond the ill-planned park, and the city, abustle, lay straight ahead. She headed downhill. Traffic, far too speedy, hurtled past. As Ellie strode she was aware of the preoccupying visions in her head, and made a conscious decision to notice more carefully where and when she was. She realised too that she was trying not to think about sex, not to be defined by her body, not to let it signify too completely.

The pavements were busy. This was the summer every young woman displayed a cleavage, and every young guy a T-shirt logo. They were amassed on the footpath and moving in packs. No mortality here, no hesitation. Vital bodies passed by like rolling surf. Ellie walked quickly. Although she had all the time in the world, something enthused her limbs and her sense of expectation, something larger than she was commanded her movements.

* * *

In the madding crowd James paused and looked around. He was at Central Station and would find the line to the Quay. He had entered under the sandstone arches at Eddy Avenue, taken an escalator, wandered around, but was already lost.

It was a confusing place. There seemed to be tunnels in all directions, tiled passages with dingy post atomic connotations and the possibility of hunched bodies, or beggars, or buskers with mournful demands, such as he had seen years ago in the London Underground. There were narrow chutes, all interconnected, which emerged at platforms outside in the glaring light, and people all-ahurry, knowing exactly where to go.

He read the signs: *Eastern Suburbs and Illawarra, Blacktown, North Shore. Olympic Park, Northern Line, Intercity lines . . . Inner West . . .* that was it: that would take him to Circular Quay.

James thought suddenly of dendrites and ganglia, all those diagrams he had seen in his one year as a medical student, all those cortical systems and webs that are our mysterious plumbing and electricity. *Choroid plexus*: why did he think of this term? Aqueducts of the brain, canals and cavities. He had forgotten most of it now.

First-year medical students cram not only images and new imaginings, but a vast vocabulary that is exquisitely arcane: from the Greek *chorion*, meaning 'membrane' and the Latin *plexus*, meaning 'knot'. Their anatomy instructor, Professor Heller, insisted on teaching them the Latin or Greek roots; that way, he said, you will learn the poetry of the body. So it was not just capillaries, but *a membranous knot*. And the linguistic body was part of the surprising loveliness of medicine.

106

'Anatomy of the Brain: Introduction': it was his favourite part of the year. Professor Heller, with his bifocals and thick mammalian moustache, was his favourite professor. When they were given a slice of cerise-dyed brain to peer at through the microscope, it was a sublime and singular moment in James's life. The channels and mounds, the trailing intricacies, they rose into focus as an entire new world. No other organ in the body looked like this. Nothing else was quite so tightly elaborated. James considered how few people had seen a slice of brain, how privileged doctors were to glance at this dark-side-of-the-moon self. He examined it fraction by fraction, forgetting that he was meant to be clarifying this or that, the purpose of the amygdala perhaps — though that was easy — or some more baroque, difficult-to-remember utility or facility. Euphonious and rhyming terms flooded his mind: *endorphin, seratonin, acetylcholine. Transmitter, receptor, mediator.* Any number of neurobiological arrangements or derangements existed in this flap of special flesh.

James tried not to think of his mother in hospital, her mind confiscated, her senses blown, dealing with the blizzard in her mind that she liked to call her 'snow'.

In his novice enthusiasm, James knocked over a pile of glass slides. He saw the glass and brain matter mash together as someone stepped backwards in surprise and crushed them underfoot. As he knelt in his white medical robe, and tried to scrape up the mess, he was overtaken with the offence of it and an intimation of vulnerability. Just as he had worked during the year, not wholly successfully, to overcome his aversion to blood, this also became an abruptly threatening substance — mashed brain spiked with glass. He withdrew instinctively, his hands visibly trembling. The others were all watching. Professor Heller was watching. James was afraid he would cut himself and add blood to the mix.

'Leave it,' Professor Heller called. 'Sally will get it.'

Sally was the laboratory assistant who cleaned up after them. She appeared from nowhere and matter-of-factly set about the cleaning. Sally was the girl who dealt with the violet-pink open cadavers and mopped the floor of its rheumy spillages after the students had left. She dealt with all the unhallowed matter of the place: waste tissue, muscle, bone, leftover humans. She was a quiet girl with auburn hair and blotchy skin, teased by the male students and ignored by the women. James felt, though he could barely concede it, a furtive affinity with Sally. He thought of asking her to coffee, or whispering to her as she passed, or pushing her against the wall and running his hands under her shirt.

Sally bent over the mess, scrabbling and wiping. James moved away. Something in the moment shamed him. He felt his throat flush and said something meaningless before he fled from the room.

What upset him was not so much the crushed brain sample, the flagrant clumsiness and ineptitude, as the evidence of his precarious grip on things. Within seconds he had moved from poetical pleasure to unpoetical bungle; he had fallen from the prodigious terminology of medical life to mute departure and a pathetic, stammered excuse. He had failed before Professor Heller, whom he most wanted to impress. He had failed before Sally, to whom he had never spoken a word.

★ ★ ★

James dropped out of university in the last few weeks of the year, just before his final exams. He had wanted once to be an artist, perhaps a figure like Magritte, who might paint with Surrealist extravagance all the anomalies of life, who might depict the illogical as though it were everyday. It would be like a holiday, being an artist. He would have a mistress and a casual, supercilious demeanour. He would wear a beret and drink toxic mixtures to excess. The clichés didn't bother him. Coming from a small country town in Western Australia, European clichés of another life carried the prospect of seduction.

Then he had wanted to be a doctor, because he was clever — everyone said so — and because this was a conventional aspiration for clever young men. He had won a university scholarship and medicine would earn him respect. James never really considered what this work might involve. He was initially shocked by encounters with gross, ruby innards and the sense that the body is perpetually prey to disorder. Against the magnificence of its system was the jeopardy of any organism. His mother and her snow dome. The list of communicable diseases. All those patients he had seen, randomly damaged and cruelly assailed. He was haunted by a young man, barely forty, with Fahr's Syndrome, a degenerative neurological disease which caused him to writhe and jerk.

Edward, his name was. Edward something. On one of his first visits to the hospital he had seen this unfortunate fellow, whose basal ganglia were crusting over, whose cells were popping away. From his wheelchair, bent over, Edward smiled up at him, feigning equilibrium beneath his acute distress. James could not bear it. He averted his eyes. Edward something-or-other.

It was rather like discovering that the boy Magritte by the riverbank was also fourteen years old, an odd sense of having one's boundary blurred, as if history or other people could carry premonition, or warning, or an obscure shared meaning. Behind his panic was the spectre of an overwhelming loneliness, but also the knowledge, then and there, that he would never be a doctor. Edward something-or-other.

⋆ ⋆ ⋆

For all this, the study of medicine had surprised him. The intellectual appeal was something he had not anticipated. The body was more improbable and fantastical than he had imagined, and also more plausible and lavishly coherent. The chemistry alone was astounding, not to mention the mechanics. Diagnostic and treatment enigmas were

111

everywhere to be found. Something as simple as laughing was physiologically complex. Professor Heller told them that the ancient Greeks had a word, *agelasti*, for those who never laughed. Once or twice, when the first-year medical students were bent in mirthless contemplation over their specimens or books, he would call out: 'Ah, my *Agelasti!*' and elicit a startled chuckle. 'The baby cries,' Professor Heller said, 'approximately 4,000 times in the first two years of its life. Enough with the crying already!' At which the class laughed again, a shudder of reply rippling through their backs.

James wondered how comedy worked, calling up a collective response. Or words, just words, joining each of them in the same moment. But the puzzle of being-in-the-world, first and foremost, was this: the weirdness of one living body, and the precipitate touch.

★   ★   ★

Ellie. How he had loved Ellie. She had gathered him in. James had been cautious at first — they both had — discovering the difference of another body still fully dressed and in outline. A tentative hand on the breast, her exploration inside his trousers. But the first time he pulled her thighs towards him and rocked into her, slowly, and then began fast-breathing and labouring for pleasure, the first time he dropped his face to her neck to whisper her name, and to gulp at her skin, and to convulse somewhere inside her, he felt astonished that no one had needed to teach them at all, but that this experience had arrived, and would arrive again, complete and intact. Ellie was kissing his damp forehead; he was saying Ellie, Ellie, and he did not want to extract himself or leave her embrace. He felt sodden, emptied, crazed by joy. He could smell the lavender scent of the powder she dabbed under her arms, and his own fluids, and hers, pungently intermingling. He could feel her breathing as though it were lodged in his own chest: the union had not broken but was there in the warm pounding of their hearts, almost pressed into each other, like a new organ shared.

When they rolled apart in their quiet, shadowy space, he felt like singing. He remembered he said it out loud, 'I feel like singing.' He had turned to her reddened face and seen Ellie smile back at him.

'Sing then,' she said.

And he had started something, probably Dylan, and ended humming deep inside, as if new knowledge rested there and a new understanding. He had heard guys talk about fucking, about the slags and the tarts, the bikes and the molls. There was a huge world out there of sticky yearning and illicit images, of schoolboys telling each other of mythical conquests, or of some girl with lank hair and bad skin who would do it with anybody. But this tenderness was not what they had described. And this correspondence was quiet, even unspeakable. He had no wish to tell anyone. His greatest fear was that, having found her, he might scare her away.

Our secret, they agreed. Like the secrecy of their hideout. It was the secrecy of singing to a girl, of tucking his mother in bed at night after she had finished her hot milk, of sitting under the standing lamp, reading a book about artists, then dreaming he wandered through the ruins of a lost city and found something unbroken.

★　★　★

James thought afterwards that the shyness of social situations — the schoolroom, the shops, even the road outside their houses — was a kind of fake distance under which this real life of connections happened. Perhaps all life was like this: affinities known but hardly ever expressed, pulsing and

114

moving beneath an everyday encounter or conversation. A man might meet a woman in a corridor, exchange a few words as they held cups of coffee, enact a punctilious and austere restraint, and know afterwards that some code had passed between them. Some sympathetic quiver of recognition that finds its completed expression like this, only like this, with two faces touching.

★ ★ ★

After the first time together they were hyper-sensitively aware. For him the brush of her skirt, the threads of hair at her nape, the way she turned away when she found his gaze too compelling, were almost unendurable. He was distracted, always waiting, for a thrilling handful of breast, for the next time she guided him into her, her hand gentle around his penis.

They sat beside each other in the class. He watched her reading and writing; he noticed that she chewed her finger-nails, and hid her hands so as not to reveal it. He saw how she yawned and sneezed and kept pushing her hair behind her ears. Everyone was still treating them the same, like kids, but between them was this hidden maturity, this adult awareness. There were twenty-eight students in their classroom, twenty-eight bodies and twenty-eight inner worlds, but James could imagine only Ellie as alike, or as unlike in ways he almost understood.

✷ ✷ ✷

At Central Station a loudspeaker somewhere was booming. The message was unintelligible. James saw signs: *Eddy Avenue Exit, Elizabeth Street Exit*, and felt disorientated. Discreetly he shifted his genitals in his pants, and tried to put Ellie from his mind. After all these years she still returned to him in this private way. Just as he held his father in a phantom dip and rise, escaping the gravity of the present, so Ellie also persisted in an earlier body and unrelinquished longings.

James stood before the ticket machine, fed it coins and pressed the buttons. When he located his platform it was bathed in full sunshine. He could not have denied there was a cheerful spirit afloat in the weather, but he still felt out of sorts and enormously thirsty. The side effects of Temazepam, taken for too long. Dehydration, memory loss, depressive withdrawal. All those benzodiazepines zapping the gamma-aminobutyric acid in his brain. He bought a bottle of water from the little stall on the platform, suddenly wondering how he might appear to Ellie. He didn't want rings under his eyes or a hung-over daze.

The doors parted before him. When he boarded the train James found he was silently chanting fragments of anatomy revision: right coronary artery, left coronary artery, anterior-ventricular artery, aortic valve, mitral valve . . . it must have been one of the early lessons. He used to chant the terms as he walked the paths by the university around the river, timing his steps rhythmically, watching light from the sunrise glance in streaks on the calm water. It was a kind of happiness. Repetition, sky, light on water. Once he had seen a pod of dolphins in the river, lazily arching, turning their sleek bodies, and all momentarily was right with the world. God-in-his-heaven. Etcetera, etcetera.

The man in front of James was wearing a black T-shirt stamped with a logo that read *teen spirit*. As James found his seat he recalled the Nirvana video-clip, 'Heart-Shaped-Box': cut-price Surrealism. There was Kurt Cobain looking crazed, shouting at the camera. There was a crucifixion, ravens, babies hanging from a tree, there was a sad little girl in white robes and a white conical cap. There was a large woman in some kind of suit that showed her inner organs on the outside.

Although James was what? — nineteen — when this video version had appeared, it left a terrifying impression. He cannot now remember when first he saw it on television, but the images gave him a nightmare. And here now, on a train in Sydney, it was still invading and upsetting him, acting like airy turbulence when he wanted to cruise.

★   ★   ★

James stared out of the window and watched inner-city Sydney slide by. He took another gulp of water, finishing the bottle. So much was playing in his head, ringing in this paltry, mortal cupola of the skull. He wanted to see Ellie. He wanted peace and quiet. He wanted not this thirst, this wider hunger, this sense of failure and shame, but whatever he had felt when twenty years ago he first fell into her body. Wholeheartedly. As a kid. Finding a true home.

It was freakish good luck, to be welcomed to the chamber she offered him. Women didn't realise this: that the noise a man made when he came was of gratitude, simply to have been admitted.

★   ★   ★

Central Station. She was almost there. The train slid to a creaking halt and a line of passengers disembarked, then came a tide of others to replace it, in a lovely long stream. It was reassuring to see so many people in the world. So many legs moving, stepping upwards, to the modern command of sliding doors.

Central Station. Pei Xing thought wryly that she would never be at the centre of anything, that her life would always be this circling around an irrepressible past. As the train accelerated away, so did her recollection. The world in a train-ride was conducive to her own speedy summonings.

★ ★ ★

Pei Xing was thinking of her family, long ago, making them reanimate. With her mother and brother Lao, four years older, they had gone together to the First Department Store on Nanjing Road to buy her a new winter coat. She was seven years old. It was 1958, the beginning of the Great Leap Forward. Every morning at school the students praised Mao, the Great Helmsman, and sang 'The East is Red' in a hearty, energetic spirit of agreement. They stood stiffly to attention, and even then, so young, Pei Xing knew of Grand

Economic Plans and carried nationalist phrases on her tongue. Her teacher was pleased to remind his class that Mao Tse Tung once worked as a primary-school headmaster in Hunan — anyone could be a Communist leader! — and each week they learnt about a new hero of the Great March of 1935, some modest fellow who had sacrificed all, melodramatically, for the People's Republic, or who had starved, or martyred himself, or believed in Mao beyond all others. In storybooks these figures always appeared in the same poses, three-quarter view, one arm raised, peering towards the future, and the illustrations of valiant deaths made Pei Xing cry. She knew she belonged to an incomparable nation with an inviolate leader, a leader, fortuitously, who shared her birth-date.

Mao's balloon face would become better known to her than her own father's, that mole on the chin, that spaced-out stare, the way the single button in head-and-shoulder portraits always looked so exact and rhymed so perfectly, so centrally placed, with his mid-chin mole. His head would float like a dirigible throughout her life, beyond gravity, weightless, in the corner of her vision, always sweeping into history with the bright awful glamour of a God.

The weather was already cold, though it was only early autumn, and the visit to the First Department Store was an outing she remembered because her mother had made a fuss. Her daughter needed a new woollen coat because, she predicted, it would snow in the coming winter. Pei Xing could not remember having ever seen snow before, but believed — in a kind of magical thinking — that the purchase of the coat would be answered by a wide white heaven. Lao also wanted a coat, and mother said she would see how much money was left. He was carrying a kite. It was a time in her brother's life in which he always carried his kite, as other boys carried books, pocket-knives and fighting crickets. The kite was homemade with a painted phoenix outstretched on the brown-paper diamond. It crackled as he held it, a fragile precious thing.

* * *

The women behind the counters chanted a greeting: *Huanying guanglin! Huanying guanglin! Welcome, brightness draws near!*

Pei Xing looked into their broad friendly faces and felt that all was right with the

121

world; it was an auspicious day, and she would choose scarlet.

She had never known before how various and how many were the products of the world. She had been to markets, of course, and to smaller local shops, those near Hua Shan Lu and further up Nanjing Xi Lu, near the Jiang'an Temple, but her first visit to a department store was a revelation. When they selected a coat from a rack of hundreds it was exactly as she had wished — of scarlet wool, with four buttons, two by two, and a neat symmetrical collar of two black triangles. There were side pockets for warming her hands and a black trim around the sleeves. Pei Xing remembers her mother standing behind her as they looked together into the long tilted mirror. She was smoothing the coat across her back and tugging at the sleeves to check that it was not too small.

There was not enough money that day for Lao to have a coat too. But he was placated by a trip across the road to the People's Park, where mother bought them onion-salted pancakes wrapped in rice paper. Lao flew his kite with other boys on a large oval of grass while Pei Xing sat with her mother on a bench beneath the shedding trees. An old man nearby was playing an erhu and singing in a thin reedy voice. He plucked at the two strings intently, as if every emotion was caught there and must be released.

'From the provinces,' mother whispered, with a hint of approval.

Pei Xing was wearing the new coat, taking care not to stain it with her snack. When she finished eating her mother leant over and wiped her fingers with a cloth. It was a moment Pei Xing would return to again and again, first when she was in prison, and later at the Cadre Camp. For some reason there was a purity in this simple touch. Pei Xing held her hands out obediently, finger by finger, as though it were a game. It reminded her of how her mother stretched and pulled her fingers before she played the piano, seeing the gift of her own hands, preparing to skim them across the keys.

She wondered if the recollection was so complete because she had been so happy. Sadness blurs and erases; it cannot bear too many details. But the sight of Lao's kite aloft, the way he turned to them and called out, wanting to show his skill, the fluttering phoenix visible as a golden mark swooping and rising in the sky, all this was preserved for Pei Xing in a kind of shining delineation.

★ ★ ★

When they rode the tram home, along Nanjing Road, it was full to bursting with Saturday shoppers and all three had to stand, packed in the crammed aisle. The vehicle rocked and shuddered. Pei Xing was wedged between the bodies of larger people, hemmed in by adult legs and arms. Lao held his kite above his head, afraid it would be torn. Mother steadied Pei Xing as they rode. One hand rested gently behind her daughter's head, the other clasped at a leather strap, so that she held the motion for both of them. All around was chatter and communality and the smell of someone's fried meat. Pei Xing loved this sense of other bodies containing and encompassing her, the muffled, animal warmth of the moving tram. She loved her new coat. She loved her family. She leant against the cushion of her mother's belly and felt like singing.

★   ★   ★

At home Pei Xing's first thought was to show the new coat to her father. She rushed into the house and found him where he should be, at his desk, translating. His face was fixed in concentration. He was somewhere between languages, in a studious and placid world. Pei Xing stood in the doorway until at last he

124

noticed he had company. Father peered at her over his rimless glasses, slowly put down his pen, then smiled and opened his arms so that Pei Xing stepped forward into his embrace.

'Ah, a new overcoat! Pretty! Let me tell you about Gogol!'

And as if the day had not enough intimate moments to fill it, he pulled Pei Xing onto his lap and told her the story of *The Overcoat*.

In St Petersburg there was once, long ago, an unhappy young clerk, called Akaky Akakievich Bashmachkin, who wanted nothing more than to own a new overcoat. He scrimped and saved — he was very poor — and at last the day arrived when he could afford a new coat, a fine-tailored garment with a collar made of cat fur. When he wore this coat he was suddenly popular and successful. But one night, after a party, two thieves set upon him, beat him up and stole the coat, leaving him alone and barely conscious in the falling snow. Poor Akaky Akakievich died, bereft. He took revenge on the people of St Petersburg as a scary ghost, roaming the snow-white city at night, spooking and attacking the people for their winter coats.

Pei Xing must have looked alarmed.

But in the end, her father said gently, he attacked one important man who had been tormenting him and then no more: justice was done. Other ghosts roamed around, playing havoc and disturbing citizens. But not Akaky Akakievich. He was not a bad man, Akaky Akakievich, and not a bad ghost, but he cared too much about his coat, and too little about the words he wrote in the office. Words, not coats, are where meaning lies.

Pei Xing told her father of her mother's prediction, that the coat would bring snow. He responded that she was a wise woman, her mother, and if she claimed it was so, she was no doubt correct. It would certainly snow.

At first Pei Xing thought that her father had ruined everything, moralising like that, wanting her to think about ghosts. He had a Russian story handy for every occasion, a literary homily for all events. But his tale added beautifully to the memory of the day. It was there, years later, like breath on a pane of glass, a human trace to see through. It added to the subtle, persisting ways in which she would remember her father, long after he disappeared.

★ ★ ★

Russia was in those days the 'Big Brother' of China, and Russian was the number one foreign language. Young sailors and soldiers were taught to sing Russian songs. Russian folk tales were taught in schoolrooms and universities. For Pei Xing, her father's knowledge confirmed his importance; he knew both English and Russian; he was internationally skilled. But with the Cultural Revolution everything changed; Khrushchev was a revisionist and capitalist roader; Russian was traitorous, English decadent. Pei Xing, loyal to Mao, was deeply confused. They had been mistaken, it seemed, in seeking other tongues. Languages were not a special capacity, as she had once imagined, but incautious assent to the wrong kinds of meanings.

★　★　★

A few weeks after the shopping excursion the three returned to the First Department Store to buy Lao's coat. By then the air was chill and sharp and everyday Pei Xing looked out the window, like a character in a book, waiting for the advent of snow.

The second visit to the Store was largely unmemorable, except that she wore her scarlet coat, clasped her mother's gloved hand, and felt proud that their family was so well dressed. Her coat by then held a scent of the camphor trunk in which it was stored; she walked in a little circle of fragrance, a small charmed embrace.

And when snow at last came, fitful at first, in the faintest disappointing sprinkle and then — oh yes — in a dense overnight fall, she believed that in some way she was personally responsible. She had woken and there it was, layering the roofs and the trees, lining the handlebars of bicycles and piling the edges of the laneways, caught on stall awnings and in the yard of the Elementary School. Whiter than rice powder, with a bluish-mauve lustre. Softer than leaf-fall and more wind-dispersed. You could taste it. You could drink it. You could swallow the sky. Flakes settled in her mouth and on her open dazzled eyes.

Pei Xing gazed with moist delight at the world anew. Her big brother grabbed snow and moulded shapes and flung it around him, or tipped the branches of trees so that he created his own snowfall. But Pei Xing wanted the snow to remain forever as it first was, a damp hush and a pale shadow, just fallen, undisturbed.

Within hours it became slippery mush, dismally dissolving. But the early morning vision was enough to confirm the bright promise of the scarlet coat.

At the beginning of the Cultural Revolution, Pei Xing's teacher who so loved the tales of the Great March was one of the first to be attacked and then disappear. By chance she had seen him in the winter of 1967, assembled with other schoolteachers on a basketball court. He had been badly beaten, and one of his eyes had been crushed. Eye matter and blood ran down his face. He wore a dunce's hat, a high white cone, and a board around his neck that announced his crime as being a 'running dog imperialist'. By then Pei Xing was no longer surprised. Her parents had been taken, the schools had been closed, everyone for whom she had felt affection was experiencing persecution. But this teacher — Comrade Lu — who had conducted their singing with such enthusiasm, who had been moved to tears telling of the 170,000 souls who died on the Great March, seemed somehow more unlikely as a generalised target.

Comrade Teacher Lu was made to kneel with the others, his eyes downcast, and a crowd of Red Guards surrounded them and shouted slogans of hate. Pei Xing had retreated. She did not want to witness another denunciation of 'black counter-revolutionaries'. Nor did she want some quiver of complicity to arise between her and Comrade Lu. Sympathy was dangerous in those dark and volatile times. Afterwards she was haunted by what her fellow students had done — so many had participated in beatings and murders. And afterwards it was not only what she had witnessed but what she had heard, that she could not forget. Her literature teacher was found dead, covered with bruises, her mouth was stuffed with torn pages from an English language book. Her arms were tied backwards in the excruciating 'flying a plane' position. With scant details, this was still unbearable knowledge.

* * *

Afraid to attract attention, Pei Xing walked quickly past the large character posters flapping in the wind, and when she was out of sight of the Red Guards broke into a panicked run. She felt she was running into shadows and from all she held dear, but she was only one of many, very many, who were told to repudiate past histories. The campaign of the Four Olds — destroying Old Customs, Old Culture, Old Habits, Old Ideas — was already well under way; the slogans of the Four Olds were daubed all over the city.

On the door of her home had appeared the

sign: '*Breaking down the Four Olds; setting up the Four News!*' after which the Red Guards had entered, tearing photographs, smashing vinyl records, crushing underfoot her parents' small collection of porcelain figurines. She heard a man call out the slogan on their door, as if reciting Tang Dynasty poetry or a line of sutras from a holy book.

Lao was not at home that day and Pei Xing had worried about his absence. Her mother was crying. Her father was brave. But she saw him tremble with distress when they pulled the books from the shelves and hurled them through the window to be consumed in a bonfire. He had always believed in ideas, not things, words, not new overcoats, but the violent destruction of his possessions must have been more painful than he could show. And they all had yet to learn that possessions would be the least of the destruction.

★　★　★

The visit to the First Department Store in 1958, the purchase of the coat and the advent of snow, was the last period, for many years, of unalloyed happiness. Years of famine followed. The snack sellers disappeared from the streets, even the markets of Shanghai became places of scarcity. Black-market trading depleted the little money her parents had saved. Pei Xing's father, always a thin man, became even thinner, living, it seemed, only on cigarettes, so that when the Cultural Revolution began and the Red Guards came to take him away, he was already half gone. As someone educated abroad and used to negotiating meanings in English and Russian, he was bound to be considered a class traitor and a running dog of imperialists. The weighty terms written in large characters on banners outside their house, the line on the door about the Four Olds, all seemed to bear no relation to her harried parents, but more especially to her father, whose skin was like parchment and who was already translating himself into another world when the Revolution began. He was already thinning in Chinese style, like lines of brushstrokes, a narrow falling vertical, and right to left.

★　★　★

On the train from Kings Cross they were sweeping around a bay. There were so many bays, peninsulas and headlands in central Sydney. The city geography was fashioned by the irregular shape of the Harbour. It was vaster than Catherine had anticipated, and an improbable cornflower blue. She glimpsed the scintillating water, and the old houses of Woolloomooloo. She saw the pearly backs of the Finger Wharves and a scarf of green grass, rising gently, that was called The Domain.

Woolloomooloo; she must look it up somewhere. What could it possibly mean? It had to be Aboriginal, she supposed. Would she Google Woolloomooloo? Brendan would have liked that: to Google Woolloomooloo. Brendan would have made a joke of it, or written a neat lyric poem. Or a song, perhaps:

I met my love, down Woolloomooloo,
I Googled her, down Woolloomooloo,
Her googly eyes, her googly hair,
I Googled my love, down Woolloo
    mooloo . . .

By the time Catherine arrived at Central Station she realised she should have walked; it was a sunny day, downhill, and with much to explore. But she found the Inner West line and set off for the Quay. This was her London habit, to assume that the Tube was the Way, to dive underground, then up again, when one might just as well have walked. Central Station was abuzz with the Saturday morning crowd. Calls rang out, loud voices, random vowels and consonants. In what must have been, she later realised, a synesthesic moment, the voices seemed orange, bright orange, and gleaming like graphite.

★ ★ ★

Patrick Kavanagh, that was one of his favourites. Brendan loved Kavanagh's poem 'On Raglan Road' and the way it was sung in pubs and by motley, all and sundry Irish bands.

On Raglan Road on an autumn day I
*   met her first and knew*
That her dark hair would weave a snare
*   that I might one day rue;*
I saw the danger, yet I walked along the
*   enchanted way;*
And I said, let grief be a fallen leaf at
*   the dawning of the day . . .*

All those Dublin poets. A'moanin' and a'groanin' and thinking forever about love, letting grief be a fallen leaf and crying into their beer.

Brendan had taught her the words of 'On Raglan Road'; it was one of hundreds of poems he had committed to memory. A 'deathless ditty,' he called it.

'When I die,' he said, 'my brain will be riddled with poetry. You should get some surgeon to cut it into lacey slices and find the poetry there.'

They talked about death a lot, when they were young. It was easy then, so daft and distant, and so unimaginable.

'It's Irish,' he said. 'We're a sad-hearted lot, it's why we sing; it's why we rhyme.'

'And you're a walkin'-talkin' all-Irish cliché,' she responded.

Brendan laughed, pleased his little sister was so cheeky and bolshie.

As a university student Catherine moved into a shared house not far from Raglan Road, just to be located where the song had arisen. Brendan said it was fucking brilliant, *fucking brilliant, it was!* to walk each day up Raglan Road, Patrick Kavanagh's road.

Raglan Road, Ballsbridge, Dublin, Ireland, the planet Earth, the Milky Way, the radiant mess of blinking stars, the deep black, the filigree night, the whole endless Universe.

She would walk up the road humming the song, turn left at Pembroke, into Upper Baggot and Lower Baggot and on to St Stephen's Green; she would waste time there when she should be studying, meet her friends at Tonehenge or at the bandstand behind the bust of James Joyce. She wandered the tidy pathways, fancy-free, gallivanting, smooching, mucking about and canoodling. With her friend Dymphna Doyle she met boys at the pub, at Hartigan's, and drank too

135

much. Her mother, had she known, would have said she had a 'reputation'. And with her brother she sat in shady corners with a packet of digestives and a thermos of tea and listened to him talk about politics and poetry.

★　★　★

Once — she must have been twelve or thirteen — they had caught the bus together to Phoenix Park and visited the Dublin Zoo to see the Giant Pandas that had arrived as a gift from China. The Pandas were called (how she enjoyed this!) Ming Ming and Ping Ping. There were images on the telly and photographs in the newspaper. Brendan bought the tickets and borrowed somebody's camera, so there exist mad snaps of them larking about in front of the imported bears.

Ming Ming and Ping Ping were melancholy in the curious way of the obese, plonked there, ungainly, stuck God-only-knows-why on the Emerald Isle. Their gigantic heads turned slowly, as though impossibly heavy, and their movements were blunt and affectionate, like those of infants. Their black eyes were Gothic, and weirdly unnatural. They sat and ate, ate and sat. But all Dublin was charmed. The crowds at the bear enclosure were well behaved and unprecedented. Everyone said so. It was in the *Irish Times*. Even Brendan, with a cynical streak as wide as the Irish Sea, loved the surreal element of displacement and the sense of exotic intervention.

'We'll go to China,' he announced. 'Just you and me. We'll become foreigners, reverse Pandas, and be ridiculously bold!'

How we cherish those who give us our dreams. In the struggle against dispersion, how we value the casual, cohering suggestion.

In a single sentence Brendan produced this wild ambition for both of them and presented his sister with wanderlust associations: the Great Wall, cups of tea, bamboo brushes, twirly noodles. *China* was a machine of formula images and folkloric associations. Pagodas with curled roofs, willow pattern plates. Firecrackers. Red banners. Portraits of Chairman Mao. Catherine loved the idea of becoming a foreigner in the faraway East. Better than a secretary or a schoolteacher, better than a shop-girl in Bewley's, serving currant buns to old farts and complaining ladies with arthritis and lipstick on their teeth, wedded to their god-awful ailments and imperfections.

Brendan asked a fellow gawker to take a photograph, there and then. To this day it was the only image Catherine possessed that contained just the two of them. There were family snaps of course, blurry birthdays and weddings and out-of-focus holy communions, but only this one, this special occasion which caught them together, vigorously happy and kooky, mugging with large smiles under a bunting of bright leaves. A piece of panda was just visible: there was one black eye, hanging like a Goth decoration in the bottom left-hand corner.

It was about that time they all realised that Da was ill. He had always been a smoker, sucking so many that the tips of his fingers looked scorched and he seemed always wreathed, like an idol, in a dim nimbus of smoke. He hacked up muck and had brass-coloured teeth. There was tobacco on his shirt-front and burn holes in his cardigans. But that was Da: they loved him just the same.

It must have been a sinister alchemy that turned the outer signs inwards, all that grubby stain and brown discoloration, because one day, after breakfast, he simply keeled over, coming to rest on the kitchen floor, clutching at his chest. Mam looked down upon the man she had shared her life with, and slowly turned him over on his back to face her. He was alive, but gasping, his face magenta and mottled like streaky bacon.

Brendan had already left home, but the girls crowded round and exclaimed, shocked to see their mother so calm and Da so unmanned, shaken by the appeal of his fear and the intimation of his mortality. Ruthy cried. Ruthy always cried. Mam called for the ambulance, knowing they came slowly to the Ballymun Estate, but without much choice; and the five sisters were posted in turns at the window to watch for its saviour arrival.

★ ★ ★

For almost two weeks Da lingered on, in the ghastly hospital. They all visited together, the mob of them, the whole Healy clan, and one of the nurses whispered 'thick as thieves' when she saw them standing together. They decided to ignore her and later mocked her moustache. They were proud and loyal and always looked out for each other.

One evening, in his extremity, Mam slipped Da a sip of whiskey from a flask, holding his head as if she were holding Jesus. Catherine could not get the image out of her mind, her father dying in a soft and helpless way, her mother cradling him, being Mary, loving him to the end. Though he was sunken and disfigured by his cruel condition, though he dribbled and could not speak and stank of disinfectant and sour breath, Mam loved him to the end just as Mary loved Jesus, full of drowsy sorrow and miraculous belief, aware of the compassionate eye of God and blesséd, as the blesséd Virgin Mary was, First Among Women, Mother of God, Cause of Our Joy and Mystical Rose, so special and so separate in her prayerful weeping.

When they arrived home it was as if all the hospital smells had followed them: Mam sprayed Lily of the Valley from a can, and placed new mothballs among their winter clothes. These were the confusing smells of her father's death. These were the smells of grief unlike a fallen leaf.

Philomena had called out 'Who's for tea?' and they had gathered then, stony-faced, in a circle at the table. Brendan was crying as much as his sisters. He was nineteen, a handsome lad and a hit with the girls, but on that day, at the table, he was returned to boyhood. Red rimmed his eyes and tears ran on his cheeks. Grief had swollen him. He carried it flaring like disease beneath his skin. Catherine loved him all the more when she knew that his grief was like hers. They shared this too, the community of sinners, the peculiar piety of atheists and of sinners unredeemed.

'Those of us that don't believe in Heaven

must stick together,' he once said, 'and believe more strongly in this world — here-now — in this gorgeous mad fuck-up.'

Mam believed: she led a little prayer. They all crossed themselves — even Brendan — and consoled her in this way. Pretending. Performing. In this gorgeous mad fuck-up. Around the table their heads were as beads on a rosary, caught in one beseeching purpose, seeming all the same.

★　★　★

The time of mourning knitted Brendan and Catherine more closely. She remembers that at the Estate there was never any privacy or quiet. Brendan had moved close to University College, using his scholarship to rent a bleak room in a grimy boarding house, the kind full of shuffling old men muttering nonsense into their shirtfronts as they fumbled for begged cigarettes and tripped on the stairs. He was studying literature by then — something Da never understood — and dressing in second-hand clothes from charity bins which he wore with a rakish and heedless flair. Women adored him. He was in love twice a week, and writing volumes of poems to girls with blue eyes and black hair, listening to dramatically unhappy songs and learning the constellations.

141

'*Our stars come from Ireland*,' he told her more than once.

For years Catherine had found this saying enigmatic and only after Brendan died did she discover that there was an American poem of this title, by Wallace Stevens. Somewhere in America some poor bastard was thinking of Ireland, thinking of distance, and the turning planet, and of the sky sliding its twinkling diagrams through the dark, lonesome night. Some Irish foreigner, gone-in-the-head, in a new far land. Some Son of Erin staring homesick at the starlit heaven.

Celestial glissade, Brendan called it, in one of his own poems. *East and West confounded.*

They spoke of the stars. They looked at and considered them. As you do. They spoke of Da and death and the absence of the hereafter. They helped each other. And although Brendan had love-affairs non-stop he seemed without intimate friends, and Catherine knew that somehow she provided this too, a kind of comfort of understanding and the forgiveness of all sins. He seemed wholly unmindful of the difference in their age; it was from Brendan she first learned of the abstract and extraordinary operations of sex, from him she heard of Marx, and mixed drinks and the relativity of time, of

Wolfe Tone, and the Easter Rebellion and the whole heartbreaking, maddening, fitful-fangled quality of Irish history. Books and music became the trade between them. Band Aid happened (how they both hated Elton John) and yet another Eurovision ('and who could forget,' Brendan said, in a high-pitched TV voice, 'the glorious achievement of Johnny Logan singin' 'Hold Me Now', bejesus and bemary, ah hold me now, in all his star-spangly, big-eejit Eurovision glory. Go hold yourself, said the tart to the bishop . . . ')

So many sentences of Brendan's speech wafted in Catherine's memory. They trailed through at chance moments, like a delayed echo. Sometimes she would be altogether elsewhere, minding her own business, getting on with her life, and Brendan's voice would softly sound; and not only the content of his funny sayings and haphazard rude wisdom, but also his timbre and tone, his particular intonation, his pauses, his sighs, his put-on accents, arriving like a breath on the back of the neck, catching her shivery and unaware.

For a long time she believed herself a derivative creature, taking all she knew from her older brother. It was a place he gave her, on the rim of his life. So much of what she knew, Brendan had taught her. But her interest in journalism and rock music — these were truly her own. These she cultivated with an exclusive, almost irrational, devotion.

★　★　★

After the death of their father Catherine felt free to worship U2. There was nothing more beautiful in the world than Bono bursting his lungs out, singing 'With or Without You'. In the black and white video-clip on the telly he wore a leather waist-coat and no shirt; his naked forearms glistened and he eyed the camera as if he was shagging it. His face advanced and retreated in a system of dark shadows, oh the plea of miserable love, oh the dank seedy magnetism. No tinted glasses; the Edge wore no cap. They were unadorned and not yet so preposterously famous, not yet kings of all Dublin and Champions of the World.

Catherine found Bono's voice deeply sexual and romantic; she played him in her head like a dirty secret. At the end of the footage of 'With or Without You' Bono emerged in half-light to swing his guitar like a madman.

Pure genius, that's what it was. Pure fecking genius, as Brendan would say.

Bono was so televisually distraught every young woman in Ireland wanted to comfort him, to drag him from the punishing contrasts of Orson Welles cinematography to the quiet soothing twilight of an unmade bed.

Catherine was fourteen years old. The passions conceived then, felt in the quiver of the heart and the unmentionable spaces of the body, experienced in dear obsessions and constant cravings, these were as significant as any adult formulation of desire, and more direct, more alive, more radically imperative.

★　★　★

The train swung in a wide arc to emerge alongside sturdy buildings and suddenly pulled into Circular Quay. She'd not noticed the journey, it had been so swift. In this new city she was still moving in guessed distances and miscalculations.

Where was her ticket? She needed it to exit.

With or without you. Jesus, she thought, still this fucking eighties' song, still a younger, sexy Bono hollering in her head.

Passengers all around her were rising to leave. There was the etiquette of standing just apart, and waiting, and a polite crowding before the doors. Catherine hitched her shoulder-bag and rose up, out of her childhood.

And she reflected then that for all her adoration of U2, for all her wish both to follow and not to follow Brendan, when she walked on Raglan, or any road, she still sang the songs that her brother loved, she still heard his voice, and thought of every damn thing that he had taught her, and all the visions he had inspired, and their sweet sibling complicity. And when she closed her eyes at night she still dreamed of going faraway, to Australia, here-now, and eventually to China.

4

Circular Quay: she loved even the sound of it. Such was the fabulous allure of the place that by noon the crowds had further grown and voices and activity were multiplied. Secular pilgrims all bent on transcendental satisfactions. Ellie realised her own pedantry, thinking in these terms, yet what moved her was the same longing for accessible wonderment.

There were streams of people walking in a kind of procession to and from the Opera House, but more still aimlessly strolling or self-amused, just hanging around, *lollygagging*, taking in the scene. And then there were the regular citizens wanting to catch a ferry, those who must encounter every day this restless quality of excitement. The mix of peoples would be everywhere — at the Eiffel Tower and the Acropolis, at the Forbidden City and Borobudur, at Niagara Falls and the Grand Canyon, at the Louvre and Uluru, at art museums that were architecturally wavy or contorted. Monuments addressed us this way: pause here, consider. What hunger is driving you? What loss? What ambition? How does this place figure in your dreams?

* * *

Ellie had not lost her thrill, or her bouncing heart. The white umbrellas were like flags, the colours of the crowd a festivity. The air still throbbed and hummed with a distant didgeridoo. It filtered and dispersed like religious communication, implying inner worlds and the dimensions of deserts. And in her camera lay the ghost arabesques of the Opera House, radiant as neon light, an image she could not quite comprehend. Photon capture and digital transfer did nothing to explain it. An idea about the thing, not the thing itself.

Ellie hesitated a moment. *Download* was not equivalent to presence. Or the same as memory, which happened in an enclosure of flesh and carried the blessings of the body, and its manifold complications.

* * *

James. She must find James.

Ellie shrugged to adjust her small backpack and glanced at her watch. Another half an hour. She decided to sit beside the water and stare into space. The ferries came and left, churning the glistening water.

Combs of light: where was that from?

148

On the water lay combs of light, shifting their patterns with fluctuations of current and wind. Ellie looked across to the Bridge and wondered if one day she might climb it. It must be a singular pleasure, with no end other than to rise, to see, to stand above the turquoise water and the green and yellow ferries and look out across the Harbour and the city spread between the ocean and the mountains. The great bowl of the water would shine up at the climbers, reflecting the sun like a giant mirror, and the faces of parents and children and taxpayers and tourists would be polished gold and transformed to mini-lights by its glare.

★ ★ ★

At first James and Ellie had groped at each other's bodies-ignorant kids, filled with vague prohibitions and sexual platitudes — just clumsily exploring. Each watched the other with an ardent and shy fascination. James's face was flushed coral, his eyes were bright.

After they discovered their hideout everything became possible. They would lie on a blanket in the dusty after-school light, read to each other and talk in soft voices. Once James spoke of clepsydra: Ellie remembered it well. Miss Morrison had told them of notions of time, and said that the clepsydra, the water clock, was one of the earliest inventions. The Chinese, she said, devised particularly ornate and complex clepsydra. The Chinese invented everything, she announced without explanation.

Clepsydra, from the Greek *kleptein*, meaning to steal.

She wrote *kleptomaniac* on the board, beside the underlined *clepsydra* and asked her class to consider how human time was measured.

'Is it really kept inside your watch?' Miss Morrison asked. 'Does time really tick? Or work by numbers? Or pass in neat measured segments? Might there be a time that flows, or indeed does not flow?'

Clepsydra involved vessels that dripped or leaked, flowed or seeped, making use of floating pointers or measures, sometimes of gears. It was a process, she said, of emptying and filling, a fluent time-passing, not one chopped into pieces.

Most of the class looked bored and perplexed. Someone was flicking balls of paper polished with spit. But for intelligent twelve-year-olds this idea was a revelation. Ellie and James truly loved Miss Morrison.

★   ★   ★

And that day, two years later, James was lying on his back in the abandoned foundry, looking at the cobwebby ceiling, all girders and split tin, and speaking, almost whispering, of the invention of clepsydra. He was recalling the year seven class and Miss Morrison with a kind of delicate affection.

That day James turned towards Ellie and ran his hand under her blue dress and she thought not of surrender but that she would gather him in. Ellie could feel James's warmth and arousal, and his body addressed and aroused her. What she loved in him was his presumption, and his lack of presumption.

That day they decided for the first time to remove their clothes. James, lying down, awkwardly wriggled from his shirt and his trousers, then kicked off his underpants, flinging them away. Ellie was slower and more self-conscious. She lifted her dress above her head and pushed it to one side, then became aware of how little her breasts were, cupped in their modest bra, incipient and girlish. But James was already pushing the bra away, so that together and laughing they managed to dispatch it. James threw it high and sideways, and something in its lacy construction meant that it adhered to the gritty wall, as if casually pinned there. Ellie hesitated only for a second before she slid off her panties.

Without a bed to lie in, with only their blanket and their randy, impatient immaturity, they wrestled for a time and then gripped each other. James's mouth was at her nipple and Ellie was moved almost to tears; it was so tender a suckle, and so gloriously wet. His hand had wandered between her legs and slipped into the crevice. She knew now, with his boyish nakedness nothing like the pictures of statues she had seen in books, with this sense of urgency and novelty and trembling delight, why adults might want to cast off their clothes and enter each other's bodies, and what the intensified, messy kisses on telly might signal and portend.

And then James drew her thighs around him and Ellie felt a sharp pain. Her face lay at his chest. She buried her feelings there. James was sweating and his scent was surprisingly lovely. He was labouring, and looking down at her, and in her inexperience she simply lay still, thinking, not thinking. She could feel the contours of his buttocks and the sensation of access.

'Ellie,' he whispered.

It was over very quickly. There was an aching pain, and a little blood, but she felt in that unlit and quiet space that somehow she had made them both coherent. Even then she was irrepressibly romantic. In the inept grapple of two children she found an exultation. Ellie kissed James's damp forehead as he lowered sumptuously upon her.

'I feel like singing,' he said. 'I feel like singing.'

'Sing then,' she responded.

That first time they heard afterwards a small animal scuttling nearby, and each flinched and looked about, conscious of another presence. A possum, they decided. They heard it invisibly skitter away. Ellie turned to James's flushed face and saw him smile back at her and laugh.

She became aware then of the twilight and the need suddenly to hurry home. Light from the evening scarcely penetrated the room. But she stayed a little longer, feeling slightly cold without her thin blue dress, one of her favourites, covered in sprigs of tiny white blossom (how these details remain), noting the seep between her legs and its unanticipated warmth, smelling the almond scent she associated thereafter with men's underwear, thinking, as she saw James flex his arms and stretch out beside her, of how vast a discovery this was, and how enticingly scary.

This cluster of illicit associations returned James to Ellie. Or meant rather that he would never be wholly released. The intimacy of their attachment was something neither could name. They did not call each other 'boyfriend' or 'girlfriend', they were too young to be 'lovers', yet they were the holders together of an intricate pact. When they met in the empty building where James spread the old blanket on the dusty floor — as if they were somewhere on a picnic, or inside a story or at play — it was the culmination of these affinities altogether unexpressed.

★   ★   ★

Her mother never guessed. Ellie was unconcerned about her father, since he looked at the world and everything in it through a scrim of shadows; but to her surprise, in that whole year, her mother didn't notice a change in her daughter or sense a new maturity. At seventeen, before Ellie left for university, Lil gave her a private talk about what boys might do, about how sneaky and downright importunate they were, about how, after all, they *wanted only one thing*. Ellie hung her head, as though reticent, not wanting to betray what she knew. And each time afterwards, with each new lover, she sought the implicated traces of her encounters with James. More than his shape, more than his touch, more than his off-hand humour and his inexperienced fervour, she wanted returned to her the ordinary astonishment of that first known body.

★ ★ ★

Ellie rose in the bright light and began to make her way to the restaurant. She felt nervous, ill-at-ease. What if they didn't even recognise each other? What if he leant across the table and tried to kiss her? Or worse, that they had nothing to say to each other, that the past was meaningless, and kiddie-romantic, and unfit for their adult-ironic thirties? What if he was married to someone called Emma or Claire, and had two delightful children, a boy and a girl?

In her nervousness Ellie decided to check her mobile: no texts, no messages. She was one of millions checking their phone at exactly that moment; she could see a dozen or so from where she stood. This community of the telephone, so pragmatically conjoined. Ellie stared at the sequences of letters and numbers. In the glowing alphabet in her hand lay every word in the world.

What was it Miss Morrison had said, all those years ago, about the invention of the alphabet? And why could she not stop thinking of her teacher?

155

Ellie walked with feigned confidence along the Quay, past the Museum of Contemporary Art, around which hung funky red banners advertising something-or-other, past the seagulls aflutter and the row of docks for small vessels, and further, towards the Bridge, to the harbourside restaurant James had chosen.

She was surprised at the size of it and would have liked something smaller. It had a wide glassy front, the better to see the operatic view, and furniture that seemed entirely to be made of chrome. Everything glittered in the noonday light. The cutlery glittered, and the crockery, and the smiles on the waiters' faces, so that Ellie was reminded of a swimming pool, the shine rocking on water and the splashy, unnaturally echoey acoustics. She stood at the doorway waiting to be noticed.

'DeMello,' Ellie said, in an apologetic voice, and a jerky impatient waiter pointed to a table. She saw James, looking away, apparently deep in thought. Her first impression was that he might be ill, or had a terrible night.

He was wearing a denim shirt and black jeans and was still handsome in the way that ageing rock stars are, slightly wrecked, but with the charm of a wild history saved by the adoration of flashbulbs. Or someone nuts about Jesus, a holy roller, wanting to convert you on the doorstep or redeem the world.

James had not seen her. He was transfixed by a distant sight, his face faraway and half-dreaming. He had the look of a man who had forgotten something important. Ellie would have found it difficult to approach had he been tracking her walk towards him.

She dived into the mock-watery world of the waiters, past the women with heads like baubles, bottle-blonde and puffed, past well-upholstered men, anticipating sozzled entertainments, past the sinuous fish-moves of figures with wine bottles wrapped in serviettes, and oversized plates held high, dodging and swerving. She emerged standing before him: well, here I am.

James was taken by surprise. He stood up quickly, bumping the table. There was a moment of hesitation before he kissed her cheek, uncertain of how formally or infor-mally to behave. 'You haven't changed,' he said.

'Nor have you,' she lied.

A waiter appeared from nowhere to pull out the chair and guide Ellie into it. He fluffed open a stiff serviette and let it fall onto her lap, as if she were an infant or in need of basic forms of assistance. With one hand behind his back he made a dainty ceremony of pouring a glass of water.

★ ★ ★

The past caved in on them. In each other's eyes they saw a dim, vertiginous slide backwards. Family. School. Small-town childhoods. The discontinuous histories each carried within them. They were part of that group for whom time past travels like a screen before them. In the opalescent day lay their shadowy hideout; in the chattering crowd a few preserved words.

Ellie thought: *no longer children*. She calculated the years that had intervened, and saw too that they were surely unknowable, each to each. Too much time between them, other lovers, other lives.

'So, here we are.'

'Yes,' Ellie said.

Oh God, she was thinking, I shouldn't have come.

But she was also thinking: it's really him. This was the James who had been a stubble-headed boy covered with blood, who had cried to see a scrawny chicken decapitated, who had been the clever one, the teacher's pet, always quick with the right answers, who had met her as a naked boy, nothing like a statue, in a filthy old foundry. She would have to make the effort for both of them. Why is it, she was thinking, it's always women who have to keep the conversation going and find the right words?

'Here we are,' she repeated lamely.

★   ★   ★

By the time he arrived at the restaurant James was nervous and moist with sweat; it was a relief, having arrived early, to sit alone in the Antarctic air-conditioning. Faux alfresco. But he had to endure a supercilious waiter, overtly insolent, and the extra brightness of spotlighting, which would surely induce a new headache.

James looked out of the window at the view of Circular Quay. From his table he could see across the water the Opera House entire. He began vaguely to wonder how the Surrealists would paint it. Magritte would place it in a forest or let it float in the sky; Dali would melt it like ice-cream, like one of his dissolving clocks; Max Ernst would use it as ruffles on the cloak around a pompous figure. No: Magritte would set it adrift in the ocean, like a rare, efflorescent species of underwater

159

life; Dali would refigure it as the chambers of a woman's body; Ernst would have children fleeing it on a sparse, bleak plain, as if it had arrived from nowhere, from outer space, as a menacing apparition. And then there was the Australian, James Gleeson. For him the smooth arcs of the Opera House would be covered with excrescences; grim faces would appear, limbs sprout out, indefinable and disgusting matter would festoon the surface.

James was surprised to have relinquished his initial aversion; it was an art-object after all, it contained multitudes, suggested metaphors.

A woman at a party had once told him that surrealism was an adolescent taste, something for lonely teenage boys wanting to do violence to the order of things — and he found himself agreeing. He had discovered the instability of images when he discovered his own body; somehow these were linked, though he could not bring himself to consider why. He had slept with the woman from the party, whose name he could not now recall, and woke in the middle of the night, his heart pounding, his forehead aflame, his thoughts in a boring and groggy loop — *surrealism is an adolescent taste* — feeling he had been criticised for his judgement, and found pathetically wanting.

160

James entered the slack reverie of the over-tired. He was thinking randomly of the patina of light on the faces of pedestrians, of the ferries, the buskers, the wake on the water; he was wondering if the seagulls ever flew sideways and smashed into the glass. He tried imagining what it must be like to live here, not simply to visit. Do Sydney-siders regularly converge on this place, as if coming to a shrine? Do they esteem this monument, that from here, receding in the ultraviolet assault of the midday sun, appeared to be constructed of ancient bone? Or was it all rugby and beaches and the Good Life with a beer? Conspicuous consumption. Unreal real estate. The aspiration to a many-roomed immoderate house, shaped like a wedding cake, with a sweeping Harbour view.

But there it was: ancient bone. *Imperishable*, that was the word.

★ ★ ★

And then Ellie was before him, appearing without announcement. The Opera House disappeared; the commotion of the restaurant subsided. He lurched upwards, bumping the table, causing a little spill. He paused, and then cautiously leant forward to kiss her on the cheek.

'You haven't changed,' James said, his voice rusty from pills.

'Nor have you,' she lied.

He was grateful for the small mercy she displayed in not confirming the wreck he felt himself to be. She had not recoiled, or thought him repellent.

Yet he spoke honestly; she seemed essentially unchanged. In her face he saw the girl he had doted on at school. She was still slim, though more womanly, and held her head just so, slightly inclined to the left, just as she did twenty years ago. And he remembered this: that she was tender, but not meek, that she had a street-tough element and a resilient streak, that she was bold and assertive in ways that had made him seem the weaker one. She wore a white blouse and a blue skirt of some filmy synthetic material. Lipstick. Pink.

'So, here we are.'

'Yes,' Ellie said.

She was stretching one arm then the other from the straps of her small backpack. James saw a glimpse of the skin on her chest as her blouse briefly gaped. A glimmer of sexual memory recurred, the moment of winsome recline, the arm cast back, the curve of an exposed breast, the unconcealed invitation. He suppressed the image almost immediately and looked away. On the path before the restaurant an overweight couple ambled past, their arms affectionately draped around each other's backs. Both wore identical baseball caps and matching loose clothes, as if belonging to an exclusive club of two. James was moved; he was sentimental. He felt the same way watching old couples walk hand in hand, or bending solicitously towards each other over cups of tea. A gentleness of bodies long proximate and wordlessly comfortable.

It may have been the sedative effect of gazing out the window; James realised that he was no longer anxious. But he was dumb-struck and feeling foolish at the paucity of his words. What to say?

'Here we are,' she repeated, and with this forgiving chime, they began.

★　★　★

Ellie took a sip of water and seemed slightly abashed. There was food to order; the waiter was hovering and insistent. They busied themselves with gigantic menus bound with gold cord, like something one might see in a church, opened slowly by a priest. Both decisively ordered the grilled barramundi.

Salad, not vegetables. And a New Zealand white. So it was quickly settled. Their instinctive unanimity made the first moments together easier.

'No entreé?' the waiter asked, in a tone that said 'cheapskate'. He was perhaps seventeen and subtly fierce in his persecuting disrespect.

James moved a small basket of bread rolls to disguise his embarrassment.

'We have enough,' Ellie said firmly. And the waiter turned away.

★ ★ ★

So they were, at last, left alone to talk. James realised that he had chosen the wrong place for a rendezvous, too noisy, too Saturday, too public, too bright, too susceptible to his sardonic turn of mind and his disdain of relaxation. A dusky bar, late at night — that would have worked. A quiet corner with a banquette and the kind of sensual confinement that permits bodies to lean seductively towards each other, to find a whispery tone and a cunning route for confidences. Perhaps a trumpet, low-playing a plangent jazz solo. Perhaps a furtive tab of pharmaceutical stimulation.

But he was here, *here-now*, and had much to say, and to confess. He must tell Ellie how he had carried her, all these years, how through everything there persisted the residue of her affinity and understanding. She was a voice in his head; she was a passenger he transported. Her shape, her face. Her grace a still incredible immanence that had tempered his fucked-up life.

Her hair was short now, James saw, and seemed a lighter brown. She was looking down at her lap.

And he must tell her of the child who died, and for whom he felt responsible. Only Ellie would understand. He must tell her of his mother, and of his long-time regret. It was a time of apology. He must also apologise. He must say sorry. He must drag sincere words from his heart to his mouth. He must say something, so that he might be cured of the ordeal of his own history, of his failings, of his loss, of his disabling culpability.

★ ★ ★

Of these things, at this time, James said nothing. In the raucous restaurant, no place for a confession, Ellie and James spoke together in a casual way, ascertaining that each was still single, no kids, that Ellie had moved to Sydney to take up a postgraduate scholarship, returning to university after all

165

these years, and worked part-time in a hole-in-the-wall coffee shop on King Street; that he was a med-school dropout but a committed schoolteacher, that he had declined the scholarship that had been proclaimed in the small-town paper, that he had bummed around Europe with a backpack and settled for a couple of years in London, that he was now visiting, just for a few days, with no declared purpose. There was a dark patch he skipped over, something he could not yet tell her. Yes, he still played the guitar, was still a crazy Bob Dylan fan; and no, he had never, never ever, returned to the old town.

The meals arrived and both were relieved to have something neutral to claim their attention. James tore at the bread, using it to mop, as his mother had taught him. Italian, *Mama*. Today she was more than usually present.

'Do you remember,' Ellie said suddenly, 'our teacher, Miss Morrison?'

'Of course.'

'The way she wrote arcane words on the board, and underlined them?'

'Clepsydra,' said James. He saw Ellie blush. 'I was cruel, wasn't I? Boys are such bastards.'

'She liked you. Both of us. Teachers always like the clever ones . . . '

James shrugged.

'Well, she liked you best, teacher's pet,' said Ellie. 'And she taught us all those fancy Greek and Latin words.'

James thought of clepsydra. Across the table this young woman was recalling their first time: he knew it. In a confused second between mouthfuls he wanted nothing more than to slip his hand beneath her skirt and remove her panties, to find himself back in the foundry, to enjoy *adolescent* lust. Their love-making had been simple, blundering, making up in lewd vigour what it lacked in sure knowledge. James had no idea then how to treat a woman's body; he entered, collapsed, found a momentary logic for his meagre boy's life, pulled into hers. Still, it had astounded him, to be alive in that way at fourteen. To enter another body.

James poured more wine for himself and knew he was drinking too fast. Ellie had barely touched her glass. James's thirst was crude and demanding. He thought of slipping away for a moment to swallow another pill, but the compulsion of Ellie's presence was too difficult to break.

Fluids, essential for homeostasis. *Polydipsia*: excessive thirst, one of the indications of diabetes. *Dipsomania*: drunkenness.

★ ★ ★

Not long after the death James considered returning to their town. His mother had died in the hospital in the city, where she inhabited her sad lonely skull full of snow, and a letter from a lawyer arrived, requesting a 'consultation'. James turned up at an office in a tower block, one of those buildings that looks like a huge filing cabinet, and found there a gloomy looking man, Mr English, with marble eyes and a touch of brilliantine in his starkly black hair. He sat behind a wide desk, his hands shaped into a cathedral. After the antiseptic formality of condolences, none of which could assuage the guilt that had subsumed James's grief, Mr English informed him that the house he had shared with his mother might now be worth something. The strip of land along the beach, once the space of outcast migrants, of *dagoes and chinks*, he might have said, was being redeveloped to construct a group of chalets for a beach resort. He pronounced the word 'chalet' as if he were eating a plum. And then there were the 'goods and chattels', he added (James wondered if lawyers lived, as doctors did, in a world of parallel vocabulary), since the house had been closed up when his mother was committed to the 'institution'. Might there be something of worth locked away? He was acting, he said more formally, on behalf of the

168

'institution', which often had cases like this, of deceased estates 'going begging'.

James sat before Mr English, noted his large brow and his clean fingernails and the hairs curling on the backs of his hands, noted the framed documents on the wall, and the imposing beige surrounds, and felt too disqualified as a son to know what to say. He resented this horrible man, with designs on their house. It had been such a poor, despised place, symbolic of all he wished to leave; now this man who inspired such distaste was urging a conspiracy of profit. James had risen from the chair and without a word, left the lawyer's office.

★　★　★

'I once thought of returning to the old town,' James said, out of the blue. 'After Mum died I considered visiting to deal with her things. To sell the house. Tidy up. And I wanted to see you,' he added shyly.

'When was that?'

'Almost ten years ago. You had left, I heard. So I never returned.'

It was as close as he would come to saying that she was his only reason for returning; or more forcefully, that she was the only past he could admit.

'Couldn't do it,' he went on, remembering the dreadful emptiness of that time, the funeral, oh God, that no one attended, the woman he was with, who found his prolonged weeping rather touching at first, but then disgraceful and unmanly. She told him so. After that they could only draw painfully apart. After his mother, the scale of his feelings shifted. After mother, the deluge.

'I didn't cope very well. The death, I mean.'

Why was he telling her this?

'I'm sorry,' Ellie said. 'I remember your mother. I remember her voice, calling.'

It was the wrong thing to say. James looked at the mess of fish scraps on his plate. Jesus, *she* was sorry.

As if telepathically called the waiter appeared to take away their plates. Coffee, yes. The waiter smirked at his small victory.

★   ★   ★

The vast white silence of his mother's death overhung their conversation. He had seen her on the very last day, summoned by a nurse at the hospital who believed in the spiritual solace of goodbye, and who, reading her details, had already called a Catholic priest. His mother was almost entirely vacant. She did not acknowledge her son. She could not

170

speak or respond. Beneath the covers of the standard issue hospital linen, pale blue blankets with a honeycomb texture, her body had never looked so reduced and so small. The outline might have been of a child, or a victim of starvation. Her spotted hands clutched at the covers and her face was closed and unfamiliar. James thought her eyes enormous, sunk as they were into their sockets, and was afraid she might open them, afraid of what they might see. Afraid for himself, perhaps, because while she lived, even in a snowstorm, he was still a little boy. While she lived, even evacuated, he need not be the grown-up and sensible one.

So he stood there listening to the disastrous ebbing of her breath, he stood there, at her bedside, giving death its dominion, he stood there letting her slip into darkness without dragging her back, or following, or pretending — for whose sake? — that there might be a glow, a release, a transformation, he stood there in blasphemous misery hearing the priest's words as gibberish and his own shabby muteness as a self-accusation, he stood there willing her to die more quickly.

Go away, for Christ's sake, go away, go away.

Overhead a fluorescent tube quietly fizzed. The light it cast was knife-sharp and almost unbearable. There was nowhere to hide. James stood in silence under the shadowless fluorescence that already signified her absence.

Afterwards the priest clasped his hands in an automatic handshake, and James found almost comical his earnest tone. 'She's with God,' the priest said. James wanted in return to give hysterical, ungodly offence, to argue for the medical impossibility of resurrection, to send this man and his ingratiating theories packing. But the nurse was beside him, with a cup of tea, and he drank down his feelings, calmed his own mutiny, grateful to have a solid object like a teacup to clutch on to.

★ ★ ★

The coffee arrived. Her flat white, his espresso. James drew his cup forward and looked up. Ellie was examining him.

'You didn't marry?' she asked softly.

Only then, hearing her blunt inquiry, looking into her eyes, seeing the slight moisture there and the intensity of her concern, did James realise there was lingering desire in her voice. Her lips were still slightly parted. She lowered her gaze and tore open a small sachet of white sugar.

'Well, you know . . . ' he said vaguely. The

noise in the restaurant rose, fell back, resumed its generalised clatter. He was distracted by the din and felt once again numb and dull. He glimpsed the threshold of what might be said, then retreated. 'So what about this new government?' He was trying to find another topic.

'I'm full of hope,' Ellie announced. 'I believe, I really do, that the Apology will change everything. It will alter history. And it can't be bad having a polyglot prime minister.'

'You think that matters?'

'Has to. Has to open his horizons.'

James was silent. Ellie was still the optimist; she believed in redemptive futures. He repressed the impulse to lecture her on the necessity for political cynicism. Besides, they had reached that point in the conversation when both were disengaging, when too much remembering had eclipsed what it might be possible to say to each other. James was confused by his own responses to seeing Ellie so unchanged, and so self-possessed. This was her beauty, he reflected, her command of her own life, her staunch independence. Something about her concentrated presence was effortless and assured. And now Ellie was turning her silver rings on her slender fingers; she had the resigned, soft gaze of a passenger on a long-distance flight. He had bored her, he thought. He was an idiot, a fuckwit.

The lunch concluded. Ellie was sending her mobile number to James.

'Let's talk again,' she said. 'In another context. Give me a call. Any time.'

James's phone rang. He silenced it. 'Got it,' he said. These were magical numbers. The code to find her by.

There was a moment of tense hesitation as Ellie looked into his eyes. What must she be thinking?

Her bright pink lips. Bob Dylan's 'I Want You'; its facile declaration.

'Of course. We'll talk tomorrow, if that's OK.' He looked down at his fingers, entering her name into the mysterious world of telephonic memory. 'Thanks. For meeting up.' He felt unworthy of her, a prisoner of his own skulking gloom and tongue-tied desire. A mug-shot of a man.

Ellie stepped forward and embraced him. This time James felt her shape, the sturdy curve of her back, the soft and confident press of her breasts. He made himself let go, made the embrace unsexual. It had been like a bad date, a couple attracted but inert, a conversation that turned from easy news to freelance unhappiness.

'Tomorrow,' she repeated.

James watched her walk away. He thought of the priest holding his hands, saying 'With God'. He thought of René Magritte's painting of the lovers, their faces smothered in cloth. Then he thought of another painting, the giant red lipstick lips, ludicrous, dream-crazy, floating like a joke in the sky.

★ ★ ★

Pei Xing disembarked at Kurraba Point Wharf on the North Shore. She stepped lightly from the ferry onto the narrow gangplank, then onto the jetty, finding her land legs. Only a few other passengers ended their journeys here. She looked up at the high row of steps and the rim of houses overlooking the harbour, some of them teetering, it seemed, with the weight of their own importance. The wind was still fresh. She held her face to it, enjoying the sweep of scented air and the deep breaths of spirit. The Harbour was magnificent, and richly blue. From somewhere among the small yachts moored in the bay there was the clink-clink of metal hitting an aluminium mast. In her sudden lightheartedness Pei Xing paused to perform a Tai Chi gesture, right there, in the sunlight. And so, after placing her heavy handbag carefully to one side, she held out her right arm, lifted her left leg, leant sideways, swung back, swooping her arms in a restrained formal elegance before her, moving into eternity for a few precious seconds. She held the pose, staring at nothing. She felt the shape of her body and the fine balances it could achieve, muscles taut, or relaxed, or forming a woven pattern of crimson chords tucked deep inside her. The left leg down, the weight moved, the arc of her arms afloat on the air. *Qigong*. The life of breath.

Then she began again, her arms upraised: the soft sway of a movement known as 'cloud hands'.

Behind her the ferry lurched away with an animist tremor of departure.

★ ★ ★

The weekly visit was a source of argument between Pei Xing and her son Jimmy. Even Cindy, his girlfriend, did not understand, but was quieter about it and less confronting. Why would a woman want to visit her former prison guard? Why reattach to that history? Why torment herself so? And Pei Xing would pause, and collect her thoughts and say again that it was something difficult to explain, but that there were forms of forgiveness that make life go on, and forms of reproach that hold history still. She needed, she told them, to live in the aura of forgiveness. At this announcement Jimmy had almost guffawed. He had been sloshing noodles into his mouth, his chopsticks quickly scooping, and he threw his head back in an exaggerated, groaning laugh. He was eating pork heart and bok choy cooked in an aniseed broth, topped with glass noodles. Pei Xing looked into the bowl at his half-eaten meal and saw before her *xin*, the character radical of *heart*. One of the very first characters her father had taught her. She must have been only three years old. Four strokes of the brush. Simplicity itself. He had guided her hand. And almost immediately Pei Xing saw the character 'heart' everywhere, in 'love', in 'mind', in 'remember', in 'forget'.

Cindy looked critically at Jimmy, but said nothing. In the restaurant in Chinatown they had been enjoying their meal; now, Jimmy implied, she had spoiled it once again with all this talk of the old country, with all this returning to the past and her refusal to let go. Pei Xing considered continuing the argument ('this is how one lets go, in sympathetic reconciliation'), but remained silent. She could not bring her words to her mouth from her own lumpish heart.

It occurred to Pei Xing that there were

177

things her son would never understand because he was not a reader. Reading had taught her that actors in history must find a logic beyond violence. When Jimmy was smaller they had watched action movies together; it was the one activity he allowed her to join. Now she wondered if, seeking his company, she had also encouraged his ignorance.

Cindy was also eating like a starving peasant. Pei Xing flinched at their manners, at the voracity of their consumption. She averted her gaze. Another dish arrived, steaming mushrooms with shallots, and Jimmy stabbed at it with his chopsticks even before it hit the table.

All around them were happy young men and women, many of them students, or like Jimmy, children of migrants who left China in the 1980s. Hong Kong businessmen, Guangzhou entrepreneurs. Dissidents, perhaps, from Beijing and Shanghai, even minority Uighars, a group of whom ran a small restaurant in a side-street not far from where they sat. They were gambling, every one of them, on another kind of life. Chinese people liked to gamble. You only had to go to Star City Casino on a Saturday night to see Chinese at the roulette tables, mesmerised by the wheel, or betting their savings on the capricious turn of a single card. They were the regulars, hailing each other in the timeless light, wandering the cavernous, cacophonous spaces, wondering what they were doing there and what happened to the dreams of their ancestors.

Pei Xing had been tempted herself when she had first arrived in Australia. Incapacitated by migrancy, she had sought a dollar-sign solution. And after her brother's sudden death, within weeks of her arrival, she lost most of her savings in a single, utterly desolate night.

★　★　★

Pei Xing began the long walk up the hill towards the nursing home. Dong Hua would be waiting. Although she had experienced a stroke, the nurses said that she could still understand what was going on. She couldn't speak and was paralysed in most of her body, but she waited, they said, she waited for each visit. The weekend duty nurse was a plump, efficient woman who ushered her in and the staff knew by now that Pei Xing visited every Saturday, bringing her lunch with her, to sit with Mrs Dong and read to her in English, or to talk softly in Chinese. They indulged and liked her; they brought her cups of green tea.

179

Hua sat propped in a wheelchair, tilted to one side. Her face was pulled back towards the bone, burnished and hard, like beaten bronze. Pei Xing saw the twitch of the mouth on the right side that indicated recognition. Hua, or one of the nurses, must somehow keep track of the days, since she was always there, in a clean blouse, with her long hair brushed, parked beside the empty visitor's chair.

Pei Xing crossed the room and lightly touched Hua's hand. Then she straightened her collar, which had folded under. A tear sprang from the corner of the patient's eye; more lightly Pei Xing wiped it away with her finger.

She did not ask the usual rhetorical questions — 'so how are you today?' — these only upset Hua. Instead, she announced matter-of-factly:

'We are almost at the end of *Doctor Zhivago*. Chapter Fifteen. Conclusion. But don't be fooled. After Conclusion there is Epilogue, then sixty pages of Zhivago's poems. So we have a few weeks yet.'

Pei Xing flicked though her book — another fifty pages of story. 'The Conclusion is seventeen chapters,' she said. 'Let's see how we go. It takes Mr Pasternak a long time to finish his story.'

In truth, she was pleased with Mr Pasternak's delay, with the story that went on and on and on. She always remembered her joy as a young woman when she discovered that after the Conclusion, after Zhivago's death, which she now approached with serious trepidation, there was the story of his discovered daughter, the laundrywoman Tonya, living in a labour camp.

Pei Xing made herself comfortable and held the large volume before her:

All that is left is to tell the brief story of the last eight or ten years of Zhivago's life, years in which he went more and more to seed, gradually losing his knowledge and skill as a doctor and a writer, emerging from his state of depression and resuming his work only to fall back, after a short flare-up of activity, into long periods of indifference to himself and to everything in the world.

Pei Xing glanced up at Hua. She was staring into the distance, but was certainly concentrating. Hua looked over as if to ask: why have you stopped? So Pei Xing resumed:

181

During these years the heart disease, which he had himself diagnosed earlier but without any real idea of its gravity, developed to an advanced stage . . .

Pei Xing read from an English edition, and in the beginning had paused every now and then to explain a word or a phrase she thought Hua might not know. But she quickly discovered that Hua preferred her to read right through. She may have been guessing the meaning from context, or learning as she went; she may have had a better knowledge of English than Pei Xing had surmised. Pei Xing recalled how many words she had looked up in the dictionary, the first time she read it, and how many idiomatic translations she had found difficult to understand. '*He went more and more to seed*': how unintelligible that had sounded. From *Doctor Zhivago* she had learnt a smattering of English phrases, formal syntax and a broad and rather old-fashioned vocabulary.

After five minutes or so they had entered their rhythm: the reader's voice in a steady current, the tone even, firm, and Russia, textual Russia, entered the room, seeping under the door, flying through the window, infusing the summer air, bringing to North Sydney the Red Army and the spring of

1922. The plump nurse quietly placed a cup of tea at Pei Xing's elbow, and she sipped as she read, kept up the cadence, and pronounced as confidently as she could all the polysyllabic names.

★ ★ ★

One day in Sydney's Chinatown Jimmy had introduced a new friend, Lin, a young man in a leather jacket and with hair gelled into a high dark helmet. Pei Xing thought he looked like a gangster from a Hong Kong movie; she imagined black dollars, heroin, bad luck, spilt blood. His family, said Jimmy, was also from Shanghai; you should meet his mother. And so to please her son, who for some reason wanted to impress this young man, to forge *guanxi*, connections, to get ahead in some obscure and possibly criminal way, she agreed.

When Pei Xing stood for the first time before Dong Hua, she felt a surge of nausea. The tapeworm in the gut. The body remembering its beatings. A shrill inner cry she had tried for long years to smother. *No, no, no.* This woman was responsible for her debasement, had been sadistically cruel, had made her consider suicide. She carried a new name and a new hairstyle and had aged stiff and metallic, but it was still the same person; it was still Comrade Peng.

The woman who now called herself Dong Hua had also looked shocked. Their sons had contrived a meeting neither would ever have wished. Pei Xing held herself together — was that the English phrase? — and made vacuous small talk for fifteen minutes, after which she invented an excuse and left. She told Jimmy she would never see this woman again, this woman who, she said, without going into details, had been her guard at Number One Shanghai Prison. It was incomprehensible, this fold in history, this diabolical return. What afterlife was this?

But within a week Dong Hua had knocked on the door of her apartment. 'I need to talk,' she had said.

'Go away,' Pei Xing responded. 'I have nothing to say to you.'

But Dong Hua had wedged her foot in the doorway — that old joke about salesmen and Jesus-people — and would not leave. Pei Xing remembered how Comrade Peng had borrowed a pair of boots to kick her senseless on Mao Tse Tung's birthday. She remembered the blow to her face that had broken her nose and the sour taste of blood at the back of her throat. She looked down at the shoe in the doorway and thought she would faint.

184

'I will call the police,' Pei Xing said weakly.

But still Comrade Peng would not leave or withdraw and Pei Xing, caught in the seizure of her former role, would not have dared to crush the guard's foot in the door.

Pei Xing thought to herself: I can never escape this, never; it has followed me to Australia. I am Australian now, and still it is here. Still it is here.

★　★　★

But they had talked, and shared tea, Pei Xing striving to maintain face for the sake of her son. Hua spoke of her childhood. Her father had been of the virtuous proletariat, working in the Shanghai Number Four Steel Factory. Hua talked about her life in the Red Guards and how exhilarating it had seemed, how she had worshipped Chairman Mao, how proud her family had been. Even with the failure of the Great Leap Forward Campaign, when their family was starving, when a small piece of pork that had been two yuan was selling for fifty yuan, she still believed everything she was told. She had been chosen in the *da chuanlian* period to travel with other young Red Guards to spread Mao's words across the country. She had never travelled before; it was an exciting time. She spoke of her years working in the prison, how she had believed the inmates were evil, dupes of foreign devils, conspiring against China; she believed too in destroying the despised Four Olds, that everything traditional should be crushed and eliminated. It was our history, she said: Red Guards, the Cultural Revolution, the thoughts of Chairman Mao. You were an 'educated youth', she said, of the bourgeoisie, a basic class enemy.

As she spoke, Pei Xing heard the same old excuse: we were all in it together. Millions were Red Guards, millions were persecuted, millions were sent to the countryside for re-education; your story is but one and worthless in the scheme of things. Guards, prisoners, all the same. It was a murderous time. Brutality occurred. The mighty dialectic of historical materialism held them all in its sway. Pei Xing felt the exhaustion of so unremitting a narrative — *a revolution is not a dinner party, said Chairman Mao* — its crass inhumanity, its dark determinism.

There was a pause.

'But my violence,' Hua added softly, 'that was inexcusable. I am sorry,' she said. 'More than I can say.' She lowered her head. There was a long, awkward silence.

It was as if the sky had fallen in. Pei Xing stared at this woman she had spent most of her life hating.

'I'm sorry,' Hua said again. 'Please forgive me.'

Pei Xing was in a turmoil of mixed responses. This woman, she thought meanly, was pleading not to be hated. An ignoble plea, a denial of her actions. A suggestion that history was essentially vague and impersonal. But this woman, she thought more generously, was asking forgiveness, had surrendered herself to another story in which she was the villain. She had no reason to ask forgiveness if she believed she had acted without choice.

★ ★ ★

Guanyin, Goddess of Compassion and Mercy. Her mother had owned a small Qing statue, of white crackle-glaze porcelain, elegant and pure, that was crushed by the Red Guards. Pei Xing still remembers the *pop!* sound as the god's head was flattened underfoot. Guanyin was first among gods, her mother declared, and though she considered herself too educated to be a sincere Buddhist, and was committed, like her husband, to staunch Western secularism, she loved this delicate figure, which she had inherited from

187

her own mother, and knew all her tales of miracles and redemption. Guanyin had a narrow, thoughtful face and an expression of loving kindness. She stood in a lotus blossom and held up one hand. The statue had rested in a small alcove by their front doorway.

Pei Xing said nothing. She would not forgive this woman. She would not befriend her or hear any more of her self-exculpation.

★ ★ ★

Dong Hua continued to visit, uninvited, and with infuriating determination. Each time she visited she repeated her formal apology. She offered gifts of ginseng, rice wine and candied ginger, which Pei Xing found easy to dispose to the garbage. She stayed only for short periods, ten minutes or so. Then she set off for the long walk back to the train station. Pei Xing was determined to remain strong and not relieve this brutal woman of the guilt she must be feeling. There was almost a pleasure in watching her walk away unsatisfied, seeing how she struggled in the heat and moved with a slow, unhealthy drag.

But the challenge of Dong Hua was to her deepest self. If there was no recovery within history there was no point to suffering. If there was no meeting, no words, there could be no escape from the hateful circle of vengeance, there could be no peace, there could be no future. After each visit Pei Xing was obliged to confront her own intransigence, to consider the dreadful power of her own stubborn reasoning. After each visit, Pei Xing wept.

★　★　★

She remembers exactly when it was she decided to forgive. It was just before sunset, the sky full of the last flickering glimmers of the day. There were puffy clouds lying stretched and copper-coloured on the horizon, looking Chinese, as they appear on watered silk scrolls. There were the distinctive calls of Australian birds, which always sounded to Pei Xing a little dejected, and she was sitting with her Dragon Well tea at the window of her apartment. Below, a boy was circling a small area of asphalt car park on a skateboard; its massive clatter and rumble — angry-sounding, repetitious — reverberated with hard energy against the brick walls that surrounded him. Looking down she saw this boy, caught in his noisy curves. He was insanely intent on his confined route, almost imprisoned, when he might have been out there, flying along the street.

Pei Xing closed the novel. 'Now we shall take a break,' she announced, 'and have something to eat.' She cradled the old woman's head in her hand and with a teaspoon fed her portions of rice porridge she had brought from home. She placed the rice at Hua's pleated lips, pushed it in, tipped a little. Then she wiped the shiny trail of food with the edge of the spoon, as one does with an infant. Hua's skull was heavy, motionless, and it was the thinness of her hair that truly suggested her frailty. A nurse came and went. Time slowed, seemed to pool. There was the drum of an air-conditioner and the minute clicking restlessness of electrical objects. There was the languid quality to time that rests in hospitals for the aged, something entropic, slightly fearful, something Pei Xing associated with worn decks of playing cards or those rust-coloured chrysanthemums that fall apart in a mess, petal by slim petal.

On the table before them lay the novel they had shared. Their reading was moving towards the inevitable conclusion. And they had been visited again by a kind of provisional peace; they had entered the fluidity that composed them; they had read their chapters.

At Circular Quay Catherine rejoiced in the sunshine.

God, it was bright. Such a shine to the world, as Mam would say, such a shine to the world and all the Good Lord's creations.

Catherine had stayed for a while in the semi-circle of people watching the didgeridoo player. He was an Aboriginal man, covered in what looked like ceremonial white paint. Like the best buskers, he paid no attention to the crowd, but entered his music as though it were a room he might rest in. Sitting on the ground, the instrument between his bare legs, held by his toes, he also paid no attention to the electronic backbeat issuing from two fat black speakers set up on a ledge behind him. He entered the autism of recital. He was deliberately alone.

Catherine wondered how authentic this performance might be, and whether they were listening to music that was wrenched from a community somewhere, and a dark night, a long history and a secret sacred purpose. CDs were on sale, and she considered buying one, but instead dropped coins into the hat splayed on the path for that purpose. It was the beauty of the sound that most surprised her. She had imagined a wearisome, uniform thrum, but heard instead a set of nuanced tones, at times like a human voice, distant, misremembered, at others like wind, or blown rain, or the amplified sighing and heartbeat one hears during illness or love-making. This was romantic, no doubt, and perhaps some honky-white fancy, Irish-inspired, but knowing nothing of the culture she responded only to the sound. This wooden tube of breath, pulsing and alive. She must tell Luc, who had an interest in 'world music' and who had once, in a similar moment, hearing the sound from a loud-speaker broadcasting to the street, considered buying a didgeridoo in Paris.

★ ★ ★

Catherine's mother had a saying: *Remember Frances O'Riordan!*

Frances O'Riordan was a thirty-seven-year-old Cork housewife mysteriously cured of her deafness when she went to see the moving Madonna at Ballinspittle. Completely deaf since twenty, she had stood before the Virgin and been touched by acoustical God. Glory be. When Catherine was listening to U2, with the volume turned up, Mam would shout out: *Remember Frances O'Riordan!* It was an ambiguous message. Catherine was never sure if her mother was telling her that hearing should be preserved for holy sounds, or that amplified U2 would drive her to ungodly deafness. She thought of it now, her mother's high call, and calculated that the good woman must be sixty this year. Happy Birthday, Frances O'Riordan.

* * *

The didgeridoo music followed Catherine as she walked towards the area called the Rocks. When she passed an ice-cream kiosk, she realised she was hungry. She walked beneath the massive train line suspended above her — just as a train roared on the iron tracks, slowing, arriving — and crossed to a street of old sandstone buildings, mostly modest and quite small, the barely preserved but gentrified remnants of a colonial city. The Harbour Bridge loomed at the end of the street; it hung against the sky like one of those dream-catchers you find in hippy homes, a net for invisible entities and the gluey stuff of the ether. Ruthy once owned one, before Mam declared it Protestant and asked her to take it down. Catherine decided to find lunch, then visit the Museum of Contemporary Art. In the rising wind fluttered red banners advertising Conceptual Art from Osaka. They depicted what appeared to be a simple black hole. A simple black hole on a bright red flag.

Give it a go, whatever. *You never know now, do you?* as Mam would say.

★ ★ ★

Up a side-street, beyond the bustle, Catherine discovered a French patisserie. It had white tables on the pavement, a busy brown interior and a courtyard out the back, surrounded by trailing vines. Couples sat close, sipping coffee and tackling baguettes and tarte tartin.

Luc. Ah my lovely, hungering for your touch.

They had met in a place not unlike this hidden-away café. She had fled Ireland to Paris after the murder of her heroine, Veronica Guerin. Though not yet finished her journalist training, Catherine was star-struck with Guerin; she wanted to be like her and to write fearless stories, to work with a risky profile on the *Sunday Independent*. She wanted to play Camogie like a demon and defeat the champion team from Cork, to expose the murdering bastards who drug-dealt junk at Ballymun, to talk with such confidence, to display blonde cool. Catherine and Brendan marched in street demonstrations after the news of her death.

Together they wrote letters against the Gardai, and felt dismally outraged.

Catherine admitted only later that she had been afraid. A coward, to be sure. It would be easier, she told Mam, to be a journalist in London. She would visit Paris first for a short break, a few days' holiday. Then London. Across the water.

★ ★ ★

It seemed that everyone in Dublin in '96 had an urban tale about Guerin. Someone had known her at school; someone else knew gossip or scandal. She was a saint or a complete bitch, or a fucking brilliant journo. Her image was everywhere. Her name was in the papers. But Catherine had never met or seen her, other than on television, and knew only in a remote way that there might be brave acts of writing, and that this murder on Naas Road, this silencing of one writer, would punctuate and determine the course of her life. *Remorseless killing*, that's what the papers said. At stake was the precarious self she had only just begun to confirm, the one that found the world comprehensible, that wished to report it to others, that wanted to be part of the great otherworld that is our lives in print. This was only a nebulous

195

understanding, and an instinct to flee. But it was enough to impel her to act decisively and finally to leave. Her sisters were married, all except Ruthy, her favourite, who seemed to be enjoying her job at the lingerie counter of Dunnes. Her Mam had settled into the paralysis of life at Ballymun. Catherine felt the need to escape the local nets they were trapped in.

Brendan was staying put. He had at last finished his doctorate, a study of Seán Ó Faoláin's editorship of the literary magazine called *The Bell*, and had just been appointed at University College, teaching literature. 'I'm Modern Oirish,' he proudly proclaimed. He had taken to wearing new clothes and quoting James Joyce to visiting Americans. They apparently found him adorable and wanted their photographs taken with him, with their jointly literary smiles and their muck-about attempts at the brogue. Catherine wondered then if Brendan would write a fine book one day, a real book, in hardback, with real ideas.

'Real life,' he once told her, 'is *really* overrated.' He said *really* with elastic and cynical emphasis, as though he was weary of the entire world.

And she remembered with heartbreaking clarity the look on Brendan's face, wide open as the ocean and joyful-miserable, as he led a farewell sing-song over drinks at the Penthouse pub. They had their arms around each other and sang at the tops of their voices. Using the excuse of her departure, friends and family drank too much and afterwards staggered addled and idiotic around the streets and the car parks.

Brendan said: 'You'll miss the piss in the lifts of the towers of Ballymun. You'll miss the screechin' of priests and the flappin' of nuns. You'll miss the seagulls diving for vomit on O'Connell Street at five on a Saturday morning.'

'Disgraceful,' Mam said. '*Disgraceful.*' She was wearing her best frilly white blouse for the occasion, and touched the frills lightly when emotion overtook her.

Catherine hooked her arm and leant against her mother's shoulder, warm and full of love. She steered her home, through the pile of rubbish and the syringes and the graffiti in the lobby, up the stinking elevator, all the way to the sixth floor. She made her mother a cup of sugary tea and put her to bed.

★   ★   ★

Brendan wept at Dun Laoghaire as she waved from the ferry; and waved to her as if he was

197

a man drowning, not waving. He made a *scene*, Mam would have said, embarrassing them all, and was foolish and emotional and brotherly loving to a fault; he shouted from the wharf to the deck that they'd meet up in China. Yes, yes, he shouted. In China, in China. The semaphore of waving continued until he could not be distinguished from the others left behind. This was ever-Ireland, Catherine thought, those departing, those staying, and the frail signs in between, resting, fading, on the cold trembling air. The Irish: always leaving.

★ ★ ★

The images on telly were all of the shot-up car, Guerin long gone. Catherine dreamed of it; it scared her. A cherry-red something or other, an unpretentious little car, with blood on the front seats.

★ ★ ★

At their first meeting Luc had seen her reading an English book and shyly struck up a conversation. She was suspicious at first, a guy with a literary pick-up line, taking a chance with tourists. We Irish girls, she thought, are wise to the pick-ups. But she was reassured by his lack of confidence and his apologetic English.

'I read it better than I speak,' he said. 'You can test me if you like.'

And she liked that too, the quiet humour, the self-deprecation. So Catherine had tested him then and there with Nabokov's memoir, and he filtered the ornate prose to say that this was a book about memory, and that the poor man was so afraid of passing time, and so confused, so desperate, that he considered the baby's carriage a sinister kind of coffin. Every shape, said Luc, was already filled up with death.

'I read it in French,' he confessed with a smile. 'Poor Mr Nabokov.'

Luc was a translator, from Russian to French, originally from Besançon. He was struggling, he said, to make a living. Russian literature was out of favour.

'But only temporarily,' he added softly. The Russians were 'eternal', he insisted, and sombre enough and broad enough to express life for all of us.

'It is something to do with scale. The consequential and the inconsequential. They are not afraid of history; or the smallest human endeavour. Side by side.'

It sounded formal, like something he had read in a book. But Catherine was attracted to the way he implied that words mattered. She saw in him seriousness of mind and an endearing manner, both youthful and old.

★ ★ ★

Catherine and Luc spent four weeks together, then parted. It was a relationship with the economy of a holiday romance, strictly contained, without obligation or the projection of a shared future. In Luc's tiny room in Belleville they had sat up in bed together eating raisins, talking of books and exchanging stories about their lives. It was a happenstance affair, genial, uncommitted, and she discovered he was another of those souls who carry the past before them, who somehow understand the compulsion to repeat and revisit. They recognised this in each other. They liked each other's stories. Into the shell of each other's ears they poured random narrative seductions. Catherine found herself telling Luc about Ming Ming and Ping Ping, as though she understood at last how so humble an excursion might bind children together. She told of the grander trip to Ballinspittle and of her mother's godforsaken disappointment. She told of her brother, how he was word-filled and crazy-like, and her best and truest friend. She told of the assassination of Veronica Guerin, Irish heroine. She told of where she grew up and of the sorrow of Dublin, a sorrowful city if there was ever one.

Luc had fewer stories he was prepared to impart. His childhood was a cloudy, obscure place, which he was always on the brink of clarifying. When he spoke of it, without fluency, he seemed to Catherine to be picking his careful way through a fog, as if he had never spoken of anything personal before. But he told her this: that his maternal grandparents were from the town of Pont-Saint-Esprit, in the south, where in 1951, in the early years of their marriage, there had been an outbreak of ergot poisoning. Infected rye bread had been sold at the local bakery, and his grandmother was among the many who suffered appalling hallucinations, most of which involved blood-letting, dismemberment and scenes of atrocious violence. Ergot poisoning, Luc explained, has effects like LSD, like a bad trip. There were only seven deaths, but there were widespread delusions of a mostly fearsome kind. A town gone mad. Everyone remembers a tailor rushing through the streets believing he was pursued by spiky devils, and a young woman who ran into the river, believing her body was on fire.

201

Grandmother was hospitalised and never really recovered, Luc said, and his mother, then a baby, was raised by her aunt. In her late teens his mother had moved to Besançon, but could not overcome her guilt at leaving her mother. When he was eight they made the only visit he can remember: they took a bus to Pont-Saint-Esprit and saw her briefly. He remembered the sound of the river beyond the window and the distant wailing of herons; he remembered how his mother's guilt transferred to him, that he absorbed it there and then, blotting its darkness in, standing before this old woman who neither greeted nor spoke to them. She had purplish-grey skin and flapped her hands like a moth, he said. He was afraid. He felt alone. He had felt the guilt entering him. He looked out of the window at the river, and wished he could dissolve there.

'And translation?' Catherine had asked.

'It could have been any language, anything other than French. I loved literature and longed to be transported elsewhere, to exist inside a language. Russian appealed because of the alphabet, which seemed to me as a child like something from a dream in which meaning was coded, but not immediately evident. Backwards-facing letters. The mystic glyphs of Cyrillic. Serifs. Ligatures.'

Here Luc paused. 'And because of the novels, of course. Those weighty novels you fell into for weeks and weeks. As a teenager, I read the classics, all the great works. I fell into Pushkin and Dostoevsky. I loved Gogol and Tolstoy.'

Luc warmed to his explanation, as if it was a summary of his passions. 'And *Doctor Zhivago*,' he added. 'I really loved *Doctor Zhivago*.'

★   ★   ★

When Catherine left for London they stayed in touch by email — thinking phone-calls were much too intimate. In this way she knew of his brief marriage, his translation commissions, the death of his mother. He knew of her job with Reuters, her ugly flat in Golders Green, the on-off affair with one of her colleagues in the office. They remained friends against the odds, practising a long distance affection.

When Luc at last visited Catherine in London, almost eight years after their friendly Nabokovian encounter, they were two foreigners who both found the English amusing, who were carrying bundled in themselves the mosaic of displaced lives, who were sentimentally fond of the unencumbered month they had once spent together. Luc looked older than Catherine expected. He had grey at the temples and deep creases beside his mouth, as if some sadness had afflicted him that he had never told her. Men have secrets, many secrets; she knew this by now.

But his body was unchanged. He was still slender and milky-white, he still had bluish flanks in the cold and a lovely tilting step when he emerged naked from the shower. She would kiss his goose-pimpled flesh and make a show of drying him, wrapping him round as if she had discovered the young boy still inherent. Beneath the towel, almost imperceptible, she felt him shiver. Kissing his neck and his shoulder, rubbing her nose down his ridge of his spine, smelling the gardenia perfume of the soap on his body.

Once, lying in her arms, he whispered: 'As a child I was really afraid of moths. There are giant moths in the south of France: they have furry grey abdomens and coarse rustling wings.'

'Moths?' Catherine asked, expecting a funny story.

'Yes, moths.'

There was no funny story but only a cosy moment, like that of the confessional in Our Lady of Victories on a cold winter's day, with the scent of damp wool, animal and acerbic, and the priest's voice, and her own, and the muffled sound of the rain, pouring in a light steady veil, washing into the shadowy car park outside.

★　★　★

Catherine was not sure now, on a Sydney Saturday, why she should remember this fragment of conversation. *Moths, fear of moths.* It was the gift of tenderness, perhaps, to persist and return like this, delivered wistfully and for no purpose other than to recall the texture of an affair. And it was a token between lovers: to confide the vulnerability that might have followed from childhood.

She rose from the table and paid her bill. Outside the light was startling and the sky avid and aflame. Catherine walked towards the Museum of Contemporary Art, breathing in the voluptuous light, thinking of the clean, sleepy body next to hers, of the melodious quality of his voice after they had made love, of a childhood faraway, in Besançon, and another parallel, in Ballymun, and thinking of the rhyme in her head, *Besançon/Ballymun*, of its inward music and the trinity syllables, thinking too how romance is no longer possible, how *Doctor Zhivago* is no longer possible, that epic perspective on history, that snow-decorated love, and she decided, there in the sunshine: I must ring Luc this evening.

5

Something in the prodigious quality of the light, the way it gathered in the Harbour, cobalt and gold and sparkly as an advertisement, made Ellie think for a moment of her father, Charlie.

He had owned an old-fashioned electrical goods store, the kind that is disappearing all over the world and which only still exists in a few small country towns. He sold cords, bulbs, lamps and steam irons; he sold switches and cables for electricians and household goods for families. It was a narrow, cramped shop, just off the main street and out of the way, and had about it the air of a forgotten or essentially forgettable place. It seemed silent, sepia and fixed in the wrong time. There was a bell on the front door and one stepped immediately into a room in which cables hung in thin loops like snakes from the ceiling and dusty objects, long neglected, lined shabby shelves. Her father sat behind the counter, reading obsolete manuals on do-it-yourself radio or adventure novels set in Africa. As she entered he would nod and smile and slowly lower his book.

Sometimes, out of boredom, or because they had little to say to each other, he would tell her the plot of the novel he was reading. There were inevitably hidden codes, or spies, or nefarious subterfuge, there were wild life encounters, there were beautiful but evil women, limply inviting, there were dashing heroes with whom they eventually entwined. Ellie loved these charming and slightly absurd meetings with her father. At some point in their conversation he would hold up his palm and say: 'That's it. That's enough. Back into the light!'

And it was true: leaving the shop was like stepping from shadows into light. Outside was a sign: *Charlie's Electrics*, painted in flaking paint, and two simple light bulbs, such as one sees in cartoons signifying bright ideas, bracketing his name. When she was a young child Ellie believed her father actually created light — something her mother said, casually vague, she had misinterpreted. They laughed about it later, but the association stuck.

* * *

Her father never played golf or joined the Rotary Club. He didn't drink at the pub and seemed to have no friends. His was a self-enclosed, modest life, the centre of which was his wife and daughter, his chickens, and a rectangle of vegetable patch, which he tended with regular, fastidious care. There was something, Ellie thought later, Chekhovian about her father. He was a man who was waiting, always waiting, for life to happen, and in the meantime was content to sit quietly in his shadowy shop, selling the occasional lamp or fuse card or extension cord to customers, whom he treated with an almost abject politeness. His only distinctive quality was the headaches he endured, a feminising trait, Ellie reasoned, which assailed him all his life. This explained the shadows. Charlie believed life in the shade somehow protected his sore brain. It was a joke in the town: the bloke who sold lights had the gloomiest shop in Australia.

★　★　★

Ellie's mother Lil was the active one. She played tennis and was a member of the Country Women's Association. She was capable, talkative and worked part-time in a bakery. Her own parents had been farmers and this showed in her body. She moved sturdily and with a strong at-home-in-the-world stride; she had firm arms and conveyed

209

a sense of ease and authority. Ellie wondered often how it is we combine our parents, how the genetic stuff of being both follows and splits us, how it is we embody them, or don't, and find our own, singular self. She wondered too how her parents had ever met and got together, and only as an adult realised how arbitrary love was, and how easily one fell into the arms of strangers.

It was to her father Ellie first disclosed her wish to travel. She could speak of other places without it seeming a betrayal.

'I *will* leave,' she had warned him. 'There is so much world out there.'

And though he couldn't understand, he loved her for her difference, and did not tell her mother nor try to dissuade her.

Ellie had a compulsively joyful disposition. She was not naively or always happy, but she was disposed to liveliness. This was something her father understood. He doted. He indulged. He marvelled at his clever girl, so unalike, and so radically separate. And knowing this, Ellie grew up secure and strong, so that when she gathered James in and made him whole, there was no girlish trepidation or glossy-magazine agony; it was an assertion of her confidence and her wish to enlarge her experience. And when James left to move to the city as a scholarship boy she was, for a time, hurt and confused, but his leaving encouraged her own volatility in the world, and made it possible for her to leave too.

★ ★ ★

Walking the path beside the ferries and the sleek Captain Cook Cruise boats, bobbing catamarans onto which a line of jolly people filed, Ellie imagined she was carrying James's gaze on her back. She would not turn and wave; let him watch her walk away. Tomorrow he would ring, or she would ring, and they would contrive to meet again, somewhere less bright and more peaceful, a wine bar perhaps, in which they might lean close together, at kissing distance, and softly confide.

Seagulls fluttered in the air, children called out. The Harbour was busy with ferry traffic and over all spangled with light. On the lawn in front of the Museum of Contemporary Art family groups and couples stretched out and sprawled with untidy snacks. Their bare summertime legs jutted from patches of shade and they tilted back water or sucked melting ice-creams or lazed torpid over the bulging Saturday newspapers. Ellie realised she could hear the didgeridoo once again; it had maintained its low reverberating drone.

She wondered how many hours the player stayed at the Quay, and how he kept up his stamina and concentration. How, indeed, he managed so much circulating breath, this strenuous inhalation-exhalation that made such continuous sound. Some people persevere, she thought; some just keep on, and on. Ellie paused for a moment, listening carefully, but then strode towards George Street to catch her bus home.

★ ★ ★

That year, their fourteenth, 1988, had been the year of Australia's bicentennial commemorations. Odd now, to think of it. Odd to retrieve it on such a day, with her lover from the past watching her walk away, with them both, she was sure of it, recalling their adolescent lust and the sweet assurance it had given them.

Into this very harbour, in 1788, Captain Arthur Phillip had sailed his first fleet of convicts. Bosomy sails against the blue. A criminal nation boldly inaugurated. Men in three-cornered hats posed before a flapping flag, shading their eyes as they squinted into the unknown future. In the history book they read at school, Captain Phillip had a poker face and tight-pursed lips, as if he held firm against whatever it was that he saw. Their town council in Western Australia arranged farcical forms of celebration. There were lawnmower and egg-and-spoon races down the main street, there was a scone bake-off to raise funds for a statue to early pioneers, and the high-school arranged patriotic rituals and historical pageants. Ellie happily missed being chosen for a landing re-enactment, performed two months late, but James found himself duly nominated a convict, which he rather enjoyed, since his main task was to steer a rowboat. A group of ethnically mixed teenagers were chosen as 'natives': it was their role to welcome the arriving colonisers, to bow, to remain silent, to be ceremonially obsequious.

Parents stood on the beach and took photographs, proud of the nationalist fuss. The shire councillor and the school principal both gave little speeches. Birds on their broad elliptical migration from Siberia, small godwits and plovers and red-capped dotterels, ran fast along the beach or swooped in speedy arcs over the sober proceedings. Miss Morrison had once drawn on the blackboard their route from the Arctic Circle, sweeping from the tundra in Siberia down through Communist China (that was what she called it, *Communist China*) and on to South-West and South-Eastern Australia.

'These birds curve around the planet,' she had announced with glee, requiring her students to join in admiration of so arduous and poetic an achievement. Ellie remembered this phrase long after she had forgotten the names of most of the birds.

So there was James standing quietly with the other convicts, holding an oar upright, his manner ironic. His trousers were rolled to resemble britches, and he wore a red scarf tied in a knot at his neck. And there were the adults, the town councillors and a row of dutiful teachers, lined up for a photograph, their faces searching for the elusive meaning of the artificial event.

Ellie all the while was distracted by the birds — their Russian intervention and their international assertion, the way they crowned the sky in spirals and cut through it diving to the sand, the way they appeared, then vanished, blurring into the sunlight.

★　★　★

In their hideout James told Ellie of the Aboriginal protests. Unlike her, he read the newspaper and listened to the ABC radio news. Elsewhere, over East, there had been demonstrations, he said, and the defiant display of Aboriginal flags. Aborigines had called Australia Day 'Invasion Day', and the year one of 'mourning'. It was serious, James said, it was like the Bolshevik Revolution. He was critical of Ellie's lack of political understanding, and for her part she was embarrassed to know so little, never to have thought about these things before, never to have considered race politics or the British-bloody-Empire, never to have imagined her nation as an entity once hypothetical and tenuous. At home her mother cut out a picture from the *Women's Weekly* magazine. It was of Princess Diana visiting Australia for the Bicentennial. She had feathery hair and wore a peppermint dress with white trim, surmounted — that was the *Weekly*'s word — by a matching hat. She looked incredibly tall, shaking the hands of short, besuited politicians, and giraffe gawky in her body as she retracted a gloved hand. Ellie could not reconcile James's opinions with her mother's monarchical gratifications.

'Brainwashing,' he declared. 'It's really that simple.'

And so Ellie was obliged to learn if she too was brainwashed — a term she had only heard in James Bond movies — and to be led, irreversibly, into the beginnings of political knowledge. James lay beside her and instructed her on the Meaning of Australia Day, as Ellie, listening carefully, absorbed with fascination these new and impertinent opinions. She wanted this bigger world, of political meanings. She wanted the experience of shouting in a street for what you believed in, of seeing oneself in a community, of being caught in deep-dreaming utopias and a benevolent love of the whole world. She would later join the Trotskyists on campus, and then the Labour Party. She would never give up wishing for the potential of solidarity and social causes, would always refuse the arch and cynical explanation, desire, at a party, the left-leaning scruffy man with buttons undone and a slight air of dysfunction.

★　★　★

Ellie's father died during her second year at university. She took her pack and boarded the bus for the miserable three-hour ride home. It was her misfortune to sit next to a pinched, unhappy woman who told her *all men are shits, all men are bastards, fucking bastards, that's what men are, every bloody one of them, shits, all shits, no bloody fucking exceptions*; and Ellie thought she would go crazy if the chatter didn't cease. At last the woman fell asleep, her middle-aged, disappointed face pressed to the glass and her mouth open, vulnerably, like an exhausted child. Her talk was replaced by whiny country and western music broadcast throughout the bus; it must have been there all along, but submerged beneath the woman's relentless complaining. The vast industrial area of Kwinana slid past, looking like satanic mills in the fading light. Flares, sulphur, who-knows-what emissions, flew up in particles and sparks from the tall smoke stacks. The journey took her further and further into country darkness and at last, by nine o'clock, to her unhappy destination.

Lil was there, patiently waiting at the bus station to meet her. She stood stiff and widow-like under the sodium arc-lights of the car park. They looked at each other, their faces crumpled, and together they cried. Lil was distant with the severe loneliness of the early stages of mourning. She was falling apart and coped by hugging herself. Her hands had disappeared into the ends of her cardigan.

Ellie had just turned nineteen years old; her beloved father had been only sixty. He'd been pissing blood, Lil said, and probably in pain, but didn't want to bother anyone or cause any trouble. It was a heart attack, in the end. Their neighbour found him dead at work when he didn't come home for his dinner.

There he was, behind the counter, still in his chair, a library book about spies lying closed on his lap. So she learned of it, her father's death, and his lonely no-nonsense departure.

★　★　★

Within a year, to Ellie's surprise, Lil had remarried. Ellie had somehow not reckoned on her mother's life continuing. He was a widower with four children, and Lil was happy to have gained a larger family. At the wedding Ellie hung in the background, trying to suppress the mixed emotions of the day, trying to control the grief that had insistently returned, trying to act cordially to the genial, nice-enough man, who confessed he'd loved her mother for years and years and was today the damn-luckiest bloke alive. He was a mechanic, a bridge player and a Grade A tennis champion.

'Put it there,' he exclaimed, and Ellie, realising her new stepfather conducted his emotions by handshake, meekly complied.

Stan the mechanic looked pleased with himself. His smile was genuine, and he wanted to be accepted. Ellie felt a clogging of feeling and a stranglehold at her lungs. She felt a misfit and ungainly, a stranger in the home of her childhood. Somewhere nearby her four half-siblings, all in high school and still unknown, looked on suspiciously as if their father, in shaking her hand, was making her the boss.

★ ★ ★

How the night had fallen. How grief had fallen. How, afterwards, she had seen her past tunnel into a blur and her father's sign, *Charlie's Electrics*, remain more vividly than the memory of his face. On her return journey after the wedding, the bus hit a kangaroo. It rose up out of the dark night in a horror-movie flash, collided, lifted higher, then fell away. The bus jolted, braked, there was a sickening, dragging sound of animal flesh upon bitumen, then it screeched to a halt. The bus reversed. In the pale headlights was illuminated the mangled carcase, still twitching a hind leg lacerated by impact or gravel, and holding its face as though inquiring what might happen next. Ellie always thought of kangaroo eyes as softly pleading, and this was no different. Its eyes, electrically red, shone with a dying address. Even from this distance the animal seemed directly to look at her. She rested her face on the window, needing to see. The corpulent driver alighted. Ellie watched him drag the kangaroo by the tail to the side of the road, then puffing climb back into the driver's seat and resume the journey, as if nothing had happened. It was at this moment, one year later, that Ellie truly wept for her father, sobbing in the barely lit bus, folded over like one broken.

'Plenty more where that came from,' said a chiding voice behind her.

Ellie understood the matter-of-fact brutality and unconcern, decreed by bush lore. She understood what it took to kill an animal, or to disregard one accidentally hurt. Tough farmers with their tough-as-guts and practical hearts. Kangaroo shooters. Butchers. And honourable folk who had to deal with creaturely lives, and not flinch, or pretend, or expect comfort where there was none, who looked at tumid fly-blown remains, muck-streaked and decaying, with neutral regard.

But this made things no easier. She allowed the dying kangaroo to stand in as her object of concern. It was her necessary cipher in the overwhelming night. Ellie hunched in the uncomfortable seat, in the bus vibrating with diesel power and pushing through the dark, and on a day marked so definitively by her mother's new joy, allowed herself to mourn.

★ ★ ★

In the shifting shade beneath the pepper tree at the bus-stop on George Street, Ellie could now recall her father with pleasure. The light bulbs bracketing his name were such a comic sign, half a lifetime away and secure in the dazzlement of childhood. Ellie loved that sign. She yearned for *Charlie's Electrics*, for his voice telling her in a serious tone the twisted plot of a spy novel set in Africa, for his calm equanimity, his routine life in the shadows. And Miss Morrison. *Clepsydra*. Her face turned to the blackboard. Her vaulting mind. Her impressive hold on words. And the touch, yes the touch, of James's boy-new body, warm in the cold space they had selected to hide in. She remembered sitting astride his hips, looking down at his face. The way his eyes shone up at her. Their interrogative candour.

A bus-stop wait could cover all this, all this complicated history. A woman standing still in a main street on a Saturday afternoon could carry *all this*: death, time, recollected acts of love-making — all together, simulta-neous, ringing in her head.

Ellie felt blessed by today, the dense here-now. She refused the bullshit theories that life these days was thinner, and denuded. She refused to be pessimistic. To want less than this complexity and emotional ravelling.

She stood for a long time at the bus stop, just near the overhead railway, listening to the community of life around her and the mechanical and human sounds that together, a rough orchestra, filtered through the streets of the city. From the direction of the Sydney Harbour Bridge noisy traffic flowed past, and in a surprise that broke her meditation Ellie saw suddenly that the bus, her number, 431, was hurtling in her direction. It stopped directly before her, expelled a low pneumatic sigh, and she climbed aboard.

★　★　★

Air. Breath. In the time-lapse of his thinking he remembered the word *pneuma*.

They had been studying asthma, lung cancer, bronchitis, pneumonia. James remembers he came in late to the anatomy session, his umbrella dripping and his mood wintry to match the season. Professor Heller was in front of the class, in full flight, pacing erratically and speaking with passion.

'Those wily pre-Socratics,' he said, 'they were interesting guys. Anaximenes believed self and reality were both air: *pneuma*, he called it, literally *breath*.'

He turned to face his class. 'Today, these neat spongy bags we carry beneath our throats,

this bubble-wrap inside, and our daily insuffla-
tion.' He paused, smiling. 'So let's all get
inspired!' He tapped at his chest double-fisted,
like Tarzan. He took a deep breath.

'Jesus,' muttered someone. 'Here he goes
again.'

'*Just as our soul, being air, holds us
together, so do breath and air encompass the
whole world*. So said Anaximenes, about 540
BC. It was a Tuesday. It was windy. It was a
very windy Tuesday in downtown Miletus.'

The class relaxed into low giggles and a
slight rustle of derision.

'*Pneuma* accounts in his work for the
functions of the soul — nutrition, growth,
motion, sensation: they all have this single
necessary condition we now think of as
breath. For Aristotle, *pneuma* was vitality, like
the fifth element, ether, which makes up the
stars. It was from Aristotle these blokes
inherited *pneuma*.'

Here Professor Heller paused and removed
his glasses. He breathed on them, wiped them
and held them angled to the light. It was
difficult not to find his theatrical turn
endearing. 'And now, my doubters of the
soul, to the twentieth century; to the
breathless cadaver.'

★　★　★

James had taken his place with the others, in his white student-doctor gown, and peered, eyes agog, into the chest of an old woman. Her thoracic cavity had been sawed open and parted like a book. It was their job to extract the trachea and the bronchial tubes, and then lift out the lungs.

The woman's face was covered with a white cloth, and so was her lower body. There was just the gaping chest in which her lungs, dark cushions, lay indecorously exposed. The body as waste. The body splayed in bright light. Clearly visible were sinews and ligaments, gaudy planes of opened flesh, the corruptible substances of which every body is composed. The phrase 'another living soul' mysteriously surfaced.

James felt he might suffocate. The grisly thrill of anatomy class had converted to nauseated recoil. It would be another humiliation. He would display once again his flagrant anxieties, how little he governed them, how futile and how foolish was his professional ambition. His own body offered a grim allegory of medical failure. The room turned before him. Faces slid away. His hands were hot, sweaty, his movements uncoordinated. So, having just arrived at the lab, James quickly excused himself. He whispered to the student beside him that he was feeling woozy from the flu and fled the room in haste, seizing his bag and his books, forgetting his furled umbrella.

Minutes later, in the rain, James realised he could not now return to claim it. The umbrella was propped where it had been left, a symbol of his absence. Some sort of panic attack, yes, simply dumb panic. Outside he was panting, choking, fighting for air. He cupped his hands under the sky and collected water for his thirst, then threw back his head, and swallowed.

★ ★ ★

James watched Ellie retreat and enter the Saturday crowds. Her body moved with an easy sway and a fast deliberate step. The back of her skirt flipped up around her thighs. She did not look back, though James willed her to do so. She charged off in the direction of the station and he assumed she would catch the train. He remained outside the restaurant, practising the deep-breathing exercises he had been taught in his therapy.

★ ★ ★

James thought often of Professor Heller. He had once gone to see him, a raw new student not long into the semester, in order to discuss his embarrassing difficulty with the inner body. His teacher had an eccentric manner and a fatherly authority that James found reassuring. There was no reproach but Professor Heller did not, as he expected, suggest strategies to cope, or the shrewd psychological games by which he might outwit his aversion. Instead, he recommended the reading of philosophy. He seemed to believe that what haunts and damages us might be defeated by thinking alone.

'A quiet room,' he said. 'It's all anyone needs. To sit alone in a quiet room. Thinking. Reading.'

It seemed such worthless advice. James left the appointment holding Professor Heller's battered paperback of Bertrand Russell's *History of Western Philosophy*, his own student copy. The book was brown-coloured with age and lovingly worn. It took James a whole year to return the volume, and then by post.

After the failed lung class, he consulted the section on Anaximenes. There he found a sentence of Russell's commentary underlined in pale pencil: *It seems that the world breathes*. A rushed asterix, a graphite star, lay in the margin.

★ ★ ★

Medical school defeated him. When James thought of it now it returned with a tang like child's vomit and a sequence of gory revelations, held back by steel implements. So many bodies, ransacked and despoiled. And that girl, Sally, cleaning the floor with a stained mop, her face emphatically hidden and turned downwards to her task. And Professor Heller, once again breathing on his glasses, wiping them, and then holding them upwards to the light. This repetitive sequence, with the implication of stench and disgust, with one face turned down and one lifted up, would summarise an entire year in which he struggled for control.

★ ★ ★

James travelled throughout his twenties, doing casual jobs, fucking around. Then, at the age of thirty, finding himself back in Perth, he enrolled to train as a primary schoolteacher. He would never be able to explain, to himself or to others, why he made this bold and improvised decision. But he did the requisite three years, working in a bar at night to pay the rent, then applied for country service, to teach in a small town. He was posted to the wheat belt, to a place that had a single main street: a general store with a petrol bowser, a pub, a butcher and a baker. There was a Returned Soldiers' club, a Country Women's hall and an eroded sandstone plinth that served as a war memorial. This was true Australia, he told himself, suncracked and quiet. The size of it slightly alarmed him, but he could rest here, become other, live in a kind of disguise; and he could drive to the city at weekends and maintain his half-committed relationship with his new girlfriend. The illusionist expanses of wheat shifting from green to gold, the wave motions of the wind and its susurration, the sense of calm labour and community spirit, these addressed, as art might, his secret insufficiency. In the windy country air, James felt ventilated, released. Most of all it was like starting again, with a brand-new boyhood.

★　★　★

There were long afternoons that might have seemed insufferable to others, in which James found himself talking with excitement to a class of young faces all turned directly towards him. Their avidity, their interest, inspired his own reconstruction. He was reminded that he possessed a sense of humour; he was reminded how interesting were the various facts of the world, first met;

he saw again the pleasure when a hand shot up in excited salute to answer a question, and the intelligent-dumb inquiry that illuminated the class.

In the town he was considered a good teacher and an alright bloke. He was a success. Everyone liked him. Bit of a loner, but OK. Wheat farmers touched the tips of their hats when they saw him, nodded a light nod and invited him to barbeques. They asked about his surname, DeMello; yes, Italian. They found him a curiosity, told him of the Italian prisoners sent to their farms, years ago, during the Second World War. Good workers, not slackers. Liked to sing in their Eye-talian. But prisoners all the same.

James averted his gaze. And now I'm free, he thought.

★   ★   ★

In the amber sunlight of before-home-time, when the class was allowed to read in silence whatever they wished, he looked out over their bent heads and felt at peace. He imagined for the first time in his life that he might like to be a father. It must be like this, he thought, casting a canopy of concern over the heads of small children, and a sense of promise, of the time that is yet to come. He read his own book, something Russian, an anti-Australia. This too gratified him. He was at one with the children, all that might be possible within words, and all these individual minds, receiving whatever provocation or emancipation might arrive innermost, easy as music, on a long melody of story.

★ ★ ★

At night James would sit on the verandah of his weatherboard Education Department house, listening to the sounds of the lives around him, feeling the cool breeze after a stifling hot day. In the apron of yellow light that spilled from his kitchen, in the shifting evening air, in the calm of his solitude, he heard the bang of wire-screens and a fridge door slammed shut, he heard remote voices travel across the broad country dark, he heard a dog bark, then another, and a sad mopoke calling, he swatted mosquitoes and drank beer and looked up at the starry sky. He played and replayed his CDs of Bob Dylan and the Triffids. 'Highway 61 Revisited'. 'Calenture'. When he slept he slept well, and when he woke he was refreshed.

★ ★ ★

Towards the end of the year, James took his class on an excursion to visit the seaside. There were students who had never before seen the sea, those for whom this would be a gift of amazement he alone would have given them. They would always remember him, offering the ocean. It was an adventure for all of them. The local cop arranged a bus driver's licence for the occasion, and he set off with fifteen children to drive to the west coast.

★   ★   ★

What James did not tell Ellie: the drowned child. Amy Brown her name was. Nine years old. *What he could not disclose*: his own dissolution.

He could barely remember the happy part now, because of all that followed. There must have been a happy part; there must have been exhilaration. There must have been children whooping for joy and splashing in the shallows, exclaiming at their experience of the Indian Ocean. He knows for sure that the first night, when they sat in a circle around the campfire he had made, they were all flushed pink with firelight and high rejoicing, singing at the tops of their voices, acting up, going silly. For some of them it would have seemed a remarkable holiday, all their

231

mates and no parents, and this single teacher who was cool. After their dinner James brewed drinking chocolate with hot milk, warmed over the fire, and the kids poked at the embers and stayed close, avoiding the black wilderness behind them. He remembers their faces ashine, and the high tones of their voices. The small hands clutching at mugs of chocolate milk and breaking their biscuits.

And when at last they bedded down James realised he had never been so happy. In his tent he listened to the voices of his students whispering after lights-out, gradually settling, becoming quiet, then entering their own dreams. The sound of waves pulsed beyond the sand-dunes, and he stepped into the moonlight just to look at them, to see the world before humans, elemental and apart. The sky was awash with constellations and the sea was lit up with moonshine. A milky mist seemed to hover just above the horizon. Oceanic repetition and extension: it was like being hypnotised. It was like having the stars to yourself, James thought.

★ ★ ★

In the morning they had begun their breakfast before they realised Amy was missing. A few kids called her name, there was a casual search, and then it came upon James all at once; his chest contracted and was fearfully tight. James bounded over the sand dunes and in panic ran to the water's edge. At first all he saw was the sea churning under a now-grey sky, but then, yes, the child's body, dragging and tipping in the shallows. She was wearing her bathers — she must have decided on an early swim — and her limbs hung loose from the neat little sheath of green lycra, decorated with a comic-book image of dolphins. James rushed head-long into the water to claim her. Her limp body was tiny in his giant arms. He tried, and tried, and then tried again, but even through his tears and his snot and his wet dripping clothes, even through his wild desperation to unmake the catastrophe, he knew enough to realise that she was already long gone.

All at once a semi-circle of children was standing on the sand before him. James shouted at them all to go away. Told them to fuck off — *fuck off!* — with a ferocity that frightened them. Then he took his shirt from his back and wrapped it around Amy's head, gently, as if she were a baby, or could still feel his touch. So that they might not see her face, and have to remember it forever.

At the inquest in the city James wore a suit and tie. Everyone was looking at him. He saw the parents weeping quietly, but at the end of the proceedings the father shook his hand and said that he understood the drowning was an accident. The mother turned away, unable to speak. Later a simple message, scrawled in an uncannily childish script, confirmed she believed that *it was just one of those things*. The imprecision was heartbreaking. The handwriting was heartbreaking. The forgiveness was heartbreaking. But in his jangled head James was hearing Bob Dylan's 'Hurricane'. It was a tormenting and crudely compelling association. He did not want The Authorities To Blame Him. For Something That He Never Done. The song repeated its screeching message and its frenzied violins. James tried to suppress it, to break its thrall, but the lyrics penetrated with taunting efficiency, so he took valium, then sleeping tablets, then uppers to stay awake in the morning.

★　★　★

Within days of the drowning the Education Department released James on leave, and arranged visiting counsellors for the children of his class. As soon as he could, James fled. He drove too fast and manically along the wide road back to the city, pressing his rusty old Cortina to the limit of its speed. Acres of wheat flashed past. A flock of black cockatoos, like Van Gogh's crows, rose in the distance like a dark presentiment. He could not still his thoughts. He could not control his instability. He hated the Dylan noise that was playing in his head. He hated the note from the mother and the stricken stares of the other children. Then there was *pneuma*, there was Magritte: his past was recurring. Everything in his wretched life was forming a pattern, preordained and imprisoning. He didn't believe in Fate. He didn't believe in these patterns, like wallpaper, shapes to cover a split surface. The very idea of a pattern was an offence to his politics and his reason. And as James passed under the blazing sky, piss-coloured behind his sunglasses, too huge to look at, he experienced once again his own physical symptom, a sense that his lungs were being crushed by an internal fist. He pulled his car to a skidding stop and threw himself from it, bent double, afraid, gasping for air. There was the ring of an empty world, a landscape so void and depopulated it hummed. When he came to his senses he was crying, like a kid just beaten.

James breathed deeply and slowly as he had once been instructed. Inspiration, expiration. *Feel the diaphragm, place your hands there.*

The world did not acknowledge private misfortune. Not this world, with its cafés beside the Harbour and the expansive delight of a sunny day. It had been four months since Amy Brown drowned in the Indian Ocean and he still thought of her, remembered her, every post-mortem day. Four months of sick leave. Four months in which his life entered a kind of free fall, like one of those universal, cross cultural dreams of falling, caught in a sensation of unreality and unbounded panic.

James moved closer to the edge of the pier and gazed into the water. A pattern resembling his mother's crochet, crafted in light, lay wobbling and shifting in light ferry-wake. Oily slicks drifted from boats and left an iridescent trail. Then he lifted his gaze and saw again the form of the Opera House, and was seized suddenly by a desire to see it from the inside. What must it be like to shelter there, within those high white shells? To look from the other direction, out across the water? To hear an orchestra, perhaps, belting out Wagner as if the Götterdäm-merung was upon us, as if it was thrash metal rock, full of multi-track fury? The US army was playing death metal to al-Qaeda in Baghdad. Nirvana's 'Tourette' was an instrument of torture at Gitmo. Where had he heard that? Could it be true?

*   *   *

What he had not told Ellie: it swelled inside him. He had expected to explain himself so that he might be unburdened. She was the only person in the world he could imagine hearing his words. It was not too much to hope for, surely, to cast off the sense of defilement that had accreted around him, to want a reciprocating tone, a haven to rest within, to say in a safe place what needed to be said.

*   *   *

After she fed Hua rice porridge Pei Xing brushed her hair. It was a kind of ritual they shared. Hua had kept her white hair long and Pei Xing sometimes plaited it. This reminded her of her childhood, of her own dark plaits hanging down her back, of her mother's deft braidwork and the neat addition of a bow. It reminded her of dressing for school, and how proud she had been of her uniform, how in middle school she was awarded the title of a 'Three Good' student, good morally, academically and physically. *San Hao: Three Good*. A shining enamel badge.

Perhaps because Hua was silent and from the same city, Pei Xing found her presence a source of remembering; it was as if she must remember for both of them, and keep spoken out loud what was locked up in paralysis. In their mysterious friendship, remembrance laced them together; indeed, Pei Xing imagined at times — since Hua could not confirm it — that they shared a few recollections that were *exactly* the same, that there was a fatedness to their meeting and a correspondence of selves.

'Do you remember,' she asked her friend, 'Double Happiness ping pong bats? How we all owned one, what a joy it was?'

Hua would blink, and it was an encouragement.

'And Golden Deer bicycles? A boy in our lane had a Golden Deer bicycle. We bribed him to give us turns. Once my brother, Lao, took off down the lane and the owner called out *thief! thief!* and chased after him like a madman. Lao came back of course, but the boy with the bicycle never gave him another ride.'

With such details Pei Xing fell back into

the swoon of her childhood, thought of the chestnut-coloured curtains in the front room of their small house that gave it a constantly shady aspect, of the milk popsicle sweets that were ten fen a piece, of the picture above her bed, a fat rosy-cheeked baby riding an orange carp, of the sound of bicycle wheels in a murmurous procession, the Flying Pigeons, the Phoenixes and the desirable Golden Deers. There was something charming in all those legs moving together in concert, the circles of so many pedals, ring upon ring. When as an adult Pei Xing saw Western futurist art, her vision made sense: the curves in repetition, the blur of speed, the pastel tones of a movement apprehended nostalgically. If she had not been a teacher she might have been a painter. She might have attempted a painting of the river of bicycles, gliding though Shanghai in a series of abstracted circles.

Pei Xing said: 'Do you remember that awful proverb from the provinces? *Women should only marry men who can provide three things that go round: a wrist watch, a bicycle and a sewing machine.*'

She did not speak of Mao. She did not mention their large-scale history, the three-year famine, or the anti-rightist campaigns; just as she did not tell the most private of her family memories, the red coat day, her mother's music, the times she had spent learning English and Russian from her father. And so it went by, the cosy lassitude of a hospital afternoon, washed in reminiscence and a snowy story from Russia.

★　★　★

When Pei Xing boarded the ferry to return to the Circular Quay, that which she wished to forget revisited her. Every now and then she forgot to forget.

What returned to her there on the deck, exposing her face to the wind, watching the steep shore recede and the water break open in a frothy wake, was that *she had worn her red scarf*. In her first encounter with Hua, whom she knew then as Comrade Peng, *she had worn her red scarf*.

After the Revolutionary Guards took away her parents, Pei Xing lived alone in their house for six weeks before she was seized. Her brother, she had heard, had somehow escaped to Hong Kong. She felt desolate, and afraid. Three families were moved in to occupy their rooms, and at this time some minor official must have remembered her existence, and that she too was a criminal. She recalled her teacher, Comrade Lu, beaten at a 'struggle session', the pitiful sight of his destroyed eye, the splashed blood on his shirt, his forehead bent to the ground and his gentle self humiliated. There were also demons in the pay of foreigners, former Nationalist Party members, rightists, undesirables, bull devils, capitalist roaders, reactionaries, revisionists, running dogs, blacks, all guilty of obscurely serious crimes committed against the Party. Pei Xing discovered she was a 'counter-revolutionary-educated-youth', and that she had somehow aided her father in spying for the Americans. Her brother, she was told, had sold state documents to the British Imperialists. She was arrested and taken by jeep to the Number One Detention House for political prisoners. There she was strip-searched, photographed, and hauled into a solitary confinement cell.

★ ★ ★

To show her party allegiance Pei Xing had worn her Youth League badge and the red scarf of her Young Pioneer uniform. She had worn it first as a nine-year-old; she joined the Young Pioneers on 1st July, International Children's Day, in 1960. How proud she had been. With the other children she chanted: *Ten thousand years to Chairman Mao!* In those days she had believed, as she was told, that her scarf was dyed red with the blood of the revolutionary martyrs.

When she was arrested at her home in Autumn Happiness Lane, later to be renamed People's Struggle Lane, she was allowed to bring her standard issue cotton quilted jacket and pants, and a few personal items, a hairbrush and some underwear. The scarf was her protection. She had once been so fond of it. In this time of profligate symbols and ideas reduced to codes, when so much depended on the mesmerising loyalty to red, here was her conciliating sign of assent. But once arrived at the prison her effort was derided. A female guard wearing a khaki cap with the red star emblem had yanked at the scarf on her neck and slapped her face.

'Radish,' the woman said with spitting contempt.

Pei Xing felt her stinging cheek and the welt where the scarf had been torn, and held back her tears. This was so small an injury, compared with what was to come. She saw a large banner — *Serve the People!* — as she was hit again.

★ ★ ★

Pei Xing no longer dwelt on the two years she spent in prison. Nor on the injuries Comrade

Peng and others inflicted. The days were distinguished only when she was submitted to meaningless interrogation, or beaten in a particularly memorable way. Her compulsory reading material was The Little Red Book of Chairman Mao, which she learnt diligently both from boredom and in an attempt to please her jailers.

When the enemies with guns are annihilated, the enemies without guns still remain.

She was an enemy without a gun, yes, she needed Communist re-education, yes. She had studied English, yes. But she did not help her father spy for the Americans, no; he had never spied, no, she had never spied. No.

Pei Xing believed that if she signed the 'confession' saying that her father, a 'member of the stinking ninth category, the intellectual class', had committed a crime, she would be condemning him to death. It made no sense to her, this story that they told. She did not recognise her family in the crude, mendacious version they offered. Only later she discovered her parents had been killed a week after they were taken; her confession was to provide a retrospective justification. For the paperwork, someone said. To show that the Party was infallible.

★ ★ ★

At first there was only retching despair and a nightmare of foreboding. Pei Xing waited to die. She was cold and cramped and could not imagine a future. She was filled with a grief of monstrous inexactitude. Day and night she heard sobbing, and random brutal shouts. But as the months wore on she found resources of solace and distraction. In her small dim cell, Pei Xing began silently to recite lines her father had once taught her:

Transparent, blackish-white, sweet-smelling, bird-cherry.

Amazing to consider these were adjectives used to describe snow. Could it be a bad English translation, or remarkable poetry?

Yet it was also the world re-created, the world linguistically new. Pei Xing was not permitted to write, but nothing could prevent her privately remembering. Over the weeks she slowly told herself the story of *Doctor Zhivago*, and when she had finished she began again, embellishing what she had earlier recalled, adding a few Chinese details of her own. *Doctor Zhivago* was her secret life, whispered not into the air, but into the cardinal recesses of her heart, held close as she had been held by her mother and her father. She saw her body becoming straw-thin, felt her painful chest filling with fluid, she forced down the repulsive prison food to

244

keep herself alive, but she also invented a counter-life of familiar characters, a story that became over time more and more incredible.

Pei Xing's *Doctor Zhivago* included her father and her mother, it included her brother riding in the countryside on a Golden Deer bicycle, it included lines of Tang Dynasty poetry, often about nature, or love. In her version Lara and Zhivago played chess and ping-pong, visited Pudong and Puxi, and were educated much as she had been. They knew the great Chinese classics, especially *The Dream of the Red Chamber*, her mother's favourite book. They knew the plots of Chinese opera and even some quotations from Chairman Mao. And of course they also knew Russia in revolutionary times, and understood the great and improbable outcomes of any fraught nation. In this way, and by small degrees, Pei Xing saved herself. In this way she kept alive in spirit what was dangerously impermissible and communed with her family, who were hungry ghosts before their time.

★　★　★

After two years, after — for a second time — she was bashed on the occasion of Mao Tse Tung's birthday, Pei Xing confessed that

245

her brother had been an Enemy of the State. He was abroad and safe, she reasoned; so she concocted a story about his extravagant anti-Party activities in Hong Kong. She was asked to write an account of his perfidy, then signed the form in her flawless handwriting and felt ashamed. It was then they told her that her parents had died. Comrade Peng stood at the door of her cell and announced in the same sentence that she would be released from prison and that her parents had died. When? How? They ignored her questions. Pei Xing felt blank, unmourning, pointlessly relieved. They were free too. They were ghosts she might meet. She left prison in the daze of one unsure of her own measure of reality, stepping into the streets of Shanghai clouded over, like a shadow of herself.

* * *

There was no rejoicing and there was no true mourning. Something was demolished that could never be rebuilt. Years later, when Shanghai was under reconstruction, when cars largely replaced bicycles and steel high-rise loomed everywhere, Pei Xing saw '*cui*', 'destroy,' written in white paint in a circle on the walls of condemned buildings. Everywhere she saw it: *cui, cui*. And felt as if she too was marked with such a sign.

*　　*　　*

Though released from prison, Pei Xing was sent to the country for re-education. One month later she found herself joining other 'educated youths' on a farm on Chongming Island, not far from Shanghai, nestled in the mouth of the Huangpo River. Their revolutionary task was land reclamation. This involved cutting reeds, laying them on salt flats, cutting reeds once again, laying them down once again. Then growing grass, cutting grass, burying grass. Eventually, they were told, this would desalinate the flats and crops would be planted. The reed roots in the bare marshes often cut their soles; some wore thick slabs of rubber tied to their feet, but most had no shoes and ended the day bleeding into the salty water. Pei Xing had not known that cut feet could cause such agony. At night, in the rickety shack that would be flooded at high tide, the young workers sang revolutionary songs, ate meagre meals, then fell into dead tired sleep upon mats of damp reed. Lice infested them, insects bit at their bodies, many became ill.

Pei Xing no longer told herself *Doctor Zhivago* stories. She was lost to herself. The stories were gone. Her life was a repetitious cycle of brute hard labour, and she was often mistreated by cadre leaders because she was of 'the criminal class'.

But there was sky and wind and occasions of numinous delight, when a kindness was shown, or solidarity expressed. There was the surprisingly open, capacious view; and here surrounded by the river there was a sense too of distended time. Pei Xing saw birds winging in from Siberia, looking like cut-paper artwork against the sky, watched the currents of water finding their shiny channels and confluences, sometimes trapped a fish, or an eel, or a soft-shelled crab. At sunrise the streaming light across the Huangpo suggested the careless serenity of heaven. At sunset one might believe in the rosy radiance of the future. It was a magnificent thing, the water beyond the marshes, extending into the sky.

Pei Xing was by then only nineteen years old. She had missed her chance at higher education and wondered, in practical terms, what might become of her. She kept to herself and survived, and when something happened to please her, like a rare bowl of fish head soup or boiled turtle, like a kind word or the tentative beginning of a friendship, she made herself remember human gratitude and the scale of what might unfold. After two years, Pei Xing's work team were moved into thatched huts with beds, and to other forms of labour. Her sense of relative comfort had so distorted that she wept for joy the first time she lay again on a bed that was dry, above the floor, and under a rain-proof roof.

★　★　★

In her fifth year on the island Pei Xing met Wang Xun. A thin man, consumptive, already chalky in complexion, he arrived wearing a badge that said '*In the Service of Chairman Mao*'. He was a low-level cadre who had volunteered to work in the provinces. He had been in the remote far north-west, a hardship post, but was then sent south, nearer his home city, when he became ill. His father was high up, they said, big time in Shanghai.

It would always be a mystery to Pei Xing that they met as individuals. She had accustomed herself to the impersonality of the crowd, to the revolutionary work unit and its indistinctive uniforms, and to a kind of habitual loneliness and self-subordination. Prison had taught her to hide inside herself. Work had abridged her conversation and the camp had narrowed and mutilated what might be said. She had not looked into a mirror or imagined herself in the gaze of another for years. That season they were assigned an easy job, the harvesting of corn, and found themselves working together, side by side, in the rustling, strangely private corridors of leaf-light.

Xun was a talker. Others were driven to silence by years of rural labour; he retained a chatty disposition and idealist convictions. He had not lost faith. He did not think the world corrupt. He wanted to be a writer, some day, and tell the daunting huge story of the great Chinese people. The peasant class, he told her, were remarkable for their courage, they persisted in the face of suffering and endured beyond all reason. 'They congregate beneath the stars,' he said enigmatically. 'They understand the sky.'

Xun talked not in Maoist slogans but in a kind of literary language. He talked, Pei Xing thought, as if words mattered, as if they might be relied upon to untie the tongue into praise songs to the world, to describe falling snow, perhaps, or the shifts in fluid light on the surface of the Huangpo River at the very moment at which a migratory flock of birds ascends.

★   ★   ★

One day Xun discovered Pei Xing had also studied English, and that she shared a love of reading. He began talking in a low secretive voice, almost sexual in retrospect, about Jane Austen. His favourite writer, he declared, of all nations and all times.

'*It is a truth universally acknowledged,*' he announced.

Pei Xing stared at him, disbelieving. What he said was seditious and ideologically unsound. This was a confidence of the most dangerous kind. Had he been discovered talking like this he would be accused of counter-revolutionary sentiments and 'capitalist-roader' veneration of the despicable Four Olds. Yet Xun trusted her, implicitly, and spoke to no one else in this way. Once he leant so close that she felt his confessional breath upon her cheek; this was the moment in which she was reminded of the softness of her own body. This was a moment — his breath — of sensual implication, and one from which she retreated at first, bewildered and alarmed.

Then there came a further literary revelation: Xun had read her father's translation of *Doctor Zhivago*. Pei Xing quietly quoted a few lines and nervously watched for a response. Xun smiled. He too knew the famous section on *inward music*.

'It is true,' he told her; '*the irresistible*

power of unarmed truth. For all the problems in our country there are still those who know this, still men and women of virtue who will not compromise. We are a great nation. We are a great and full-spirited people.'

Pei Xing had thought this a redundant rhetoric. It gave her pause. She knew that she was not a woman of virtue; she would never tell Xun that she had constructed a false story about her brother. That she had lied, just to save herself. That she had blackened his name.

But still they grew close, in shy and tentative increments, and began to see in each other not only words but a sensibility in common, miscellaneous likes and dislikes, lost and found attachments and expressions. Xun told her that when he went to the North West Provinces the only personal object he had taken with him was a favourite shuttlecock, a Swift Pigeon, slightly damaged, that he had kept from his childhood.

This was the moment in which Pei Xing realised she loved him, when she imagined the man with a handful of ragged feathers, invaluable, saved from the past. The moment when just one toy from his boyhood alighted in her mind, soft and affirming, with a candlelit glow.

In the Museum of Contemporary Art Catherine stood before a huge installation in perspex and steel labelled *Cosmos 4*. She had moved from a room in which all the artworks appeared demolished and ruined, mere scraps assembled with proud disarray and charmless autonomy, and found herself now confronted by a sequence of objects that might have been constructed by robots. They were of space-age substances and undetectable handiwork. They had a technological sheen and a kind of high unheard frequency; a dog led to this place might suddenly begin howling. Catherine leant forward to read the little caption pinned to the wall and discovered that the artist was younger than she and had been born in Berlin. But she was none the wiser about the artwork and felt excommunicated. The sanctimonious tone of galleries often distressed her; she felt once again like a working-class girl from Pearse Tower in Ballymun, that she knew nothing, really, that she was ignorant, stupid. She had studied, as one does, potted histories of art; she had read the currently fashionable coffee table books on art movements and styles (it was cool to adore Gaudi, Boltanski, Bourgeois and Viola; Fluxus was back in, and posters from

Cultural Revolution China), but faced with unfamiliar works she often found herself dispirited.

This gallery seemed also to have within it a hidden hum, as if circuits were at work in cables and grids, and technicians, invisibly efficient, were twiddling knobs and keying symbols behind the scenes to keep the electric lights low, the temperature moderate, and the atmosphere one of a lost city newly discovered with all its indecipherable artefacts. A sculpture of multiple breasts in pink neon drove Catherine from the room.

*   *   *

She took the lift to the third floor and there she was humbled. On the walls were Aboriginal paintings from all over Australia and though these were also in a strict sense incomprehensible, she could see in the patterns of dots the suggestion of lavish effort and deeply responsive notations of the world. There was a group of works by women with mellifluous names — Kathleen Petyarre, Gloria Petyarre, Emily Kame Kngwarreye — these she found particularly compelling. These women seemed to believe that pattern was everywhere. Pattern was thought, and spirit, and land, and time. Here were no portraits or conventional depictions of objects, but something aquiver, energetic, like human activity seen from the sky. Australian earth from the sky. That must be it. Dirt-coloured: ochre, iron, quartz.

Catherine recalled the ring of the angelus, how Mam had made them stop still at 6 p.m. when it came on the telly or the wireless.

She did not understand her own response. She was addressed by these paintings as a stranger, but it was a welcoming address, and in order to be receptive she had to quell her own Irish scepticism. When at last she moved on she realised she had felt, or had imagined, a fellowship with the images. And she thought for the second time that day: *beauty as a kiss*.

★ ★ ★

Catherine stepped into the sunshine. She would take a ferry ride, she decided, for no reason other than to cross the Harbour and come back again in such splendid weather. And she was thinking once more of Brendan, and how he would have loved this, the mysterious paintings, the light, the unruly adventure of Sydney. Before her the water in the Harbour shimmered. With the change of light it reminded her of sugared ginger. How could anyone, no matter with what burden, bear to leave this world?

When Catherine boarded the ferry she remembered the unbeautiful kiss, the last time she had seen Brendan, lying in his coffin. She had flown in from London and the business was already done; there he was in the funeral parlour, the smart one in Finglas, in a suit of new clothes she'd never before seen, 'all done up like, and fancy', Ruthy said, 'and dressed to kill.' Catherine was surprised to see that his face was at peace and unmarked, but for a small yellow bruise in the centre of his forehead. She leant down to him and kissed. It was true what they said: the dead are cold. Her sisters and Mam also kissed Brendan's cheek; each in the ritual was saying goodbye, each was silently weeping.

★ ★ ★

The accident was commonplace. Traffic. It happens all the time. A car crash on the M50 and probably no one to blame. Brendan had hit another car and both drivers had died, the other two days later. There was no explanation or meaning. No point, none at all, not a skerrick of making-sense she might present to poor Mam, sobbing her eyes out at the kitchen table, wringing her apron as if she would tear it in two. A paramedic Catherine tracked down said that when they pulled Brendan from the wreck he was already dead, and Charlie Mingus — he recognised the track — was still playing from the car speakers. Catherine was not sure why this musical detail had been mentioned, except that the fellow was keen on displaying his knowledge of jazz. She hated to think there was a soundtrack, a Mingus riff on bass saxophone, sad and sultry, to accompany Brendan's premature and smashed-up dying. She had liked Mingus too, and knew then that she could never, never again, listen to him play.

★ ★ ★

At first she coped. It was Mam who went to pieces. Catherine was so preoccupied holding her mother against loss that she would not allow herself to feel what might break and undo her. They were a community now of women, the two men of the family gone, and they were like a Greek chorus, wailing in harmony, sounding ancient and forlorn and meanly damaged by the gods. They even moved in concert, all bending at the same time, reaching at the same time for the pot of tea, rising up as one body when the phone rang, or there was a knock on the door.

The accident offended each of them by its ordinariness. They thought differently of Brendan, that he was special, and clever, and had been a centre to each of them, that he was solid, more defined. So that when they were telling people at the estate it was a dull-as-ditchwater story; nothing they said could make Brendan's death even halfway worthy, or rescue him from the awful banality of his fate.

A fuck-up on the M50? Ah, for fuck's sake. Wouldn't you know it? Another one. And him so young and sprightly, apple of his dear mam's eye.

⋆　⋆　⋆

Within a week of the funeral, in a snowy winter, Mam decided on a pilgrimage to the Holy Mother at Loreto. She asked Catherine to take her and Ruthy, then still living at home. Mam had been educated as a child by Loreto nuns, and had always loved the story: the little house in Nazareth, simple and pure, where Mary was visited by the multifeathered Gabriel, had been lifted up and flown around the planet by a team of angels. First to Croatia — 'of all places!' said Mam — then on 10th December, in the Year of Our Lord

1294, the angels lifted the house once again and flew it to Loreto, in Italy. Mam loved the fact that they knew the exact date. This seemed to her unimpeachable evidence of the truth of the matter. She always celebrated the Feast Day of Our Lady of Loreto on 10th December and she kept a card from her schooldays that the nuns had given her — of broad-winged angels fluttering in the sky around a little stone hut from which Mary, dressed in blue, with her shiny halo, peeked. The sky was awhirl with diaphanous gusts and the soft breath of God, a splendid lapis screen, with a sprinkle of stars.

★　★　★

Neither Mam nor Ruthy possessed a passport, so Catherine's stay in Dublin was longer than expected. After the funeral she rang Luc to explain and he told her to take the time she needed, not to fret or worry. He would ring her office and plead for an extension of compassionate leave; she could accompany her mother and sister to Loreto. He would join them, if that helped. But Catherine said no, just as she had not wished him to accompany her to the funeral. It was difficult enough hiding her apostasy from her mother, and her sense of helpless loss, and this slap-bang wallop of grief. Luc belonged to another history. Luc was another world.

★ ★ ★

Catherine arranged the photographs and passport applications and visited a travel agent in the city who specialised in 'holy tours'. He gave her a handful of pamphlets and said he was sorry for their loss, but that the Holy Mother in Loreto would surely console.

'I doubt it,' said Catherine, and she realised she had spoken her disbelief out loud to the man, who had a mild and unassuming manner and a crucifix above his desk, and who would not understand, *could not* understand, what vast hollow in herself she might be implying. His round face looked like the surface of the moon, remote, pitted, without any connection.

'Well, you never know, now, do you?' he calmly replied.

★ ★ ★

So here, on the ferry, bobbing past the Opera House, Catherine remembered her brother yet again, and the wake of his death. *Wake*, the parting of water, this design of ripples

260

they are making. This pattern on pattern made in the shock waves of uncompleted mourning. *Brendan's Wake*, she was thinking, by Mr James Joyce. Undiscovered manuscript by the master, rollicking portrait of the artist as a young man untimely ripped, set in the fluid anachrony of elegy and the lonesome no-tense of remembering. Or the movie, starring a younger-looking Gabriel Byrne. Young genius of Erin, ladies' man and ultra-literary, visits China to protect good-looking, adoptable orphans, all of them wide-smiling, from an epidemic of typhoid. Dies a heroic death: *Brendan Hero*. Toga and sandals man on mythic travels with his sister around Dublin and the Globe. Exploring *this gorgeous mad fuck-up*. Ballymun is Ithaca, Ireland wins the World Cup and the Eurovision Song Contest, the Celtic Tiger roars: *Brendan the Sailor* by Mr James Joyce.

Rejoyce, rejoyce. Catherine smiled to herself. Like Brendan, like Joyce, she enjoyed the opportune pun. She watched the wake on the water, the decoration of where they had been, the backwards vision of any journey.

Brendan the Voyager, Apostle of Ireland, Saint's day and his birthday, 16th May. With you in spirit, my brother, I ride across water.

★ ★ ★

261

Mam had hated the flight, but enjoyed the train journey from Rome, and the three nights they stayed in a pensione in Loreto. Ruthy read out segments from a guidebook and remarked on the food. Too much garlic, she said thrice. And all so oily. She was perplexed to discover that Italians seemed never to drink tea. And that every bar had a television, and that every television showed a football match, at all hours of the day and night.

★　★　★

In the bright pilgrim morning they woke to the sound of bells. Chimes broke in trembling circles through the chilly sky. Catherine lay awake with her eyes closed, listening to her sister and mother stir. Ruthy had risen first, and was splashing her face at a basin. Mam was already stripping from her nightgown and dressing for the day, hurried by the ascetic, unwarmed air. Catherine thought of Antonioni's movie, *L'avventura*, and the scene in Noto, beautifully filmed, when bored lovers overlook the city from a church roof and begin to ring bells, then hear answering peals echo from somewhere invisibly afar. A rare moment of intersection, a criss-cross of yearnings.

The movie had stayed with her. In the pallor of the world seen in black and white, Italy was a country of languid desire and unhappy women. Monica Vitti, starring as Claudia, leant in her petticoat with sexy despair at an open doorway. Emptiness, suspension, a vague searching that led nowhere. Catherine rose, shivering, and unfolded the city map on a brecciated marble table. She planned their visit, but was quiet and subdued, confused as to whether what she felt was grief or self-pity.

★ ★ ★

When they arrived at Santa Casa di Loreto, Catherine felt sure her mother would be disappointed. There was no quaint modest hut, but a marble Basilica, Renaissance on the outside, Gothic within.

'Could this be it?' Mam asked.

The white marble edifice, of pillars, columns and chunky seated saints, was not what any of them had expected. But inside, yes, sheltered a small brick building. Mam exclaimed quietly: 'Mary's house'. To prove it was so there was an inscription etched onto the altar, *'Hic Verbum Caro Factum Est'*: Here The Word Was Made Flesh. The walls were rough and brown, with the remnants of

263

worn frescos, abraded almost to nothing by the soft rub of time; and there was a statue of the Virgin, quietly looking on. She was high up, with the infant Jesus, and both were black-faced and solemn. Mam fell to her knees and silently prayed. In that chamber within a chamber, in that space that looked nothing like a poor family's house from year zero in Nazareth, or in the Bible, or depicted on the nun's card, or envisioned circling in her schoolgirl head, Mam talked to her God. Ruthy knelt beside her and Catherine, standing apart, watched them both with love. In some odd way the lunar travel agent was correct. There was a sort of solace here, in seeing her mother and sister placated, in witnessing how confirmed they were by this imitation of imitations. Kneeling in dim candlelight they expressed the ardour of their faith. Prayed in grave tones to the mother of their religion. They stayed long enough somehow to know when to rise and leave, and slowly, with heads bowed, followed the other worshippers from the church.

* * *

Later, in their shared room, Catherine summoned her courage and said: 'I don't believe any of it, Mam. Not a word. Nothing.'

She was sitting on the edge of Mam's bed, trying to sound reasonable.

And her mother took her hand and replied that she knew, of course, and that she prayed for her, daily. They would all end up in Heaven, with dear Da, in the shining golden light.

Sweet Jesus, Catherine thought.

★　★　★

They spent the next day eating gelato and photographing the town. Though it was winter the sun was out, and it felt like a holiday. A stern, unsmiling nun shepherded a class of rowdy children in the direction of the Santa Casa. They ran about, all alike in sunflower yellow T-shirts proclaiming their confederated devotion, laughing, calling out, acting naughty and irreligious.

'Brendan would have liked this,' Mam said in a shaky voice. And then Ruthy again cried. They would say this all their lives: *Brendan would have liked this*. He was already a kind of slogan.

Perhaps her mother was thinking 'fruit of the womb'. Perhaps the chamber within the chamber was a recess that recalled her own body, and all those babies that had lived there, Catherine, her four sisters, Brendan,

265

and the two that died.

Bambino: a soft word, a whisper at nighttime.

Catherine wondered for the first time what it must be like to have children and whether she might feel this hyper-maternity and mystical satisfaction. This sense of enfolding and of pattern's repetition, unwound in DNA and nose-shapes and the colour of skin, unspooled more subtly in all that a family might hold in common, those little knots of wordplay and jokes and memories, those occasions of joint sorrow and pleasure so easy it's unnoticed.

Stray kids ran through the streets of Loreto, playing kiss chase. Their calls seemed to bounce off the stone walls and fly further than voices could. Catherine found herself watching them as they darted and hid. Remembering her own childhood. Joyriding at twelve years old beside her brother in a stolen car, playing silly buggers, breaking rules, sweeping through the streets in a hoax death-swerve that would one day come true.

★   ★   ★

When the ferry arrived at the North Shore Catherine waited one stop, then two, then disembarked for no particular reason at the third. A small Chinese woman with a sunshade and large handbag passed her on the gangplank. Catherine felt like seizing her arm and asking her to sit for a while, to describe China in honour of her dear dead brother, who had wanted to go there, and would have, but for a crash on the M50. The woman looked directly at her and nodded and smiled, as if she had read her thoughts, but then passed onto the ferry and took a seat inside. Catherine watched the ferry pull away and was surprised to see the Chinese woman wave at her, a slight but definite wave, through the grimy window. Catherine waved back. Perhaps the woman had been born in Australia, she thought, and she had only imagined a native Chinese person arriving at that moment. Perhaps she was from Malaysia, or Canada, or any of a hundred thousand other places Chinese immigrants now lived. Like the Irish, dispersed. Flung like snow-flakes in a flurry, like particles motioning through water.

★ ★ ★

There were high steps behind her but Catherine lingered, watching the departing ferry move outwards from Kurraba Point to the open harbour. She decided to sit on the jetty. She removed her shoes. There was a wind rising here, carrying the briny scent of the water. A turquoise sky. She heard the chink-chink sound of wire rigging against an aluminium mast, and looked among the moored yachts to see if she could locate it. It reminded her of the triangle she played in the convent band in grade three. Not selected to learn an instrument, she had been deemed unmusical and was given, at the last moment, a triangle to hit and a place to stand at the very back of the junior musicians. Nonetheless she'd felt proud. Brendan teased her about it, but Mam said she played beautifully, that beyond all the other sounds, even beyond the violins, and the shrill recorders and the heavy-handed drumbeat, you could hear Catherine Healy in the background, and the triangle's shiny tingle-ring.

6

Strange how time seemed now and then to reverse, patterns to flip over and resume in another life. The quirk of any story, the element of return.

It was getting dark by the time Catherine made her way back towards Darlinghurst. In the twilight there were flocks of bats flying away from the botanical gardens; Catherine could see them silhouetted against the amethyst sky. What a primitive life form they were, especially here, in the city centre, flapping awkwardly into heaven. They implied tales of dark metamorphosis and entrapment in creaturely life, early childhood fears, storybook trepidation. There were also loud, insistent bird calls Catherine could not recognise, squawks and warbles and full-throated chimes; she hadn't heard so many birds in a big city before. The sky was full of alien and animated life. As she climbed the steep steps at Woolloomooloo, Catherine huffed and puffed but felt pleased with herself for the effort, and for the muscular sensuality of her working legs. Pausing on a landing, she looked briefly behind her: the centre of Sydney hung like a vision in a silver panorama — the towers, all arrayed, the canyons between them, the Bridge in faint outline and the Opera House now obscured. The scrolling night would soon leave only the lights; the city would forget itself, become another kind of abstraction.

★   ★   ★

Catherine reached a street of backpackers' cafés and small open-fronted restaurants just as the lights switched on, casting a cadmium yellow shine, a painterly tone, over the diners sitting at tables outside. The meals looked good, generous servings of unspecific provenance, mostly some kind of mix-up of Thai and Australian cuisine. A sign read: *Kangaroo stirfry with hot chilli sauce*. Catherine paused, considering. But since she'd not yet seen a kangaroo, a *real live* kangaroo, big-eyed and cutesy, fetchingly iconic, one she could photograph or write home about to Ruthy, she decided that her first meeting shouldn't be a feast.

The long climb from the Harbour had left Catherine feeling flush with the heat and in need of a drink. But she didn't want to enter a wine bar or sit conspicuously alone at a pub, so she found a liquor store further up the street and bought a cold bottle of riesling to take back to the apartment. Then she selected a Chinese takeaway, aware of its sentimentally vague connotations, and ordered ginger fish and a portion of fried rice.

★　★　★

On Darlinghurst Road, though still early, it was an edgy Saturday night. There were sex clubs with flashing lights, young travellers already drunk, and a kind of hot human energy, sparking up currents of desire and frustration. Rowdy pubs were spilling their patrons, who swung groggy onto the street. Restaurants were like televisions, boxes of fluorescent encounter and hyped possibility. Everything, every surface, appeared glossy and over-bright. Catherine saw the junkie postures she recognised from her childhood, and the sly handshake that exchanged folded money and small plastic bags, a furtive glance, the slinking away. She noticed an Aboriginal beggar, sitting with his back against a pole, and a group of five young women, laughing and life-filled, heading in scanty dresses for a night on the town. A young man, shirtless and covered with blue tattoos, was shouting obscenities from a street corner to everyone and no one, waving his arms in a kind of violent, useless, feint.

City-ravage, pagan and awesome, on a humid Saturday night. All at once Catherine wanted quiet, and to be hidden away. She wanted to sit alone, in a kitchen, to rest her elbows on a table, and to eat her take-away meal in silence.

★   ★   ★

It had been a haunted day. Some days were better than others. Sometimes Brendan rested in peace, safely interred, but on others, like today, he hung around, insinuated himself into the spaces that broke open between now and then, turned up with his dead man's words and his unextinguished charisma. Yet it was not a mournful day. There had been a jaunty and delectable newness to things, and Catherine still felt the cheery elation of all she had seen: the didgeridoo player, the Opera House, the Aboriginal paintings, and then the supernatural ferry ride, without destination, from Circular Quay across the Harbour and back again. There was the moment, some-where in the middle, when standing at the bow of the ferry, high up in the breeze, she could see the smiling clown-face façade that formed the entrance to Luna Park, nestling right there on the shore, tucked in one

272

corner; she saw the Bridge on the left and the Opera House on the right and felt located in space by these three incomparable monuments. She was thinking of Brendan the Voyager, seeking paradise with his disciple monks in ancient Ireland, and though this was a nonsensical analogy, she had thought to herself yet again. *Brendan would have liked this.*

★　★　★

Catherine sat cradling her second glass of wine and played a CD of Sinéad O'Connor singing 'On Raglan Road'. Darkness had fallen. In the apartment she heard the lovely voice ring out, resonant and yearning, and felt wreathed around and caught up in its sweet lamentation. She rose slowly and walked outside, onto the small jutting balcony on this, the fourth floor. Ahead was the back of the Coca-Cola billboard: its jazzy illumination showed from the rear as a quivering rectangular nimbus, outlining a black building. There were other apartments nearby, and other people enjoying their breezy balcony on a summer's evening, but only Catherine had the sound-track of 'On Raglan Road', only she had this accent of herself summoned and this particular Dublin romance. At the end of the track she switched off the music, wanting no other layer of words to fall where it had been.

Catherine sat on a metal chair on the balcony, staring into space. She sipped her wine. She considered her good fortune and looked upwards for stars that came from Ireland. In the centre of the city you couldn't really see the stars. But she knew they were there. They were new stars, new, southern hemisphere stars. There must have been convicts who looked upwards in the early nights and felt entirely confounded. They must have felt that the very heavens had changed, that the all-mothering and humbling darkness had let them fall away, had released them into disaster. Mere perforations of a night curtain that had fallen over their heads. Poor buggers. Stranded. No direction home.

★ ★ ★

Ah, but she would have liked now to be lying in Luc's warm arms. She would ring him soon. She must not ring too early and must not drink too much in the meantime, lest she sound boozy and needy, or maudlin and mean. Her sexual loneliness was profound, and she had not expected it. When they were together, in the time of mourning, it had been easy to remain self-enclosed, because pleasure seemed so unlikely, because she did not consider she had a right to joy in the time of her grief. Luc was patient, remote. There settled between them a strained and uneasy quiet. But now, in another world, there seemed more reason to believe in secular redemptions, in gestures by which the body delighted in being alive. She had never before been so unclothed in January, felt this kind of warm sensual night just a few weeks after her birthday, sitting with bare arms and bare legs and a cold glass of wine.

St Catherine, St Catherine, O lend me
 thine aid
And grant that I never may die an old
 maid.

The air had become dense and seemed to shudder with rising wind. Catherine looked down William Street and saw there entrammelled car headlights, all pushing at even intervals to and from the city centre. White spots in one direction, red in the other, and she was baffled again by the paintings she had seen that afternoon, all those massing dots from the central desert, spin-drifting, swirling and anti-representational. She was not good at abstraction: perhaps that's what it was, perhaps something in her childhood in the tower, with too little private space to see her own life clearly, had left her depleted in her capacity to appreciate visual art.

* * *

As a child she has been taken on a school excursion to the National Gallery of Ireland. The students were led in obedient lines before august portraits and historical scenes, instructed to admire. What had claimed Catherine, what had most commanded her attention, was a melodramatic late Victorian picture called *The Wounded Poacher*. She still remembered the name of the artist: Henry Jones Thaddeus. They had been asked to choose an image in one of three rooms and write a story about it. Most of the convent girls dutifully chose biblical genre paintings, by which they might display their spiritual goodness. But for Catherine the wounded poacher was inexplicably alluring. It showed a man, stripped to the waist, collapsed on a chair and in the care of a young woman who bent tenderly above him. She dabbed a cloth at his chest and he appeared to be in a faint, his mouth slightly open and his posture abandoned. At the poacher's feet lay two

276

dead rabbits and a gun, and it was a poor house and gloomy, with a little still-life bottle and bowl sitting on a table in one corner.

Only as an adult did Catherine realise how sensuous the image was; and how the woman leaning over the prone man suggested sexual touch. His head leant back against her breast; her arm encircled him. Catherine's schoolgirl story had been rather dull, but the erotic impression of the tableau had vividly persisted. When at their lunchbreak a nun chided her for choosing to write about a sinner, Catherine had not felt ashamed. She fiercely consumed the jam sandwiches her mother had made for her and sat slightly apart from the other girls, *tough as a tart*, one of them said.

★   ★   ★

Catherine glanced up at the clock and decided to watch the television news. She found the remote and flashed the severe world into vision. There were the usual foreign wars, tribulations, massacres, collapsing economies, there was global warming and economic downturn and apocalyptic predictions. The war in Iraq: never-ending. Afghanistan: never-ending. Somewhere beyond balmy Sydney on a Saturday evening in January, the world was heartsick and haywire.

When the local news began, the opening story was located at the Circular Quay. A little girl, eight years old, had gone missing from her home — a suspected abduction — and was last seen at the Rail Station at the Circular Quay. CCTV footage had found her small face in the crowd, identified by her mother. On the screen Catherine saw a still shot of a blurry child, and around her were five heads, a young man, a young woman, an older woman and *herself* and then the man who must presumably be the abductor, his hand on the girl's shoulder, bending to whisper something in her ear. Catherine leant in trepidation towards the screen. One face was remarkably like the Chinese woman she had seen on the north shore, boarding the ferry — could this really be so? Yes, there was the handbag. And yes, it was definitely her, Catherine Healy of Ballymun, next to the little girl. The others were apart, at each end, and seemed to be diverging. The newsreader voice-over said that police would like to locate the man standing directly behind the little girl, with his hand on her shoulder. Others in the photograph — and here red rings magically appeared around the four nearby adults — should contact police immediately to help with their inquiries. The young man was looking down — would he have noticed anything? — but the three women were all looking alert and ahead. Catherine saw her own nebulous head in a noose and marked out. She leant back on the couch and felt slightly ill. She pressed the off button and the newsreader, now speaking about taxes, was sucked back into nothingness.

★   ★   ★

It seemed impossible to be caught in public time like this, and in elbow-rubbing proximity to a mystery crime. It made no sense. Why would an abductor take a child to a busy tourist site on a Saturday morning, and not stash her away somewhere, and act in a more evil way, more dastardly and more truly covert? Was he convinced one could hide a small child in a crowd? Catherine was struck by the poor quality of the CCTV image. There was hi-fi, hi-def, high-bloody-everything; might not the techies be able to produce a clearer photograph? It was in black and white, almost unheard of these days, and grainy, as if glimpsed and recorded underwater. The little girl might have been any little girl. Was the mother sure? How could she be certain? Perhaps the plaits were a giveaway. All the other faces looked stark and similar. The two young people appeared her age, mid-thirties or so, and so did the now suspicious man leaning towards the little girl. The Chinese woman was perhaps sixty, sixty-five, and yes, it was she. As she boarded the ferry she perhaps recalled seeing Catherine earlier in the day, at the train station. And then she waved.

Catherine waited thirty minutes, her hesitation inexplicable, before she rang the police. Her heart was heavy. She was asked: what department? And blurted out in scrambled syntax that she had seen herself on telly, there she was, next to the child, and commanded by the newsreader to get in touch. There were clicks and pauses, then a gruff voice came on.

Catherine collected her thoughts. 'It's about the abducted child,' she said clearly. 'I am one of the people in the image broadcast this evening. The CCTV image at Circular Quay.'

'Name and address?'

'Don't you want me to come in?'

'Name and address? I'll take your details, luv, and we'll send a police car to pick you up. Right away. OK? Ten minutes or so.'

Catherine left her name and address and

then the policeman hung up.

She was shaken by what seemed the dark undertow of the day, a child lost, perhaps a death, and nothing was noticed. There was just this imprecise still from a lazy camera, this unremembered coming together of four visitors to the quay, ordinary people like her, with their own purpose in being there and their own hidden histories.

Brendan would have liked this. Brendan would have seen the drama in being caught unawares adjacent to criminal intent. He would have found thrilling the accident of her appearance and the coalition of unknown faces, the preposterous coincidence, the terrible forces beneath the everyday suggested in this naff red outlining of passing faces. Faces that shared, inadvertently, in something unknown.

But it could be nothing, she told herself. The story was incomplete. Images told you nothing. That was why she was a journalist, why she loved but finally distrusted Henry Jones Thaddeus, why she was moved, but remained ignorant, looking at the Aboriginal dot paintings, why she wanted to get behind the image of the car with blood spatter on the front seat to the still-alive body of Veronica Guerin, to the woman before the blood, and before the police, and before the journalist

281

herself was the story. But the red-ringed heads in a photograph were perhaps the beginning of an explanation.

* * *

When two policemen knocked on the door Catherine leapt to attention. They were uniformed and young. The taller one, poorly shaven, with a small nick on his chin, held up a card as they do on television, and the other, vaguely handsome, was already turning back towards the elevator. They descended together in the brown light, standing too close to each other, and at the ping of the lift door Catherine saw the police car parked directly in front, brazen and bright in a no-parking zone. All she could think of was that she wished she had changed her clothes; her indigo sundress and open sandals were an offence to the gravity of their errand.

'Here on a holiday, luv?' The tall one had noticed her accent.

'Working. Just arrived.'

'So what do you think, eh? God's own country or what?'

Catherine was taken aback by this casual chit-chat. Australian men were always seeking forms of verbal confirmation.

'It's lovely,' she said weakly, sounding more foreign than ever, and all the time she was thinking: the little girl might be drifting in the harbour, eyes closed, face down. She might be turning slowly in the currents, her plaits waving like sea life, her tiny lungs, oh bless her, flooded with cold water, and her poor mam somewhere out there, completely distraught.

The indecency of small talk irritated and pained her.

★ ★ ★

Central Sydney flashed by. A flow of lights, barium, sodium and fluorescent, then deceleration. Workers in reflecting, lime-coloured vests attended a rough hole and a mound of rubble by the roadside. Sad bastards, road-working on a Saturday night. Their faces zipped by, dazed, then fell away into darkness. Orange traffic cones surrounded them, like an artless installation.

There were white taxis everywhere, and crowds jerking on the pavement, intermittently merging, or separating, or lit by pulses of headlight. Every large city is lurid on a Saturday night, Catherine told herself. Flashy, heartless, swaggering, cocksure. Every large city has its adrenaline overdrive and its regions of darkness, where one might be lost, or found, or entirely disappear.

★ ★ ★

In the reception area of the police station Catherine was told to wait a few minutes. Night settled around her. She sat on a sticky vinyl chair staring at a missing persons' poster. Squares of blurry faces in rows, six by six. Thirty-six missing people. The poster was mounted on a pale blue wall and Catherine leant forward in the jaundiced light the better to examine it, as if convinced she might see there someone she knew. She became aware of the policewoman behind the reception counter watching her with disdain. A bit like her oldest sister, Philomena, sharp-faced and mousey. The low wattage illumination flattered no one. When at last she was asked questions in the interview room — regulation grey, denuded of features but for a distracting crack in the wall above the door — there was really nothing of worth or substance to say. She disappointed the two detectives. No, she had not seen the man and child on the train. No, she could remember nothing at all unusual. She saw them when they alighted. They looked like father and daughter. Unremarkable. Quiet. No, she couldn't say which direction they took. No, she didn't notice anything, really.

But Catherine had. There had been something, something that called forth within her a momentary and ineffable tenderness. What was it, then, that the child had evoked?

And yes, if she thought of anything further she would get in touch.

It was a pointless excursion. The detectives were courteous, but bored. Why had they bothered to bring her in? She had been mildly excited at first, thinking herself a special witness, able to help solve a mystery; now she felt like the schoolkid ashamed because she had raised her hand with eager confidence and had no answers. It was nothing like television. There was no resolution and no plot.

★ ★ ★

When Catherine left the interview room she saw before her the Chinese woman who was also caught in the CCTV image. She was short, well dressed, and still carrying her bulky handbag. She sat where Catherine had earlier sat, and was examining the thirty-six missing persons photographs. Catherine sat beside her. The thirty-six faces looked oddly similar, an under-nourished, pale tribe. They were mostly young. Didn't the old go missing? Did police only search for the missing young?

'I saw you today,' she said. 'At Kurraba Point Wharf.'

'Yes.'

'You waved.'

'Yes.' The Chinese woman smiled. 'She's safe, you know, that little girl. She is safe.'

Catherine sat beside the woman. They stared in the same direction.

'She was happy, not afraid.'

'Pardon?' The accent was unusual.

'She was happy, not afraid.'

'Ah,' said Catherine. 'I didn't really notice.'

The Chinese woman touched her hand. The fabric of her dress was shiny, Catherine noticed, *oriental* perhaps, and covered with small mauve buds of cherry blossom.

'Safe,' she said again.

★　★　★

Catherine's name was called. A taxi had arrived to take her back to the apartment. It seemed too soon. She wanted to speak to the Chinese woman who had mysteriously intersected her path three times — three times — in a single day. She leant forward and kissed the woman's cheek, then embarrassed, emotionally fumbling, Catherine turned and stood. Had they been elsewhere she might have stroked the woman's hair or laid her face in her lap; this woman inspired solicitude, this woman had the composure of one who knew the pertinence of details, the solution to crimes, the way the future might ripple from a touch or a single word.

'Well, good luck,' Catherine announced. She had no idea why she said this. A formula saying. The Chinese woman raised her hand in a small precise wave. Behind the counter the Philomena look-alike made a sniffing, dismissive sound. On her high horse, as Mam would say. As you do. *Lady Muck.*

How inconsequential it felt, all this coming and going. It was maddening to be implicated, as though there was a mystery to the day, then to have the possibility of significance rendered trite and officious, a kind of bureaucratic transaction, a woman picking at her teeth in bad light behind a distant high counter.

★ ★ ★

In the half-lit apartment Catherine felt lost. She paused in the bathroom, looked in the mirror while she rinsed her hands, then pulled back from her own image, which

287

appeared weary and aged. She scooped water for her face, splashed it, and looked again. No improvement. She lifted her hair from her neck, fanning it. Catherine could not help feeling a vague prickling of panic. She was in Australia and it was not all sparkles and sunshine. *Remorseless*: the word surfaced. It was surprising to think again of Veronica Guerin, after all these years. Might there be *remorseless* crime in this country? Catherine patted her face dry. Held it in the towel, smothered. She closed her eyes into an awful solitude, which suddenly felt unendurable.

When Catherine walked into the living room she glanced at the clock and decided that it was time to ring Luc. She would not, resolutely not, tell him of the supposed abduction, but must talk of her job, and the fine weather and their tentative future. Would he join her here in Sydney? Would she be able to persuade him?

★   ★   ★

Catherine dialled and heard the phone ringing into the chamber of Luc's sleeping, on the other, now-awakening side of the planet. He took a while to pick up. She wondered if he was hushing another woman resting beside him, or if there was just this unbreachable gap, this global distance a single voice might never quite cover. Catherine, close to tears but determined to be chatty, held the receiver to her face and waited.

'Oui?'

Hearken. It was his half-asleep voice, his mother tongue, in which the wisp of himself as a boy, afraid of his grandmother and of moths, was still touchingly apparent.

'Sorry. I just wanted to hear your voice.'

★ ★ ★

And when they had talked Catherine finished the bottle of wine. And when neither had said what the other could not bear to hear, she had turned out the light. And when in darkness the little girl reappeared before her, shining in photographic silver, televisually fallible, a relic of herself and possibly now dead, Catherine tried to turn away, pretending she didn't care, into the tunnel of sleep, that sweetest regression.

But she lay in the dark and what came to her wakeful imagining was this: an altar boy swinging a censer and smoke filling the transept of the church, and her mother's face, and Brendan's, peering half disappeared through the cloudy air, and the godless and the god-fearing all together in one place, and the mystery of any family, and its assorted pieties and devotions. Any family, anywhere, its assorted devotions. Any child. Or that child, that lost, particular child.

★   ★   ★

Pei Xing rode the ferry back to Circular Quay thinking of her husband, Wang Xun. She recollected his hands, his eyes, the timbre of his voice. The shape of his back and his buttocks, and the touch they invited. There was a form of memory, yes, that resided in the cells of the body.

They were married for seven years before he succumbed to the tuberculosis that he contracted in the north; and these were her years of recovering a self. She had been effaced in the prison, but for a concealed, dim life, lived almost entirely in foreign vocabularies; and then again in the labour camp, where she learnt how physical exhaustion might wear a woman to a mere shape. This was how she had seen herself, as hopeless, insubstantial.

When Xun arrived, Pei Xing had not understood at first what it was he was offering her. She had closed down so much, and was so wholly dispirited. She was a woman composed of vacant spaces. But the first time he held her face in his hands, tilted it to look at him, leant to kiss, she discovered a flourish of inner liveliness and a remnant of self undemolished. They sought permission to marry and had to wait a year; there were many political impediments, given her family's 'crimes'. But Xun's father loved his only son and knew of his illness, and so was persuaded to make an intervention in Shanghai. They were authorised both to marry and to return to the city.

With four other families Xun and Pei Xing shared a house near Suzhou Creek and lived in one tiny room, with a communal kitchen and latrine. It was a kind of liberty neither had dared to anticipate. They woke in each other's company. They ate together, just the two of them. They had private, intense, searching conversations. The rapture of sexual experience was also unexpected. Pei Xing could hardly speak of it, even when they lay in each other's arms. Both learnt not to make too much noise in their love-making and the quiet time afterwards was eloquent enough. Pei Xing had been surprised to discover how warm a human body was, and how the need of love-making brought its own climate to their bed. And she was surprised to be reminded of the existence of laughter, that there was another faculty forgotten and a body pleasure neglected. There were the tremendous histories of nations, and the vast movements of peoples, there were collective orders of brutality and the crushing of those deemed dissidents; and there were also these more subtle and modest measures of life, the preparation of a meal, a whispered conversation, a suggestive kiss. When Pei Xing discovered her pregnancy there was more rejoicing: his face at her belly, listening to the third life growing between them.

★   ★   ★

Pei Xing was contented and at peace as she moved over the water. Looking back, she could see the smiling-face façade and Ferris wheel of the amusement park, the bridge overarching, the miniaturising North Shore. She loved these ferry rides. She was like a child with a treat. When Jimmy was little she was interested to see the emotional range of children, how profound were their pleasures, how quickly removed, how everything seemed tuned to a pitch of exaggeration. Children had a vehemence and volatility that transfigured the smallest moment. A toy removed could betoken funereal wailing; a toy recovered, a whoop of instant bliss. Now, in

Australia, she allowed herself wider feelings.

She had not thought of it before: from here the Sydney Opera House looked like folded paper, like one of those shapes children produce under instruction from a teacher. Cranes. Frogs. Lotus blossoms. Airplanes. And there was a game she had seen Australian schoolchildren play: they folded paper into little peaks, inserted their thumbs and index fingers, and counted out numbers and fortunes, opening and closing the paper object like the mouth of a bird. What was it called, she wondered. The paper House sailed by. It was achieving a golden sheen in the late afternoon light, its shells polished in the setting sun, responsive to the sky.

*   *   *

Pei Xing was hungry. At the hospital Hua had eaten most of the rice; her appetite seemed huge. Pei Xing thought often of her mother's cooking. On the day of the new scarlet coat, the exemplary day, the day she returned to again and again, her mother had cooked her favourite dishes: steamed sea turtle with fried ginger and spring onions, peppery carrot broth, tofu stuffed with pork, and for dessert, balls of sticky rice shaped around sweet sesame paste. She cannot now remember why the festive meal had been prepared, but liked to think it was purely in honour of her coat. Her parents had toasted each other with Shaoxing rice wine and she questioned now, after all these years, if it had been an anniversary of some sort. Their wedding, perhaps. She would now never know.

Gan bei! Her father's voice was still there, his glass was still raised in a toast.

★ ★ ★

Less than a year before her parents were taken, Mao had famously swum in the Yangtze River. It was 1966, he was seventy-three years old, and there he was, plunged into the brown water near the Wuhan Bridge. Posters appeared everywhere: Mao chubby-cheeked and tubby-shaped, beaming robust health and totalitarian command. He was reputed to have swum thirty Li, fifteen miles, in only sixty-five minutes. Pei Xing remembers the figures exactly, because her father had scoffed, doing a quick calculation.

'Our leader is indeed superhuman,' father announced with a wry smile.

They were happy then. The darkness had not yet fallen. They had not yet been swallowed into the belly of a giant man. In documentary footage Pei Xing saw years later, Mao was floating on his back, simply bobbing in the water, relaxed and unstrenuous. He was surrounded by five thousand young swimmers who all adored him, and who would appear lined up, in their bathing suits, in hundreds of thousands of posters. Public management jubilation. Ten thousand legs.

Why had she thought of this? Because her joy was small-scale. Because China had taught her the tyranny of scale. Because in her hunger, on the ferry, she remembered the dense and distinctive pleasure of one single day and the fact that she had never, at her peril, learned to swim.

★　★　★

There it was, Circular Quay, slowly floating closer. As the ferry moved towards its berth Pei Xing glanced across at the façade of the Museum of Contemporary Art, one of her favourite places in Sydney. Marvels, full of marvels. She loved to see what visual fictions human beings might fabricate. She had spent many hours there in a trance of pure happiness, wandering the hushed high rooms, overtaken by visions. The staff there knew her, greeted her, took her coat and hung it safely in exchange for a coin-sized token, asked in a soft voice how she was going. They welcomed her rapt gazing, her lingering arty wander; they watched with casual beneficence as she circled an installation or halted forever before a particular object or painting. It was there Pei Xing first used the English word 'fabulous', only one month after her arrival in Australia. She still remembered the moment: the delight of an unlikely, spontaneous exclamation. It was a difficult word to say out loud. Though she knew the English in her head, in her mouth it was a heavy and formless shape. *Fabulous*. One of the gallery attendants had heard her; it occasioned her first local exchange of English language conversation.

*   *   *

On the pier Pei Xing thought suddenly of Aristos, who would have finished his work by now and perhaps, at this very minute, was sitting on a bus, gazing out of a window. His face appeared in her mind, shifting even as it arose, sped away behind slick reflections.

Aristos, whom death was stealthily following.

Pei Xing looked at the sky. It was shifting colour once again; there was a fine salmon streak to the west, and a change in the weather coming from the east. Beneath omnipresent human speech she heard the murmur of wavelets and flags and the cloth domes of umbrellas. Pei Xing crossed the concourse beyond the five jetties of the Circular Quay to check on her friend Mary. There she was, sleeping, nestled in the home she had made beneath her hoarded plastic bags. She was returned, safely returned. Mary snored a little and looked content and comfortable. She was secure in her own world, blindfolded into sleep. She bore a ravaged face, deeply creased, and her hair was grey and matted with dirt and leaves. On the surface of her tired skin lay a glaucous bloom, and there was something, some kind of note, clutched in her sleeping hand.

How the poor of any city vanish and reappear.

Respectful, quiet, Pei Xing stood for a moment, offered Mary a blessing, then rode the escalator upwards to catch the train.

★　★　★

The Bankstown Line formed a stylised map in her head, a little train track in black, and a series of perky station names: Redfern, Erskineville, St Peters, Marrickville . . . Lakemba, Wiley Park, Punchbowl, Bankstown. They were a chant she had learned, and a series of familiar vistas. As she rode through the damp twilight Pei Xing dozed a little. Then she roused herself at her destination and prepared for the walk home. She thought of food as she trod the lit footpaths to her apartment block. *Xiaolongbao*: steamed dumplings. Bamboo shoots. Moon-cake. Peking duck. She recalled her mother standing outside Old City God's Temple, waiting in a line for crab *xiaolongbao*, warning 'Too much crab will make you cold inside.' Food lore: Chinese knew all the secrets of the body. Xun had brought her snake's head soup when she was breastfeeding their son; to this day she does not understand how he procured and afforded it. But she had felt instant strength and her milk flowed swiftly.

★   ★   ★

In her apartment Pei Xing brewed herself tea. She selected and played a favourite CD: Liu Fang's pipa solo, '*Fei Hua Dian Cui*' ('Falling Snow decorates the Evergreen'). In the strings plucked forward and backward she heard the descent of the snow, there was lightness, pause, there was the floating of single flakes and their moist feathery touch; there was the sense of stilled time and Buddhic possibilities. She imagined Liu

298

Fang's beautiful fingers sliding the neck of the instrument, playing, her eyes closed, on a concert stage in Germany or Canada or France, spreading notes as if snow, falling faintly through the universe, and faintly falling.

Pei Xing felt calmed and returned to her self-possession. Some of the pieces on the CD were hundreds of years old. This was music that had endured; this was sound ever-flowing, ripple-effecting, beyond clock-face time.

★　★　★

Over a large bowl of beef and noodles, Pei Xing listened carefully to several pipa recitals and when she had finished she managed a plate of vanilla ice-cream topped with chocolate sauce. It was a satisfying meal. Not turtle, but satisfying. Instead of cleaning her dishes Pei Xing unlaced her shoes, eased them from her feet, then reclined on the sofa. She switched on the television to watch the nine o'clock news.

The story of the abducted child at the Circular Quay seemed to Pei Xing unreal. The ringed heads, in which she saw herself and the woman who exchanged glances at Kurraba Point Wharf, and a young man and

299

woman, neither of whom she could recall, was a kind of adventitious device, surely not useful in solving a crime. But calmly she rang, and calmly she received word from the policeman that a police car would come and collect her for questioning at the station. He noted her name — asked her twice to spell it — took down her address and her phone number, then thanked her for taking the trouble to call.

Pei Xing had not really noticed the man caught in the photograph with his hand on the girl's shoulder, but she remembered the child, a pretty girl with Chinese-style plaits. She had been attracted to the girl, who seemed unsure, somehow, and a stranger to the Quay, but also filled with the excitement of novelty and apparently unafraid. She had wanted to say this to the policeman: *she seemed unafraid*; but was not given the chance. So she thought that perhaps the child was in no danger at all, there had been a domestic argument, some misunderstanding; her father — for so he seemed — had simply wanted more time alone with his estranged daughter.

In her fretful imagining Pei Xing wanted to save the child, to think up a narrative, and an ending, in which she would be vouched safe. At the police station she would say this: *she seemed unafraid*. She would dress well, and look serious. A reliable witness. *She seemed unafraid*.

★ ★ ★

After Mao died in 1976, China began rapidly to change. By the time her husband had died, in 1982, Shanghai was well into its transformation. There were gangs, she heard, who kidnapped children for ransom. They had a test. They let the child grow hungry, then offered them fish. If the child plucked the eyeball with his chopsticks and tried that first, he was a rich child and it was worthwhile pursuing a ransom. However, if the child reached for the body of the fish and a mouthful of flesh, he was more likely to be from a poor family and hardly worth keeping. It may have been urban myth, but stories sprang up of precious offspring of the one-child policy being stolen away and huge sums demanded for their safe return. Sometimes the stolen child was never seen again. Pei Xing had warned little Jimmy — or Lun, as he then was — to stay close by when they went to market, and if offered fish by a stranger to eat as if he were starving. This way, she reasoned, he might be let go. It made her afraid, the idea of stolen children. And she had made her son afraid too. Even now he ate greedily, as if vigorous consumption was a test of his permanence.

★ ★ ★

When Xun died Pei Xing was working as an English teacher. Those skills once despised as corruptive were now regarded as essential. She gave classes at a middle school, and taught private students in the evenings. It was hard to make ends meet. Xun's father had also died and there was no provision made for the grandson, or for her, nor did she have any remaining family in Shanghai to support her. She waited, just waited, to see if her parents would be rehabilitated, to find a way to join her half-forgotten brother, now living in Australia.

For years after his death crowds visited the embalmed Mao Tse Tung in his crystal coffin. They lined up for hours around Tiananmen Square, just to file past and pay their respects. Mao persisted undead, his bubble face waxy, glimpsed through the casket manufactured by Beijing General Glass Factory, Number 608. He hadn't disappeared; he was just more object than ever. He was the emblem of the Chinese capacity for glorification, the great face-object of a monstrous fame.

Pei Xing believed that history was still uncertain and China might, without warning, again turn violent. She returned to habits of quiet and careful circumspection. She would lay low and hide out and disappear if necessary. She would guard her child. She would practise discipline and survive. No degree of caution seemed too large. But Pei Xing enjoyed being a teacher, being out and about in the city. And when she looked over the black-haired heads of her students, all of them reading silently, all of them inward and quiet, she felt that they existed within the compass of her care, and that she might love, if permitted, each and every one of them.

★   ★   ★

The telephone rang and Pei Xing leapt up, startled. It was a nurse from the hospital saying she had left her plastic rice container behind, and would she like them to hold it for a week or post it in the mail? Pei Xing was touched that so trivial an object had prompted a call, that someone had bothered whether or not she might be concerned at what she'd left behind. She suggested they hold it, thanked the nurse sincerely, and replaced the receiver.

When the policeman knocked on the door

Pei Xing was ready. There was a man and a woman, both very young, and she was touched to see that the man had the marks of adolescent acne still apparent. Just a boy, as Jimmy was. A blemished, particular boy. He had the slightly abashed manner of adolescents, not sure exactly where to put his hands, looking away to remember what came next. Pei Xing was not afraid as she allowed herself to be guided into the police car, and was pleased that the officers were unenthusiastic and wished for no small talk. They were no doubt bored with this errand — treated like taxi drivers, taking an unimportant Chinese woman all the way to the central police station. For Pei Xing it did not feel compulsory; she felt she was doing the police a favour.

★ ★ ★

Predictably, they took the M5 route into the city. Pei Xing rarely had a chance to fly like this along the freeway, since she owned no car and went everywhere by public transport. But it was almost exhilarating, the speed at which they moved, the dark night flashing by in a neon rush of even-spaced lights, the glassy effect of staring through the window, alone with her thoughts. There were long and sinuous tunnels, foggy with chemicals, like something she had seen in a car chase in a Bruce Willis movie — all that thunderous truck-tonnage ready to detonate in a fireball, or replayed again and again as Princess Diana's final moments — the artificial quality of the light, a pinkish gel, the way the fast-shifting walls swung distorted and dangerously close. Pei Xing was relieved when the car shot out of the tunnel, back onto the open road. When they passed the airport, and entered the short tunnel beneath the runway, there was the thrill of proximity to aircraft landing and taking off. All that activity in the sky, all that national and transnational coming and going. The paranormal roar of the planes set off a tremble in her body; the boom of machinery lifting into the air, the improbability of it all.

I am young, Pei Xing thought. I am still a young woman. She turned to look out of the back window to see the jet angling away.

★　★　★

At the police station she was asked to wait a few minutes. On the wall in the waiting area was a poster asking in many languages, including her own, if she needed a translator. There was another of missing people, six by six squares, melancholy portraits garnered from albums and passports. Pei Xing leant forward to examine them. Some were trapped in dead-eye snapshots, eternally misrepresented, some were animated at a party or cutaway from an embrace, some were neutered for passport protocol, lured prematurely to anonymity. The stylistic incoherence of the photos — when so much these days was blandly standardised — seemed to Pei Xing especially poignant. For one man the sign of his existence was a bleached, almost featureless face, resting like a mushroom in an unlit hollow. How could this image possibly help find him?

The door opened and the woman Pei Xing had seen at the wharf was shaking hands with a detective and being thanked for helping with their inquiries. She leant back from the portraits and saw the woman recognise her.

'I saw you today,' she said. 'At Kurraba Point Wharf.'

Her accent was what? Irish. A tourist, perhaps.

'Yes.'

'You waved.'

'Yes.' And Pei Xing thought: she is seeking reassurance. This is a young woman, far from home, who cannot bear the thought of a lost child.

'She's safe, you know, that little girl. She is safe.'

The woman sat beside her. They stared ahead.

'She was happy, not afraid.'

'Pardon?'

'She was happy, not afraid.'

'Ah, I didn't really notice.'

Pei Xing imagined she could hear the breathing of the woman beside her. They sat close, like relatives awaiting bad news. Like mother and daughter. The policewoman behind the reception counter shifted in her seat, to remind them both that she was there, superintending. Pei Xing gently touched the Irish woman's hand.

'Safe,' she repeated.

The word would make it so. And then the young woman was called to a taxi and rose in a hesitating manner, as though she had a confession she was anxious to impart. In an instinctive movement she leant down and kissed Pei Xing on the cheek. So much, apparently, lay beneath this clumsy gesture. So much beneath a few exchanged words. It was the contraption they worked with, words, and it was insufficient.

'Well, good luck.'

It was effortless good will. Pei Xing raised her hand in a small wave and watched the woman leave, half-turned back to her, through the sliding glass doors. She readied herself for the interview: to say *she seemed unafraid*.

★ ★ ★

When, half an hour later, Pei Xing was driven home in a taxi, this time feeling disappointed and subdued, she reflected that she had not persuaded anyone at the police station that the child would be safe. They were already writing in a file somewhere that she was an unreliable witness; they were already tagging her as a helpless optimist, unrealistic and deluded. Chinese. *The Chinese woman was no help at all*. Perhaps the Irish woman had seen something meaningful. She had appeared burdened and in need of solace; perhaps she had already imparted some crucial information and was dragging sorrow and a surer knowledge of what might have happened. Pei Xing leant her tired face against the cool glass of the car window. The night was humid, electrical. There was the buzz and hum of imminent lightning and a wavy disturbance in the sky as the weather assembled and shifted. Soon the wind would whip up, the sky become ocean, the streaming rainstorm obliterate all one might see.

Back through the perilous tunnels. Back towards Bankstown. This time she closed her eyes.

★ ★ ★

In her reading that day of *Doctor Zhivago*, Pei Xing had paused after the drawn-out account of his death. Hua was weeping through her expressionless, frozen face; a line of tears soaked her collar. Yuri Zhivago had a heart attack on a stalled tram. Feeling faint and in need of air, he had pulled and pulled again at the leather strap on the window, first down, then up, then roughly towards him, even though the crowd shouted at him that the windows had been nailed shut. He was so confused and in such pain that he did not understand. Something inside him simply broke. Somewhere in the heckle and jeer, his heart was bursting. He could hear nothing. He stumbled from the tram and fell beside it onto the hard cobblestones. A crowd gathered and someone announced that his heart had stopped.

Pei Xing knew what Hua was thinking, that it was an ignoble death. But they were both moved, and it was not possible to read any further. Pei Xing was not weeping, but felt choked and tight in the chest. She tended to

Hua as if they were both bereaved, talking to her of other matters, fussing a little in her ministrations, pulling the hospital shawl closer as if wrapping her body against the chill wind of mortality.

But now, after the worrisome television news and her general unsettlement, after the futile trip to the police station and her implicit disqualification, Pei Xing opened the novel to read what she had not read to Hua, the Conclusion, and its redolent, distressing last paragraph. It concerned Zhivago's beloved, Lara, who had returned to the city to try to track down their lost daughter.

> *One day Lara went out and did not come back. She must have been arrested in the street, as so often happened in those days, and she died or vanished somewhere, forgotten as a nameless number on a list which later was mislaid, in one of the innumerable mixed or women's concentration camps in the north.*

It was this section that prompted Pei Xing to weep. This paragraph summoned the fate of her mother and her father; this was the proxy tone of unremarked death, the impersonal sweep of fate and the atrocities it enacted. It was not all 'struggle sessions' and mass criticism and public executions, sometimes there was just this, a quiet disappearance. A number mislaid. One person gone. Two.

★   ★   ★

In the inhuman dark Pei Xing could not sleep. The encumbering past was too much with her. The little girl on the television was too much with her. In the unresolvable story she had been given to live there was no guarantee that everything finally and securely would repair. She realised too what it was in the television photograph that had bothered her: it was the four heads, ringed so emphatically in red. Four was a bad luck number in Chinese, four was the homophone of 'death'. *Four people*, the television announcer said; *four people*, he repeated. *Four.* So she must remember *five*. There might be four adults, all come together in failed witness or a momentary pattern, but there was always too a fifth, a child who must be disposed finally to life, not death. She was aware of her casuistry, her number superstition, aware she wanted, in her sleepiness, just to make things settle and become right. But it seemed to her a neat formulation. *Five.* Only the inclusion of the child promises something in the future. The humid darkness held Pei Xing in her bed. She lay still, quiet, sifting her day. She could hear traffic on the M5 and the distant sound of aircraft. So many were lost. So many.

But there was snowfall, and the Opera House, and *Doctor Zhivago*. There was the sound of the pipa, ever so lightly plucked. Not everything, surely, was known through *four*. Every pattern broke open into mystery, and what is yet to come. She told herself this, still anxious in the darkness. She told herself *five*.

★ ★ ★

After the inquest into the death of Amy Brown, after the scrawled, childish-looking note from her mother, James decided to write a letter in reply. He was unable to face the parents, unable to drive out to their dusty farm and knock on the door, bend to pat the dogs, smile weakly in embarrassment at the dire cause of his mission, fumble for words while Mrs Brown offered tea and cried. So it was the least he could do. In the little wheat-belt town where he had known such happiness, he sat in his room and composed a note to try to make things right. He can still see himself in the act of writing the letter, sitting on his bed with his knees pulled up and a pillow tucked behind him, hunchbacked, sleepless, half-destroyed.

Dear Mr and Mrs Brown,

I am writing to express my condolences over the death of your daughter, Amy. Amy was an excellent student and much admired by her peers. She was always helpful, courteous and well behaved. She will be missed by her friends and those who loved her. As her teacher I want to offer my deepest sympathy at this time of loss.
James DeMello

He sent the letter, and almost immediately regretted its inane formality. He had made grief tedious, had stuffed it like a cleaned corpse into a freezer of stiff words.

James had wanted to say: *Forgive me, forgive me, something went wrong. The world collapsed and Amy was under it. There is no word I can offer, there is nothing I can say, that will make things right. I, a poor son, who ceased visiting his own mother, can only tell you that I tried on the beach to bring her back, I tried and tried but she was already gone, and I shall never forget this, oh God, oh God, this wanting to breathe into her and bring her back, and the desperation I felt and the God-awful failure. And my own grief, I know, is nothing compared to yours, but it is huge and it is dark and I am not sure how to go on.*

If he could have retrieved the letter, and sent a symbol or an image or some other wordless emblem, he would have felt more honest. At the funeral there were flowers, and suddenly it made sense, why this might be so. In this town with no florist, this tiny town on the edge of nowhere, somehow roses and lilies had turned up, somehow there were elaborate wreaths and cellophane-wrapped bunches, and he had no idea how or from whence they had arrived. Yet it made sense. Something offered so that everything did not have to rest inside words. Something silent delivered from the living world. Something with no purpose other than to declare that the beautiful exists and will not last.

Rough farmers were standing around in hot suits; many, James guessed, retrieved the suit they'd been married in, and left it unbuttoned to accommodate their older body. The women were also dressed up, and some wore hats that looked as if they too belonged to an older generation. Mr and Mrs Brown, broken-hearted, stood silently holding hands.

James does not remember anything that

was said, not a single word. Only this: the flowers wilting beneath a sheen of sunlight and cellophane, and what people wore, the way they stood looking down, and the heat on their heads, and the absence of children.

★ ★ ★

At Circular Quay James was now at a loss. Having met with Ellie, having gulped back the words he might have said, he felt aimless and without purpose. All around him were families in a kind of festive mood, and couples strolling together, looking at the sights. He glanced up at the Sydney Harbour Bridge and could see a line of people, barely visible, climbing its bow. What must they see, he wondered. There would be the Harbour below them, and all the wake-patterns on the water, there would be a bird's eye view of boats and of the meringue peaks of the Opera House, and perhaps there would be a view much further, out eastwards to the ocean. Flags flapped on the summit, in a playful image of triumph.

★ ★ ★

James's attention was caught by a family he overheard to be Italian. They had spread a rug on the grass and were unloading a late picnic, and there were three generations, a Nonno, a Nonna, a Papa, a Mama, and two small children. One of the children, a boy about four, kept breaking away and chasing seagulls from the grass, so that they flapped messily about him, rose upwards and squawked. The little boy was pleased to have such evident effect in the world, to stir birds into the sky and scare them with his arms. And then the Nonna called out: *Matteo, Matteo,* and the boy turned and ran on his fat little legs into her arms. She said *Matteo, bello; Matteo, bello,* and the child sank into her lap with a lump of bread she had torn for him. His little sister, about two, reached over to take the bread, and he pulled it back, kicking and wriggling, setting off a squeal. But then the mother intervened and found bread for her daughter. The child flopped back into her mother's lap and Mama cuddled her, and blew on her hair, and took up her toddler toes and sucked them.

It was a simple little drama, everyday, unremarkable. But what had snagged in James's heart was *Matteo, bello*. It was as if he had heard it before, in the distant past. His own true name, given by his father, was *Gennaro, Gennaro DeMello*.

He had never told anyone, not even Ellie.

At some stage his father had left and when he was enrolled in school someone persuaded his mother to call him James. And so he became James, a fake Anglo translation. But on his birth certificate and passport, there it was, *Gennaro DeMello*, symbol of something he had one day lost. The sing-song of someone he used to be, but now orphaned and contracted and misidentified.

Si parla Italiano.

James thought of lingering longer near the happy family, but was afraid he would look suspicious, a guy just hanging around, a guy seedy-looking and ill. They would think he was a druggie, or someone who liked to look at small children. James gave Matteo a little wave as he walked past the family, and to his great surprise, Matteo waved back. *Ciao!* the child called. He waved in the Italian child's manner, closing his hand and opening it, closing and opening. In that second James lost his miserable nonentity. He became the man heralded by a child, caught in the egalitarian affirmation a small child might bestow. James smiled. Spent as he was, alone, the small wave moved and pleased him.

Auguri, he thought.

★ ★ ★

It was the wine, James decided, that made his mind swim in this way, and caused him to feel sleepy at only four in the afternoon. He considered visiting the Museum of Contemporary Art, but decided instead to take a short nap in the sunshine. He found a spot on the grass, on a slope, and laid himself down. He closed his tired eyes. He could hear a didgeridoo playing, a muffled soothing sound, and the distant busy din of traffic and people; he could hear the whole world jangly and abuzz on a Saturday afternoon. But he slipped away within seconds into a dreamless sleep, his body finally yielding to bone-aching tiredness. It was peace, it was retreat. The oblivion was sweet.

★　★　★

When James awoke it was just after six o'clock. Surprised to have slept for so long, he glanced at his watch a second time, for confirmation. It was as if someone had scissored out a slice of the day, destroying time. So he rose and sat for a while, calculating the shift of scene. The light had altered to what painters used to call Naples Yellow and the air had turned unusually humid and heavy. A change in the weather had begun to travel in from the sea. The crowds had thinned a little. The didgeridoo hum was gone. The non-stop faces and noises were less invasive and compelling. No sign, anywhere, of the Italian family, or the boy who had offered such an innocent and easy salutation. It was good to have slept, after so much wakefulness. James's mind felt clearer; he did not have a headache; he was relocated in the present tense, here and now.

James stood, shook off his doze, and set off in a semblance of true volition to visit the nearby Botanic Gardens. Inattentive to the crowds, conspicuously alone, he walked once more around the circumference of Circular Quay, crossed in front of the Opera House and headed up a hill, finding himself in a space of leafy parklands and wide expanses of grass. A strong wind flew in off the ruffled waters of the Harbour, and James, with no reason to be there but to wander and look, simply drifted between the trees, followed the winding paths, read the Latin tags affixed to little signs below exhibitions of plants and bushes. In dwindling light he saw there was a native garden, marked with a placard that acknowledged that the land was first possessed by the Cadigal people; there was a begonia garden, a rose garden, an oriental garden and a succulent garden.

At length James arrived at something called Mrs Macquarie's Chair, a bench carved by convicts out of sandstone in 1810. Mrs Macquarie, wife of a colonial Governor, liked to sit here, the sign said, to watch tall ships enter the Harbour. He imagined a woman in Regency dress, like someone in a television drama, decorous, prudish, moving with stiff reticence. She would speak in posh tones and gaze into the far distance, her tendril hair blowing.

There was no one else present, so James sat down on the chair, displacing Mrs Macquarie's ghost and acting colonial. He stared at the water. It was bucking under the wind and iron-toned with the coming night. Almost at once a kind of aggravated disquiet assailed him. James could not release himself from the pressure of absent others, Amy Brown in particular, and the tragedy of her death, Ellie and all that she urgently signified, his mother, vivid still and intolerably memorable. So long in inertia, so long sealed away, he was now made restless by his understanding that there would be no conclusion to all this, and that Amy's death had punctured or ripped something, had opened him both to devastation and to revisitings from the past. He was oppressed, all at once, with a sense of her plea from beyond the grave, as if she were a vision, transparent, with the world shining through her. Ghosts disobeyed time. Their flimsy bodies were interminable. They were at once long-lasting and bizarrely sudden. Afflicted by what he could not name or speak, James needed once again to move his body.

★ ★ ★

With dusk the light had become purple; yellow was draining to the west. Bats rose in flocks from the Botanic Gardens and were streaming across the sky; though distant and high above, they were a loathsome presence. With no plan, with no purpose, James began the walk back towards Circular Quay. In the twenty minutes it took, night had fallen; out here, in the open, it was like parts of the world silently ceasing to be, a downward bending to nothing. The sensation of disappearance was contiguous and threatening. James quickened his pace, almost afraid.

★ ★ ★

But as he approached the Quay he saw that everything was transformed. The Opera House was illuminated against the dark sky and looked still and shiny, like something made for a church. It seemed to bulge in his direction, as if it had grown in his absence and possessed an organic life he'd not noticed before. Beads of light picked out the shape of the Quay, most of them ornamental and over-powered; so too the Bridge was visible as a pattern of dots following its shape, the faint outlines of girders and struts, the honey-coloured pylons, a single crimson light blinking at the high point of its arch. Beneath the Bridge, far to the north, James could see the shimmering icon of the amusement park: a face hideously smiling, its lit hair in afrighted spikes. Along the near side of the Quay the white umbrellas were still up, massing like wings over the heads of customers now beginning to gather for dinner outside. High palms were moving slightly in a rising breeze. Most impressive of all was the Harbour itself, which was black now, pure metaphysical black, and covered in a net of broken light. The ferries were still heading out and returning, their beacons shining, their little windows lit. And there were red buoy lights on the water, showing the way.

★   ★   ★

322

All this came towards James in a lustrous rush. He couldn't help thinking of the adjective 'cinematic', the way everything with perceptual force, everything city-scale and spaced out, was nowadays described. There was flicker and montage; there was the strangely versatile and celluloid shine of the darkness. It was so: *cinematic*. Faces manifested before him, veering in and out of focus, and a continuous ribbon of activity seemed to catch at his vision. The crowds had grown once again, and included the smart set heading for dinner and those anticipating a night at the theatre or the Opera. The elevated train rumbled and raised voices sounded. Everything was converging, everything was ample and ablaze. This was one of those parts of a city that passes for a myth.

★ ★ ★

James walked along the Opera House side of the Quay and took a seat under one of the umbrellas for something to do. A waiter appeared instantly, bending like an actor taking a bow. There was generosity in his manner, a calm assertion of connection. James was not hungry but he ordered a meal and a bottle of wine because he wanted to prolong whatever abnormal feeling this was, waking to a new time, into this *cinematic* illusion, waking into the visionary present after so much smothering past. His steak came, dribbled with sauces, and he looked at it without interest, but he began drinking almost immediately, feeling the Cabernet Sauvignon suffuse his body, falling into him, warmly, like a familiar drug. His metabolism recognised the stimulant whizz in the bloodstream, the cheap revival of chemical life.

Oh Ellie. The ledge in time that was their bed had forever gone. He realised he was leaning on the table, drinking alone, looking to all the world like some miserable bastard whose girlfriend had just left him. An *Agelasti*, that's what he was. James could not remember the last time he had laughed.

★   ★   ★

After the unfinished dinner he rose wide-awake, and walked, wishing to lose himself, into the streaming crowd. James made his way to the steps of the Opera House and sat looking at the sky. Then, as the numbers swelled, arriving for concerts and plays, he walked back again. He might have been floating, the loose crowd parting before him, voices circumambient, a sense of idiosyncrasy to his sensations and being in the world. Faceted faces drifted past, the crowds moved gently around him, he saw figments, apparitions, as an artist might have seen. Magritte. He was Magritte, who had lost his mother.

* * *

At a small liquor store facing the city James bought two large bottles of whisky. These were of thick glass, expensive, and reminded him somehow of a fist. The young man who served him thoughtfully put each bottle into an eco-friendly bag. Drug of choice for the evening, James thought, for a silhouette of a man, false-hearted, misnamed, thinly sketched in graphite by a schoolchild in another time and place. He was not worthy of Ellie. He was too wounded, too lost, too finally disconsolate.

He thought of his cock in a woman's hand — any woman — as she guided him in. A woman's mouth half-open, and the carnal, comforting sigh as he fell into her body. This was the imprecision that desire might become, the unbearable paraphrase and substitution.

A drum of voices hung around, creating the resounding white noise of a busy Saturday night. James wanted silence. He sat on the ground in a dark corner behind the ice-cream stand and took a few gulps of whisky. Then he retrieved pills from his jeans' pocket, and complicated his tox result. Slurred his sick-drinking self, destroyed his sexual imaginings, wanting the peaceful ruination of not having to remember. And though he'd given them up long ago, he was desperate for a cigarette.

★ ★ ★

On impulse James bought a ticket and boarded a ferry, any ferry. Randomly chosen. He was not sure where the ferry was headed as it surged into the night. It was like entering a small, unstable and generalised world: the rocking seemed exaggerated and the passenger compartment confining. He couldn't bear the overhead lights and the neat little seats, the young people talking in puerile witticisms, the mobile phones and the texting and the Saturday night excitation, so he moved to the back, outside, into the moist gusting wind. It was like being alone, being wholly alone. His nerves settled, he felt himself return, he began again to look. There was the wake, lush white and sucking under the black water; there was the Opera House sliding its great and singular form, and the reflection of the Opera House, which looked thin and unabiding and made of snow. And there was the city, retreating, all those towers of lights, all those engineering wonders, high-rising and firm.

★ ★ ★

It was not a decision, but an act. James slipped over the edge and the whisky pulled him down. At first it was a bounteous wash of dark and light, the water colder than he had expected and covering him quickly. The Harbour seemed to throb around him as the ferry pulled away, and then slacken and gently take him and require his surrender. There were verticals of filmy light and fish-shapes breaking open. There was a winding embrace so that he opened his arms like a lover. There was pressure. There was night, the tide of night, flowing in. He was thinking of his true name, Gennaro DeMello, which came to him as a song, *Gennaro bello*. He imagined singing from the Opera House penetrating the water — *Gennaro bello, Gennaro bello* — an extended melisma, a round pure moment.

He felt the water of the Harbour enter his body. His chest was filling. The black wet pushed its thumb-balls in. He felt the sad sinking of giving up and letting go.

He was washed and washed into the mothering darkness, a release, a release, as sound releases; into the wake, Gennaro's wake, and into waves, in waves.

★ ★ ★

The market was a joy. Ellie had caught the bus up Glebe Point Road and disembarked before her stop when she saw the market. It was near closing time, so stallholders were looking rather hot and bored, but pleased too to see browsers still wandering about and relaxed into friendly chit-chat and casual light banter. The market was a mixture of craft, new goods and second-hand junk — clothes, knick-knacks, books and collectibles. Ellie walked past the vendor roasting caramelised nuts in a big open pan at the entrance, and headed straight for the second-hand stalls and the trays of old books.

The sunlight now was orange and the day was drifting away; it gave the shoppers a healthy non-commercial glow. They were defeating all market predictions by their delight in trash and treasure; they held up crumpled cast-offs and cracked old teacups; they leafed through children's books from the 1930s, they paused over someone's collection of rusty tools, most superceded these days by something electrically loud. Ellie bought an old hammer so that she could hang a small print on her wall. The man who sold it was pleased, he said, to see that his hammer was going to a good home: it was a small courtesy he offered her, a sweet civility. He reminded Ellie of her father. He wore a scraggly cloth hat on his thin white hair, and read a novel, self-contented, when he did not have customers. She saw that his hands were callused; he had been a hard worker.

Ellie moved then to rummage through trestle tables piled high with discarded clothes. They gave off a slight whiff of naphthalene flakes and were remnants of every era and style, mostly retro-shaped and of fabrics one no longer saw, velveteen, chiffon, Crimplene. She extracted a cheongsam dress of a dense woven silk, covered by tiny emblems of cranes and pagodas. It was of shiny teal blue, with cloth fasteners at a slant and a small mandarin collar. Ellie stretched it across her breasts and hips to gauge if it would fit and decided yes, it was worth a try. She would wear it when next she met James so that he might remove it slowly.

★　★　★

Though he had looked nerve-wracked and bloodshot James still carried timeless appeal. Ellie was not sure how much this was overcoded by memory, but there was a charge to his presence and an arousing promise. His proximity in the restaurant had made her want to lean closer. She could feel her naked thighs beneath her thin skirt and had imagined his hand there, gently exploring. Her sexual fantasies all had this efficient simplicity. She would ring him in the morning and arrange another meeting, possibly at her apartment, with a bottle of wine. She would have indirect lighting and a melodious CD.

★ ★ ★

At fourteen they had been inept but lusty lovers: they didn't know what was what. But they knew that there was a world of feeling awaiting them, and the opportunity to talk. The space of disclosure, when they lay in a sweaty embrace in late afternoon, was a sort of second home, so that they were homesick when they were apart, needing the wrecked foundry to rest in, and their own rug upon the floor, and the way light flowed and settled there, needing the bare talkative intimacy of one other person. The meaning of their meetings eluded them, but there was a sufficiency, a self-sufficiency, and a kind of sensual arrogance. Some afternoons they had thrashed about, in sheer heedless pleasure, and it took months before they each learned to slow down and take their time, and for Ellie to learn that she might instruct and more fully participate.

★ ★ ★

She remembered when James first discovered that women menstruate. He had not known how clandestine women were obliged to become, how curved around their own bodies. He told her then of the terrible shame of his nosebleeds and how he feared that he would never outgrow them. Imagine an adult, he said, bleeding from the face like that. Ellie had gently reassured him. It would pass. Everything passed. They were kids, just kids. No one, she told him, would remember his nosebleeds.

They had sex, but they did not know what 'sexy' was; their responses were untutored and without any deception. They shared pleasure and discomfort. They told each other funny stories. They discussed books they had read and whacky teenage ideas. Together they enjoyed unusual words, those

331

that described something in the world of ravishing or antique particularity.

The word 'clepsydra' became a kind of code between them, an erotic trigger and a flag of assignation. No one else knew. When she leant over in class to whisper it, James would respond with a little nod, and sometimes reach, surreptitiously, to squeeze her hand. Neither she nor James had ever uttered the word 'love'. Both were too shy. Both were troubled by what might dissolve if they dared to name it. Neither wished to alarm the other, or to reach and find their hands empty.

★   ★   ★

Clepsydra, the water clock, time rendered continuous. Time in transient light, talking softly about everything they were and might be. And now he was returned, her James, the body remembered above others, and in the saturated time of his return Ellie felt something open before her, another scale, a refashioned future, the glimmering of something half-concealed up ahead. She had always hated driving along country roads in the dark, seeing only in the pale stereoscopic limits of the headlights, sure only of things weakly illuminated, shapes, barest presences, rushing forward in the dark, atomised, gone. Now, looping back to the past, everything had changed. It was like recovering sight. It was like moving more slowly, watching objects solidify, and seeing the way. With her father they had driven cautiously, to avoid hitting kangaroos. 'See?' he once said, when they braked in time. 'They rise up in the dark and you have to be careful.' From the passenger seat she had watched the animal bounce off into the night, a silver outline, a mobile arc, energetic and unharmed.

★ ★ ★

Some of the stallholders in the market were beginning to pack away their wares. There were Turks selling Gözlemes; they had turned off their hotplates and were scraping leftover tabouli into plastic containers. There was an African man wrapping wooden statues, elongated human figures and animals with horns; there was a Hungarian baker, over-supplied with poppy-seed cakes, and a Thai woman who sold jewellery made from sea shells. Merchants of many parts of the world were here, in a hippy leftover rehearsal of united nations. Ellie found heartwarming this Sydney of mixed populations. As she left the market — how everything converged — she saw a little stall behind which a Chinese woman sat. It occurred to Ellie she might discover a trinket to go with the mandarin dress. The woman was sixty or so, and sitting by her side was a girl about eight, who was likely her granddaughter. Her stall was a fold-away table covered with oriental odds and ends. There were jade charms, pink coral ornaments and a few hexagonal coins; there was a row of brass-handled magnifying glasses of different sizes; there were small cut-paper pictures in crimson and embroidered silk dragons. Objects from another world. Objects from *Communist China*.

Ellie picked up a magnifying glass. No reason, really.

The little girl said gravely: 'you can make fire, as well as see,' and she held a glass to the fading sun to show Ellie how rays might concentrate. Ellie pretended she didn't know and tried to sound amazed. The girl was pleased. She beamed at her grandmother. So Ellie left the market with a hammer, a Chinese dress, poppyseed cake and a magnifying glass, and walked up the hill and a few blocks further, back to her apartment. She was sweating when she arrived and unlocked the door. The air was heavy with the threat of a coming storm.

★　★　★

It was difficult to filter all she had remembered that day, all that circulated around seeing James again, after so many years. Ellie took a shower, dressed in a sarong and prepared herself a gin and tonic. Then she sat for a while in front of a small electric fan, letting it blow cool over the damp surface of her hair. Miss Morrison had taught them about birds that came from Siberia, migratory birds that flew through China, then continued all the way to south-west and south-eastern Australia. *These birds curve around the planet*, that's what she had said. They had chanted out the names of the birds in a sing-song fashion, the way they had been taught their maths times-tables, and Ellie had loved the way the listing and repetition became a kind of music. She must ask James if he remembered the chant. She would ask him to do the sing-song of the birds that curve around the planet, to give voice to the vectors Miss Morrison had described. James had talked of this once as they lay on the blanket; he had chanted the names and then turned to embrace her. These fragments they shared. They were more plausible, more secure, less private and idiomatic, now that he had returned to her. And it seemed to Ellie that there was an unexpected profundity to these recollections, as though they portended the completion, at last, of something long ago begun.

★　★　★

Ellie found the print, an old one and foxed, of native Australian flowers, and standing balanced on a chair hammered a nail into the wall, taking care not to make the plaster crack. Then she hung the picture. It was the simplest of pleasures and she loved the feel of the hammer in her hand, the warm wood, slightly concave for a labourer's grasp. Lovely old bloke, he was, who wanted his hammer to go to a good home. And the print of a bunch of flowers, *dryandra*, another item she had rescued from obscurity at a market stall, here glowed in the pallid twilight and was suddenly redeemed and beautiful.

★　★　★

Ellie made herself a snack of cheese and poppyseed cake, opened a bottle of red wine, and decided against turning on the television for the news. Instead she stretched on the couch and resumed her reading of a Russian novel, one she was hoping to write about in her thesis. She took notes as she went, placing tiny coloured stickers on significant pages, so that the book was already looking half-transformed, an oddball art object, sprouting a rainbow of rectangles. If she were to write on this book, she reflected, she would have to learn Russian, and in a casual half-serious way entertained the idea of looking up courses on the internet, before the weekend was over. It appealed to her, the idea of learning the Russian language. There might be curiosities of translation that would remake the novel and transport her to a different kind of European otherworld. The novel was called *Petersburg*, by Andrei Bely. It was written in olden times, in 1913. The young revolutionary, Nikolai Apollonovich, must assassinate his father, Apollon Apollonovich, with a complicated time bomb. Wonderful names, these Russians. Ellie would compare it, she thought, to James Joyce's *Ulysses* and find intelligible links between cities rendered in words. The intellectual adventure of comparison excited and moved her, so that when she returned to her Sydney world it was thundering outside and it was eleven, perhaps, or nearing midnight. Time had leaked as she read, time had lost its authority, the peculiar duration of reading had entirely taken over.

Ellie stood up and slowly walked to the window. In the distance she heard the low rumble of a storm, and saw flashes of lightning tearing the sky. There was sublimity to thunderstorms and a sense of barely withheld threat. She watched for a while as trees sparked into seconds of existence, then fell back into darkness; she saw the ragged skyline in electric shock; she saw the undersides of clouds illuminated, like surreal creatures floating there; she saw the city take on a quality of abstraction, doused with crude light. Then the rain broke and fell heavily, in loud-roaring sheets. The air was filled up with noise and agitated presence. Each raindrop a small lantern.

Ellie closed away her book, undressed, and went to bed. In the darkness she lay listening to the sound of the flooding rain. It was a betokening, somehow, of another kind of engulfment, one of time, of memory, and of James returned.

★   ★   ★

And they are sinking now, all of them, into the wet sleep of the city. Rain is falling all over Sydney.

★   ★   ★

Catherine is still mourning her dead brother and still speaking to him in silence, summoning his company in the torrential night. An altar boy swinging a censer and smoke filling the transept of the church, and her mother's face, and Brendan's, like faces in an old film. She is remembering the summer he made a trolley-cart from a broken-down pram; it was the summer, light-lit, of her holy communion, and her little communion bag with the rosary beads in it, and a fiver, a gift from her parents; and everything then was white, her knee-socks were white, and her dress was white and her gauzy veil, white as those petals at the Quay, perpetually subsiding; and now she is seeing no floral emblem to carry her feelings, but enormous white eyelids, one resting upon another, the rims overlapping in a bulbous, rhyming fold, and the eyelids are closing, slow-motion, closing into dreaming; and she is thinking, so she will remember, so she will remember in the morning, *must Google Woolloomooloo, must Google Woolloo-mooloo* . . .

★ ★ ★

Pei Xing is preserving the lost child on television by magical-thinking the number five: *Wu, wu; wu, wu; wu, wu; wu, wu*; and remembering ancient men painting with

339

water on the footpaths of People's Park, practising calligraphy. The signs disappeared almost as they produced them, elegant broad flourishes with oversized pens. And returning half-sleeping in rain-sound to the park in Shanghai, she remembers old people performing *cloud hands*, swaying their bodies in the air, then walking backwards, stepping carefully, stepping beautifully solemn. It was another Tai Chi practice, walking backwards, backwards. And before she slips into dreaming Pei Xing realises this is her: some of us walk backwards, always seeing what lies behind; and she falls asleep like this, reversed into her own history, seeing her own childhood and what she has lost, walking backwards, and backwards, walking forwards backwards . . .

★ ★ ★

Ellie is thinking of rainfall over the Opera House, thinking of the Harbour swept shining and mystical by rain light, thinking of the time-lapse of all that she has known and read, and of James, and with James, ever and ever and abiding. The night has gained an enormity with the coming of the storm and in the drench she imagines it out there, Circular Quay, the vast dark water, the rain-glazed tide, the Harbour buoys with their red flares tossing messages across the water, seabirds rising up and rain coming down and the falling, falling, upon the living and the dead, ever and ever and abiding. There is the musical sound of rain on her roof and Ellie is thinking, so she will remember, *must ring James, must ring James, must ring, ring . . .*

Acknowledgements

The first debt of this project is to Kenneth Slessor's elegiac poem, *Five Bells* (1939), which returned to me, like a remembered song, one midnight on a ferry in the centre of Circular Quay.

I wish to thank my colleagues at The University of Western Sydney, especially members of the Writing and Society Research Group led by Professor Ivor Indyk. The solidarity of members of this group is deeply appreciated. Thanks to the Shanghai Writers' Association (SWA) for sponsoring my residency in Shanghai in 2008; Madeleine Thien and Yukiko Chino had coterminous residencies and were both congenial and supportive companions. Particular thanks to Claire Roberts and Nicholas Jose, for their patient kindness and circumspect advice on Chinese cultural matters. Hu Peihua, Rowan Callick, Wang Anyi, Ye Xin, Antonia Finnane, Guo Wu, Julia Lovell and Jiang Liping have all offered Chinese advice of one sort or another. Thanks to Jia Zongpei (my Chinese publisher), Zhao Lihong and the SWA for arranging my visit to Chongming Island. Jang Luping (Lucy) was a wonderful translator; Hu Peihua (SWA) was tirelessly wise and helpful; Francine Martin offered hospitality in Shanghai; thanks too to Michelle Garnaut, for her friendship and advice. Thanks to Paddy and Clare Callanan for hospitality and good-humour in Dublin, Fiona Wright for the clepsydra image, Fiona Stanley for medical knowledge, Kathleen Olive and Melinda Jewell and Suzanne Gapps for collegiate generosity and support. Special thanks to Geoff Mulligan for editorial advice and to Meredith Curnow and Catherine Hill, two extraordinarily gifted and sensitive readers. Rebecca Carter and Laurence Laluyaux have been especially kind. I have the good fortune to work with Zoë Waldie, my wonderful agent. Victoria Burrows, Susan Midalia, Prue Kerr and Michelle de Kretser have each offered utterly essential moral support, as have Robyn Davidson and Drusilla Modjeska. My daughter Kyra has made this book possible.

Among textual resources, the works of Gelin Yan, Qui Xiaolong, Yu Hua, Ha Jin, Xinran and Yiyun Li have been helpful. Nien Cheng's *Life and Death in Shanghai* (Penguin Books 1988) and Anhua Gao's *To the Edge of the Sky: A Story of Love,*

343

Betrayal, Suffering and the Strength of Human Courage (The Overlook Press 2000) are two fine memoirs of women's cultural revolution experience. Wang Zhousheng's story 'The Beautiful Mushrooms' is the source of some of my knowledge of labour conditions at Chongming Island. It is in *Selected Short Stories by Contemporary Writers from Shanghai (II)* (Better Link Press NY 2008). I also consulted Feng Jicai's *Ten Years of Madness: Oral Histories of China's Cultural Revolution* (China Books and Periodicals Inc. San Francisco 1996), the website Morning Sun http://www.morningsun.org/and Li Zhensheng's *Red-Colour News Soldier: A Chinese Photographer's Odyssey Though the Cultural Revolution* (London: Phaidon, 2003). Simon Leys' work, most recently a return to articles in *The Angel and the Octopus* (Duffy and Snellgrove 1999), was also inspiring.

The opening stanza of 'On Raglan Road' by Patrick Kavanagh is reprinted from *Collected Poems*, edited by Antoinette Quinn (Alan Lane, 2004), by kind permission of the Trustees of the Estate of the late Katherine B. Kavanagh, through the Jonathan Williams Literary Agency. The stanza of 'Five Bells' by Kenneth Slessor is reprinted from *Five Bells: XX Poems* (F.C. Johnson 1939), by kind permission of Paul Slessor. I thank Paul for his warm-hearted and affirming response to this project. The quotes from *Doctor Zhivago* by Boris Pasternak (Harvill Collins Edition 1988) are reprinted by kind permission of the Random House Group Ltd.

We do hope that you have enjoyed reading this large print book.

Did you know that all of our titles are available for purchase?

We publish a wide range of high quality large print books including:
Romances, Mysteries, Classics
General Fiction
Non Fiction and Westerns

Special interest titles available in large print are:
The Little Oxford Dictionary
Music Book
Song Book
Hymn Book
Service Book

Also available from us courtesy of Oxford University Press:
Young Readers' Dictionary
(large print edition)
Young Readers' Thesaurus
(large print edition)

For further information or a free brochure, please contact us at:
Ulverscroft Large Print Books Ltd.,
The Green, Bradgate Road, Anstey,
Leicester, LE7 7FU, England.
Tel: (00 44) **0116 236 4325**
Fax: (00 44) **0116 234 0205**

Other titles published by
The House of Ulverscroft:

THE RAGING SPIRIT

June Gadsby

For a woman in 1890 the journey to the wild archipelago of St. Kilda, off the coast of Scotland, is hazardous. Untroubled and underterred, Meredith accompanies her naturalist father on his expedition, knowing she may have to endure a long stay. But then she meets the renowned Professor Fergus Macaulay and soon has cause to fear him. As their boat flounders in savage seas, Meredith is jettisoned overboard. However, she is saved by a young man called Logan, who bears an uncanny resemblance to Macaulay . . . and Logan's dark and terrible past is slowly revealed — at great cost to them all.

FOLD

Tom Campbell

It's 2009 in Reading. Five men, each in their forties, meet monthly in each other's houses to play poker. Doug shows off his new-minted wealth, Simon insists on serving only red wine and goats' cheese, and Nick tries, desperately, to end his losing streak. While Vijay records every game on his spreadsheet, Alan frets about his inability to get his wife pregnant, and Nick becomes obsessed with the idea of engineering Doug's downfall. Aiming to triumph over his nemesis in poker as well as in life, he comes into troubling proximity to Sophia, Doug's clever and beautiful wife.

IN THE SEA
THERE ARE CROCODILES

Fabio Geda

One night before putting him to bed, Enaiatollah's mother tells him three things: don't use drugs; don't use weapons; don't steal. The next day he wakes up to find she isn't there. They have fled their village to seek safety outside Afghanistan, but his mother has decided to return home to her younger children. Ten-year-old Enaiatollah is left alone in Pakistan to fend for himself . . . Fabio Geda takes the true story of Enaiatollah's remarkable five-year journey from Afghanistan to Italy and shapes it into a beautiful piece of fiction.

THE HOUSE OF HOPE

Audrey Willsher

When Marianne goes to Hope Grange, it's to take up her job as a maid in the household of Hugo Lacey. But it is not the grand house she is expecting. Hope Grange is a crumbling wreck and a house of ghosts, whispers and secrets. Living there are seven-year-old Gerald and his grandmother. Forced to sell his home, Hugo's behaviour becomes more irrational and descends into madness. Marianne finds herself in a perilous situation and, fearing for her safety, she decides to leave. Then Franz, a German prisoner of war, comes to work in the garden and everything is changed.

HILL FARM

Miranda France

Hill Farm tells the story of what appears to be an ordinary farming family living in a perfect village in an Area of Outstanding Natural Beauty. It feels like a place that will never change. Its farmhouse is crumbling and the same bric-a-brac has been circulating the village jumble sales for decades. But change does come, that summer. It comes in different guises: a handsome farm hand, a deathwatch beetle, a scented bosom, a lost hedgerow, a disused water tank. But finally it comes after an explosive argument in the tractor shed — and nothing will ever be the same again . . .

THE SONG HOUSE

Trezza Azzopardi

Kenneth Earl's memory is failing, so he advertises for help to catalogue his vast music collection and create a record of his life. He takes on his final candidate, Maggie, unaware she's been to Earl House before ... As a child, Maggie and her mother lived near the river that runs past the house. Her memories of that time are vague. There was Kenneth's son, William ... a boat ... children singing. She was alone — afraid — and had returned home, refusing to speak. Returning to Earl House as an adult offers the chance to fill in the gaps, and finally lay to rest her childhood ghosts.